THE SLEEPER

THE SLEEPER

Clive Egleton

This title first published in Great Britain 2005 by
SEVERN HOUSE PUBLISHERS LTD of
9–15 High Street, Sutton, Surrey SM1 1DF.
Originally published in 1971 in Great Britain
under the title *Last Post for a Partisan*.
This title first published in the USA 2005 by
SEVERN HOUSE PUBLISHERS INC of
595 Madison Avenue, New York, N.Y. 10022.

British Library Cataloguing in Publication Data

Egleton, Clive
    The sleeper
    1. Espionage, British - Fiction
    2. Espionage, Russian - Fiction
    3. Suspense fiction
    I. Title
    823.9'14 [F]

    ISBN 0-7278-6243 X

Printed and bound in Great Britain by
MPG Books Ltd., Bodmin, Cornwall.

AUTHOR'S NOTE

All characters and events in this book are entirely ficti-
tious, with the exception of Mathilde Carré, whose
activities as a double agent after Ramon Czerniawski
was arrested in November 1941, are briefly described in
Chapter XIII. A more detailed account can be found
in *Inside S.O.E.* by E. H. Cookridge, published by Arthur
Barker.

1

TYLER OPENED THE wardrobe and checked his appearance in the full-length mirror on the back of the door. His shirt sleeves, rolled up above the elbow, were folded to the correct regulation width and neatly pressed back in place, and the black Sam Browne belt and holster, which hugged his flat stomach, shone like patent leather. Satisfied with his turn-out, Tyler absent-mindedly patted the thinning blond hair on the crown of his head before closing the door.

Tyler was rising thirty-two, married, with a son aged nine, and most mornings he woke up with a sinking feeling in the pit of his stomach, because it was no joke being a policeman. It was no joke being cold-shouldered by your neighbours, no joke when your son came home from school with a black eye and his hair caked with excreta, no joke when your wife was pestered with obscene telephone calls while you were out, and no joke to know that there was a chance that some day, somewhere, someone might just shoot you in the back because you happened to be a policeman.

Given the choice, Tyler would have resigned from the Police Force long ago, but he had had no choice. He was a policeman before the Soviet occupation began, and the Government said he was going to stay a policeman until they decided his services were no longer required. And as long as he was a policeman it was to be clearly understood that if he performed his duties negligently, disciplinary action would follow, and that meant a term of penal servitude. He was therefore as much a prisoner of the system as any inmate of the Scrubs.

He trod a narrow path aiming to keep his nose clean, while at the same time taking care not to fall foul of the Resistance. He had been told that he had nothing to fear from the Resistance as long as he turned a blind eye to their activities, and Tyler took their advice to heart. He had become adept at ignoring those things he was not supposed to see or hear—like the man in the basement flat, for example.

Tyler had never seen the man, but he had heard him moving about during the night, pacing up and down the narrow confines of his room, one footfall sounding slightly heavier than the other. He had no desire to meet the man because he knew that the Resistance used the basement flat as a safe hide.

He took the ·38 Lee Enfield revolver out of the holster, broke it open, and fed five rounds into the chambers leaving empty the one under the hammer, and then carefully put the pistol back into the holster. Tyler sensed, without looking at the double bed, that his wife, Marge, was watching him closely, and he could read her unspoken thoughts. There was nothing remarkable about that because she had but one idea in her head of late.

She seemed to think that all their troubles would be solved if he could wangle a move to another district where nobody would know them. He had tried hard enough to get himself transferred, but his present District was under-manned and the Station Officer wouldn't hear of it. Unfortunately, Tyler had failed to convince Marge that he had done his best, and, as he reluctantly turned to face his wife and met her speculative gaze, he tried to think of something to say which would get her off the dangerous subject of his transfer. He was unlucky, she got in first. In a quiet voice she said, 'You won't forget to see about your posting, will you?'

'No,' he said dully, 'I won't forget.'

His lack of enthusiasm irritated her, and her voice rose

in anger. 'All right then,' she snapped, 'just make sure you don't take no for an answer.'

Tyler picked up his hat from the chair and left the room without saying another word. He slammed the front door behind him and ran down the steps into the street, anxious to get away from the atmosphere in the flat. He wondered if the man in the basement had heard Marge shouting; not that it mattered a damn anyway. He squinted up at the sun and knew that it was going to be another stinking day in more ways than one.

At 7:45 am Tyler reported in for duty and attended the daily briefing by the Station Sergeant. It followed the usual format—a general run-down on the list of men and women wanted for Resistance activities followed by the occurrence report for the previous twenty-four hours. There was scarcely a man present who didn't carry a detailed mental picture of the known Resistance leaders, and Tyler was prepared to bet that most of his colleagues would do absolutely nothing if they met one of the wanted men face to face. There was, he thought, no percentage in being a dead hero.

Shortly after eight o'clock, Tyler, accompanied by Police Constable Hayes, began his eight hour tour of duty. The rush hour was just beginning to build up in the High Street, long queues forming at each bus stop, and pedestrians jostling each other on the pavement as they hurried towards the tube station. Hayes said, 'That's the third possible I've seen in the last ten minutes.'

'What?'

'That man in the lightweight suit who just passed us.'

'What about him?'

'Where were you this morning? Didn't you hear the Sergeant read out the description of the man wanted for the Parkhurst job? Age believed to be between thirty-six to thirty-eight, black hair beginning to fleck with grey, weight about one hundred and seventy-five pounds, strong square-shaped face, cold blue-grey eyes.'

Tyler said sarcastically, 'We'll go a long way with that kind of information,' but for some unaccountable reason

9

he found himself wondering what the man in the basement flat looked like.

The man in the basement flat was thirty-six, his black hair flecked with grey, his eyes a cold blue-grey, but the strong square-shaped face was pale and drawn, and there were deep marks under the eyes. He weighed one hundred and seventy-five pounds and a grenade fragment in the left leg still gave him slight trouble. He was pale because he had spent the better part of four months indoors, and the dark circles under his eyes betrayed a lack of sleep. He did not sleep well at night because he had a vision of a girl lying on the platform at Portsmouth Station with her legs drawn up to her stomach, surrounded by a crowd of curious onlookers who were staring at her and wondering why she had felt compelled to take cyanide. And every time he thought of Dane he wanted to be sick because death is so final, and she had died because he had let her go on alone when she needed all his help.

In the weeks spent waiting for his turn to be fed into the escape pipeline, Garnett had found that the only way to get rid of this black mood of despair was to walk it out of his system, but his room, which measured eight paces long by five paces wide, didn't offer much scope as an exercise area. It was as bare as a monk's cell and as functional as an operating theatre. There was a bed to sleep on and a basin to wash in—no Hilton Hotel, but a safe place to lie up in. Room-service was a watery-eyed old man with decaying teeth and bad breath, who came down the back stairs carrying Garnett's meals on a tray. The food was invariably cold.

Garnett had the clothes he stood up in and a battery-powered shaver. Travelling light meant that he could clear out fast if he had to. In the event of trouble he had two things going for him—a telephone number and a fail-safe rendezvous. He hoped he would not have to make use of either facility. On this hot, still, quiet August day such a contingency seemed unlikely.

He was a man hardened by nearly five years of Soviet occupation, who had lost his wife and son in the ten megaton strike on Bristol. He had known the humiliation of serving in an army ordered to surrender to the enemy, and he had seen friends taken out of PW Camps and executed with hundreds of other officers because the Russians were afraid that they might form the backbone of a Resistance movement. Five years of being the hunter and the hunted had left their mark on him. Garnett was a man who now found it easy to hate.

Tyler finished his tour of duty at four, and slowly made his way back to number 36, Elm Hill wondering if Marge would still be there when he arrived home. He wouldn't blame her if she wasn't; London was one hell of a place to live in under Soviet occupation. Tomorrow, he promised himself, tomorrow I'll put in for a transfer.

The street was quiet, almost too quiet. In another part of the town this silence might have worried Tyler, but he lived in this street and here he felt safe, because knowing what he did he enjoyed the protection of the Resistance. A six-year-old girl in a bathing suit sat on the front step of her house playing with a rag doll. She tried not to show it, but she wanted to join the group of boys further up the street, who were huddled in a circle on the pavement outside number 28, but of course she knew there was no chance that they would invite her to do so, so she pretended to ignore them.

The boys, four in number, aged between eight and ten, were playing with an egg-shaped object which they had found on the waste ground behind the railway yard. The outside casing of the egg was encrusted with dirt, and most of the paint had flaked off. They had discovered that there was a plug at one end, which was rusted solid, and a key-ring and a pin at the other which they had removed after a bit of a struggle, with the result that a pitted lever had fallen off the side of the egg. By rights, the plunger should have thumped down the sleeve and ignited the four-second safety fuse, but dirt in the sleeve caused it to stick. One of the boys picked up the hand grenade and banged it on the pavement. The blow freed the plunger, the safety fuse began to splutter and a thin spiral of black smoke escaped from the sleeve. There was a split second of uncertainty, and then the eldest boy, acting instinctively, picked up the grenade and lobbed it down the street. It bounced twice before rolling to a stop at Tyler's feet.

He turned to run for cover, saw the child playing with her rag doll, and hesitated. The grenade exploded behind him, the base plug smashed into his spine and his back looked as if a bacon slicer had run amok. Tyler lay on the pavement, the blood running out of his mouth and slowly forming a halo about his head. The small girl hugged the doll to her chest, stared wide-eyed at the dead man at her feet, and then started to scream. The street suddenly came to life as Garnett emerged from the basement. The woman from the flat above hurtled down the steps and ran towards the body, and, in seconds a knot of people had gathered on the opposite side of the road. There were two choices open to Garnett; he could either stay and chance to luck that Tyler's wife wouldn't talk to the police when they arrived, or he could make a run for it. He chose to make a run for it.

2

It seemed to Garnett that the next street was a hundred kilometres away at the far end of a long sunlit alleyway. Behind him he could hear the bleep of a police car siren getting closer, and he was tempted to break into a run. He did not, because to have done so would have attracted attention, and so he ambled along trying to look unconcerned. He turned off into a quiet, tree-lined avenue and slowly made his way up to the High Street, unable to shake off the feeling that, behind the lace curtains in the upstairs bay windows of the terraced houses, inquisitive eyes watched him closely. It was imagination, of course, but it gave him a prickly feeling down his spine and he became unnecessarily conscious of his slight limp.

The crowds in the High Street gave him a temporary feeling of security, which had been missing from the instant he had walked out of the basement flat, and he felt absurdly grateful to them. Garnett went into the tube station, got himself a 10NP ticket from the slot machine in the booking hall and passed through the gate on to the platform. Five minutes later he hopped a train for Earls Court, changed to the Piccadilly Line, and got out at Leicester Square.

He rode the escalator up to street level, surrendered his ticket at the barrier and then looked for, and eventually found, an empty phone booth. He closed the door of the booth behind him and dialled the number he had been told to use in an emergency. The phone rang a couple of times, and then the receiver was lifted and a male voice answered.

Garnett said, 'Hullo Tim, this is Mark. I'm afraid we'll have to cry off coming round tonight.'

'Oh?'

'It's Chris, it looks as though she has picked up a bug or something. She's running a temperature.'

'I'm sorry to hear that,' the voice said in a soothing tone, 'I expect Jill will call round in the morning to see if she can do anything—run errands, that sort of thing.'

'That's very kind of you.'

'Not a bit, it's the least we can do. Give our love to Chris and tell her we hope she will soon be better.'

'Right,' said Garnett, 'I expect we shall see you next week as usual. Our love to Jill.'

He hung up, left the call box, and walked out into Coventry Street. He had an hour to kill before making for the rendezvous. He bought an *Evening News* from the vendor at the street corner and turned into the nearest coffee bar. He got himself a cup of pale, lukewarm coffee and a leathery hot dog, and then sat down in an empty booth facing the street. It always paid to watch the entrance just in case the Special Branch made a snap check. He glanced through the paper, which, for once, contained news it could be cheerful about—the Government had announced that motorists were now to be allowed fifty litres of petrol per month for pleasure purposes. It was a great step forward as the leader writer was so eager to explain, and one that would be welcomed by all sections of the community. Petrol rationing had never bothered the Resistance; they simply printed their own coupons, but at least more cars on the road meant less risk of detection. He folded up the paper and laid it to one side.

In the booth across the aisle, a young man was in earnest conversation with a girl whose face was half-hidden behind a veil of mouse-coloured hair, and, looking at her, Garnett remembered Dane, and the lost feeling came back again. Dane, who had filled a gap in his life after his wife, Liz, and his son had been killed in the thermonuclear strike on Bristol nearly five long years ago; Dane, whose blue eyes could reflect the warmth of sunlight or the chill of a glacier, depending on her mood. Dane, unfashionably tall and shapely in an era of 'Twiggies'; Dane, whose shoulder-length hair had slipped through his fingers like golden silk. He could picture her so clearly in his mind, but he would never see her again. She had died, alone and frightened on a crowded railway platform, and his chance of happiness had died with her. For some utterly incomprehensible reason his mind suddenly recalled Kampfert's arrangement of Bye Bye Blues, and he couldn't shut the melody out of his head. He pushed the half-eaten hot dog and the tasteless cup of coffee to one side and left.

He walked slowly, whilst around him the rush hour crowds moved with purpose towards the Underground. He had no need to hurry. He had no home in the suburbs to go to and no one waiting to greet him. He wondered what the future would hold for him once he got into the escape pipeline. Garnett tried to visualise living in New York or Toronto or Gary, Indiana, and he couldn't imagine what it would be like. He shoved both hands into his jacket pockets and realised that he had left the battery-powered shaver in the basement flat, and after a momentary stab of fear, he was surprised to find that he no longer cared; perhaps because he was tired of running.

He turned into the subway by the London Pavilion and became another insignificant figure in the hurrying crowd. He fed the automatic vending machine, and clutching the pasteboard ticket between thumb and forefinger, passed through the barrier and took the escalator down to the Bakerloo line. Uncaring, he allowed himself to be herded into the compartment, where he stood braced against a glass partition as more and more commuters pressed into the carriage.

He got out at Kilburn, feeling as if he had just stepped out of a Turkish bath, and walked down the steps to the street level. As he sauntered down the High Street in the direction of the cinema, yet another train thundered over the viaduct above his head.

The cinema hadn't had an outside facelift in twenty years. The concrete façade was covered in a layer of grime and soot. The interior wasn't very much better; the carpeting was threadbare, the stuffing oozing out of some of the chairs, and there was a very powerful aroma of Jeyes fluid.

The film was one of those Swedish epics, shot in almost total gloom, where the heroine was a good-looking lesbian school teacher tortured by a hopeless love for one of her fifteen-year-old pupils. The background music was suitably soulful. He sat through a whole half-hour because those were his instructions, and then Garnett got up thankfully and left by a side exit, and found himself in an almost empty car park.

He stood by the exit gazing across at the parking lot, wondering which of the three men could be his contact. He decided it couldn't be the attendant sitting in his hut reading the evening paper, nor the youth in the black leather studded jacket tinkering with the valve lift on the Honda 250cc, and that left the third man sitting in a grey Mini-van. Garnett clutched the lapels of his jacket briefly, in the way that a parson hitches his surplice before delivering the Sunday sermon, and the man, recognising the signal, got out of the van and came towards him.

The man was dressed in a snugly fitting dark blue suit and dark brown suede shoes. A mass of black wavy hair was held immaculately in place by a surfeit of hair cream, and sun glasses straddled a prominent hooked nose. He was a big man in his late twenties but already running to fat. He extended a fleshy hand, and in taking it, Garnett noticed that the back of his wrist was covered with hair. He smelled of after-shave lotion, hair oil and deodorant.

'The name's Katz, Bernie Katz,' he said, flashing a broad smile. He steered Garnett towards the van. 'It's a pleasure to meet you, Mr Abel.'

Garnett got into the van without saying a word. If Katz wanted to call him Abel, then that was all right by him.

As he swung the Mini-van out of the car park into the High Street, Katz said, 'I expect you're glad to be on the move again.' It was one of those questions which didn't need an answer. They were moving through a neighbourhood which was foreign to Garnett. A maze of high Victorian tenements stood shoulder to shoulder in drab uniformity, and it seemed absurd that these mean streets should have such exotic names as Mogadishu, Asmara and Keren. Katz twisted and turned through one identical street after another, often doubling back on his tracks, crossing and re-crossing the main railway line until Garnett was convinced they were going round in circles.

They passed but one vehicle, a Mr Whippy van, trying to drum up a little evening trade. And then, when he was least expecting it, Katz turned sharply across the road and shot into a narrow drive in front of a semi-detached house and went straight into the open garage, which was barely large enough to swallow the van. He slammed the brakes on just in time to prevent the van piling into the work bench at the back of the garage. Katz got out, closed the garage doors, and then tapping on the side window, signalled Garnett to follow him. There was a small door, next to the work bench, which opened out into the back yard; and skirting the coal bunkers on one side and the apparently empty house on the other, they made their way through an overgrown garden, which was enclosed by a tall privet hedge. There was a padlocked wooden shed at the bottom of the garden, and in the gathering dusk, Katz experienced some difficulty in fitting the key into the lock.

The floor of the shed was littered with garden tools, bags of fertiliser, and old newspapers. Katz heaved them to one side, raised the trap door and shone a torch into the open shaft. He grinned at Garnett and said, 'Mind how you go—it's a long drop.'

Garnett sat on the lip of the hole and eased himself into the void. Katz was right. It was a long drop, and in the feeble light it seemed even further. He landed awkwardly and pitched forward on to his hands and knees, grazing his face against the earth wall. Katz laughed softly. 'I told you to watch it,' he whispered. Katz followed, landing efficiently. For a big man he was surprisingly light on his feet.

The tunnel was narrow and they were forced to walk in a stooped position, shoulders brushing the dank earth on either side. After fifteen metres the tunnel merged into another larger one, which crossed at right angles, and it was possible to stand upright once more.

Katz said, 'Turn right.'

'Where are we?' Garnett's voice sounded unnaturally loud in the chamber.

'In a disused GPO tunnel. You go ahead, I'll follow.'

A faint light flickered ahead of them, which had nothing to do with the torch Katz was holding, and then, as they came closer to the source, Garnett saw that a blanket had been crudely rigged to the roof of the tunnel in an effort to seal off most of the light. He pushed the blanket to one side and stepped into the alcove. Katz followed him.

The smoke, given off by the flickering yellow flame of the hurricane lamp which hung from a nail driven into the wall, drifted up to the curved red-brick roof, mingled with, and finally absorbed, the smell of the tobacco fumes. The smaller of the two men facing Garnett was leaning against the wall sucking on a Dunhill, and the spittle in the stem of his pipe produced a noise not unlike water gurgling down a waste outlet. He was about five feet eight inches tall, stockily built, badger-grey, and his face was weather-beaten. When he spoke, it was with a deliberately cultivated Dorset accent, for it amused him to be taken for a farmer. He was, in fact, a Superintendent of Police; his name was Endicott, and he liked Garnett about as much as a mongoose likes a snake.

The other man was much taller, but failed to give the impression of commanding height. The years spent in hiding had left their mark on Vickers; his hair had turned silver, and his bloodhound face was lined and drawn. But for the war and the Soviet occupation, he might have joined the fraternity of retired admirals and generals who used to live in and around Salisbury. Now he had to keep running in order to stay alive.

Garnett said, 'Hullo General, I didn't expect to see you.'

'No, I don't suppose you did.'

Garnett moistened his lips. 'I presume everything is still okay? I mean you haven't changed your mind about sending me out of the country, have you?'

The assumption seemed to amuse Endicott. He snorted and almost choked on a lungful of Balkan Sobranie.

Vickers said, 'We have a problem.'

'I didn't think it would be easy, but the accidental death of a policeman shouldn't throw a spanner in the works.'

'That isn't the problem.'

'No?'

'No. The problem is that we appear to have a split in the Movement, and Coleman isn't available to deal with it.'

'Why not?'

'He's had a coronary.'

'How bad?'

'It killed him.'

Garnett leaned back against the wall and lit a cigarette. He supposed he ought to feel some regret, but he felt nothing. The news didn't altogether surprise him, because Coleman at sixty-three had been overweight, suffered from high blood pressure and chronic asthma. The best that could be said for him was that he had been a ruth- lessly efficient head of Security. There had never been anyone quite like Coleman in the Resistance, and with any luck, they would never see his like again.

Garnett said, 'I suppose I should say I am sorry, but

in the circumstances, that would be hypocritical. He did his level best to get me killed.'

Endicott tapped his pipe out against the wall.

'That's past history,' he grunted.

Garnett said, 'You may think so, but what happened a few months ago is scarcely ancient history to me.'

'We are not really interested in your persecution complex, David,' Vickers said in a mild voice, 'the fact is we have a split in the Movement and I want you to look into it.'

'Is that a request or an order?'

'A request.'

Garnett dropped a cigarette on to the stone floor and crushed it under the heel of his shoe.

'Well now, General,' he said pleasantly, 'I don't want you to think I am unco-operative, but, as I recall our last meeting some four months ago, you said, and I happen to recall your exact words, you said, "I promised to get you out of the country and I will". So, to put it in a nutshell General, I want out.' There was an awkward pause while Vickers let his gaze travel from the top of Garnett's head down to his feet and back again. Katz coughed nervously and scuffed a foot on the uneven concrete floor. Endicott took out his tobacco pouch and began to prime his pipe again.

Vickers said, and there was a silky edge to his voice, 'I didn't set a date for your departure, did I?'

'You're about to tell me the escape route is still closed.'

'As a matter of fact, I am.'

'I'll wait until it's re-opened.'

'That's your prerogative,' Vickers said calmly, 'of course, it may so happen that you will lose your place in the queue.' A droplet of water fell from the arched roof, hit Garnett on the nape of his neck, and slowly trickled down his back.

'You bastard,' Garnett said quietly, 'I don't really have any choice, do I?'

'Let's say I'm glad you volunteered.'

'All right, so I've volunteered—so what do you want me to do?'

Vickers cleared his throat and said, 'I don't know how familiar you are with the history of the Yugoslav Resistance in World War Two, but we have the makings of a parallel situation in this country now. Initially, the Yugoslav Resistance was organised by General Milhailovitch, a right wing, pro-royalist officer, whose followers were known as Chetniks. Round about 1943 a Communist called Tito emerged on the scene with his Partisans. Tito had a wider appeal than Milhailovitch, and his movement expanded rapidly. It wasn't long before both Resistance organisations were accusing each other of co-operating with the Germans. We, in Cairo, had to decide which organisation to back—the Chetniks or the Partisans. We plumped for Tito, because he was the more effective of the two, and there was some foundation to the story that Milhailovitch was more interested in fighting the Communists than the Fascists. Endicott can bring you up to date on our situation.'

Endicott struck a match against the wall and lit his pipe. Getting the tobacco to burn was a long-drawn-out process which irritated Vickers.

'For God's sake,' he snapped, 'get on with it. We haven't got all night.'

The rebuke had no effect on Endicott. In an unruffled voice he said, 'The trouble at present is confined to the south-west, where for the past three and a half years, our Head of Operations has been Richard Olds. Olds is a thirty-four-year-old building contractor, height five six, weight one forty, thin fair hair, no visible distinguishing marks, married, one son, two daughters, ages eleven, seven and six respectively.'

Endicott paused and shook the spittle out of his pipe. It was part of his make-up to imitate a computer; the only trouble was that, in Garnett's experience, you could never be sure whether he was talking in centimetres or feet, pounds or kilos, until you applied the law of probability.

'Olds was a hard-liner like you, Garnett; he believed in hitting everything and everyone in sight. Until eighteen months ago, his deputy was Colin McDonald. We don't know too much about McDonald, except that he is a liberal-minded man who favoured a more selective terrorist campaign. He didn't go along with shooting people just because they were in police uniform. Anyway they split up over this and other issues which we are not too clear about. McDonald went his separate way and formed his own organisation, which until a few months ago, was of no great significance. We've no reliable estimate of his strength now, but it could be between three fifty and a thousand active members. Until just over three months ago both organisations more or less rubbed along together, and then the situation changed.' Endicott reached inside his breast pocket and brought out a manilla envelope which he tossed across the room to Garnett. Garnett caught it one-handed and ripped it open. The envelope contained four photographs.

Endicott said, 'The man lying on the pavement with his legs still in the car is Danny Sykes, a taxi driver, who was killed outside Swindon station with a sawn-off 12 bore shotgun a few minutes before midnight on 16 May. The three men lying in the debris of a coffee bar in Trowbridge were killed by a hand grenade on 3 June at about 9:30 pm; the man and the woman hanging from a tree were found near Chitterne in the early hours of 17 June. The house in the last picture used to be in Amesbury. It was dynamited at 8:20 pm on 2 July; five people were killed. McDonald's people were the victims of the first three incidents; Olds' lot were on the receiving end of the fourth. You can guess the rest; McDonald accused Olds of selling out to the Russians, and Olds virtually says the same of McDonald.'

Endicott stopped talking abruptly. It was just as if somebody had switched off the current and the machine had come to a grinding halt.

Vickers selected a filter tip and inserted it in a black

22

holder. 'An interesting situation,' he observed mildly. He lit the cigarette with a gold lighter and blew a smoke ring towards the roof. 'You might say that there is something in what McDonald says, since he appears to have suffered the most. On the other hand, it is just possible that the Russians have infiltrated both organisations. I want you to check it out; start with Olds, find out whether or not he is getting paid off; then switch to McDonald if you draw a blank there.'

Garnett said, 'Do I get any help?'

'Certainly. Tomorrow you'll catch a train to Salisbury where arrangements have been made for you to stay with Walter Dinkmeyer. He's an American who runs an employment agency. He lives at 19, Wimbourne Street.'

Garnett said, 'It's no go, General. Just over three years ago, I shot and killed a man in the city centre. Maybe Willie Vosper didn't have many friends in Salisbury, but I wouldn't like to put it to the test.'

Vickers stared at Garnett, and his face slowly took on a pained expression, which was meant to convey that this was not the sort of defeatist attitude he expected of his subordinates.

'I'm disappointed in you,' he said, in a voice tinged with sadness, 'frankly, I expected a more pragmatic outlook. Who now remembers Commissar Willie Vosper? And who would connect you with his assassination? No one, because you were in Salisbury for less than twenty-four hours when you did the job. The risk in going back there is insignificant.' He paused, before ending on a firm note. 'I'm afraid your objection is over-ruled, Garnett.'

Garnett said dryly, 'You've no idea how relieved I am to hear that the risk is insignificant.'

Vickers raised one eyebrow, looked as though he was going to rise to the bait, and then changed his mind. He ejected the burning cigarette from the holder and crushed it underfoot. 'Katz will tag along with you,' he said, 'he's fluent at Russian and a trained interrogator as well as being a chartered accountant. He'll be staying with friends in Winchester. You can call him on 56995 when you want him.'

'Anything else I should know?'

'Keep in touch with me, don't take any corrective action without first obtaining my approval. Is that clear?'

'Absolutely. How do I get in touch?'

'You'll have a communicator. She's waiting for you at Brockenhurst Farm in Sutton Veny, a small village just outside Warminster.'

'She?'

'Dane,' said Vickers.

For a moment Garnett thought he was mistaken, but there was a tentative smile on Vicker's lips, which confirmed what he thought he had heard. There was a peculiar feeling in the pit of his stomach, not unlike the sinking sensation a ride on a roller-coaster can give you.

'Just four months ago,' Garnett said in a cracked voice, 'you told me she had committed suicide. Now you tell me she is alive.'

'I lied to you four months ago.'

'Why?'

'Because it was necessary. I told you that, when we moved Dane from Portsmouth to London, her papers were in order ... they weren't. Our people slipped up, and as luck would have it, she was stopped by the police at the railway station. She didn't panic, in fact she kept her head remarkably well. They arrested her, because as a visitor, she had failed to register with the local police. She went up before the local beaks and got two months' detention.'

'You could have told me that much,' Garnett said harshly.

'And what would have been your reaction? You'd have gone after her and done something bloody stupid. Her chance of survival lay in not being connected with the raid on Parkhurst, and we knew there was not much chance of that happening, as long as you kept out of the picture. As soon as she was sentenced, I knew she was safe. They shave their heads as soon as they get them inside the Detention Centre, and it's surprising how much difference a bald head can make to a woman's appearance. Believe me, the best possible solution was to let Dane do bird, and allow you to assume she was dead.'

The smile was warm on Vickers' face, and it had a goading effect on Garnett. He balled up his fists and took a pace forward, 'You fucking bastard,' he said thickly.

Vickers knew what was coming, and he spoke quietly to Katz, and Katz did the rest. Big, hairy, lavender-scented Katz sank a fist into Garnett's kidneys, and the world was suddenly a dark and painful place. As he went down on to his knees, he heard Vickers say, 'I'm awfully sorry about that, Garnett,' and then the light went out.

3

THE TRAIN CURVED into the station, and a Wiltshire voice, its accent amplified by the tannoy, announced, 'Salisbury, this is Salisbury.'

Garnett stood up and reached for the suitcase in the rack above his head, feeling a twinge of pain in the area of his right kidney, a positive reminder, that Katz was Vickers' man. He opened the carriage door, dropped down on to the platform, and walked to the barrier. There was, as usual, a policeman on duty inside the entrance hall, but, apart from a cursory glance, he showed no interest in Garnett.

Heat waves shimmered above the Cathedral spire in the distance, and the tarmac in the station yard was tacky underfoot. A taxi driver in shirt sleeves caught his eye, and eased his Vauxhall Cresta forward until it was abreast of him. Garnett slung his case into the back and got in beside the driver. As they moved off Garnett gave him the address in Wimbourne Street.

At the bottom of the road they turned into Bridge Street and headed towards the Poultry Cross. The taxi driver was the talkative type. A mine of information, he had missed his vocation as a guide for the State Tourist Board. 'Been here before, have you?' he asked.

'No,' said Garnett.

'Well, it's a grand place for history is Salisbury. The Cathedral now, took thirty-eight years to build and was finished in 1258. The spire was added on in the fourteenth century, and it's the tallest in England—four hundred and four feet it is. Constable loved that church, he did.'

'Did he?'

'Oh yes, he painted lots of views of it.'

The crowds were thick on the pavements as they neared the centre of the City, and Garnett saw a number of stalls around the Poultry Cross. 'Market day?' he asked casually.

'Yes, every Tuesday and Saturday; Wednesday's early closing day.'

The traffic circuit led them round the Market Square, past the Guildhall, with its clock face showing 12:30, up Winchester Street, along Rampart Road to Fowler Hill, and then across to Wimbourne Street. Garnett paid off the cab outside number 19, a detached three-storeyed red-brick house dating from the middle thirties, and which now sported a signboard in the privet hedge bordering the front garden. The signboard said Cranleigh Guest House.

He pushed open the front gate, walked up the concrete path, read a sign in the downstairs bay window announcing there were no vacancies, put his suitcase down and rang the doorbell. The door was opened by a slender, flaxen-haired, teen-age girl; a listlessness of expression and a curious blankness in the blue eyes suggested to Garnett that her IQ did not match her shapely figure. Garnett picked up his suitcase and slipped past the girl into the hall.

'Hey,' she said slowly, 'where do you think you're going; can't you read the notice—we're full up.'

'You have a room reserved for me,' said Garnett.

A voice from the back room said, 'What's the trouble, honey?'

The man appeared from the kitchen. He was powerfully built, broad across the shoulders and narrow hipped, but the years had caught up with him in the form of a sagging waistline, and his curly red hair was beginning to take on the shade of pepper and salt. His sleeves, rolled up above the elbows, revealed forearms covered in freckles, and a matt of hair peeped out above the V of the open-necked shirt. He had an open, youngish, good-humoured looking face—Hollywood's model of the boy next door in middle age.

The man said, 'I'm Dinkmeyer, what can I do for you?'

'You have a reservation for me. My name is Abel, George Abel.'

'Of 10, Temple Gardens, Kilburn. Right?'

'Right,' said Garnett.

'Room 14, third floor back. Have you eaten?'

'No.'

Dinkmeyer took the suitcase out of his hand. 'Tell you what, honey,' he said to the girl, 'suppose you fix Mr Abel a couple of sandwiches and a cup of coffee, and bring them up to his room on a tray.' He turned away and started up the staircase; Garnett followed him.

Dinkmeyer said, 'Have you been to Salisbury before?'

'Fleetingly,' said Garnett.

'Enough to know your way around?'

'At a push.'

Dinkmeyer stopped before a white painted door with a brass door knob. 'This is your room,' he said. He threw open the door, walked inside and put the suitcase down on the floor. The windows overlooked a large back garden, secluded by a high privet hedge. The lawn was well kept with neat borders around the rose beds. A couple of apple trees, heavy with fruit, grew in one corner of the garden directly opposite a greenhouse full of ripening tomatoes.

'You like the view?' said Dinkmeyer.

'It's very peaceful.'

'I guess it is, we like it anyway.' He paused, and then with a conscious effort became more business-like. 'I'll run you down to the office when you've had a bite to eat. Might as well see the place where you're going to be working for the next few weeks.' He walked out of the room, leaving Garnett to unpack.

A few minutes later, the flaxen-haired girl brought up a plate of sandwiches and a cup of iced coffee. The coffee was refreshing, but the sandwiches were made of thin slices of tinned meat and the bread was curling at the edges;

all the same, he was hungry enough to ignore the cotton-wool taste. He finished eating, put the cup and the plate on the bedside table, and went downstairs. Dinkmeyer was waiting for him in the hall—he obviously didn't believe in taking long over lunch. He said, 'I thought you'd gone to sleep on me. What kept you?'

If he expected a reply, he didn't wait for it. He opened the front door, ushered Garnett out of the house, down the front path, and into a sky-blue Volkswagen parked by the kerbside. Dinkmeyer got in behind the wheel, started up and raced the engine until it almost seemed to shriek with agony, and then let the clutch in with a bang. The car reared like a startled horse. With a broad grin on his face Dinkmeyer said, 'Say what you like, this bug may not look up to much but the Volks is a glutton for punishment.' Garnett didn't doubt that statement for one moment.

The office was located at the top of Castle Street, south of the railway bridge and facing a garage. Painted a dun colour on the outside, the interior was equally unimpressive. The distempered walls looked in need of a touch up, and there were dirty marks on the off-white skirting boards. A varnished counter, the top of which was covered in cigarette burns, divided the room in two, and kept the office staff and clients apart. The staff was a prim old maid with a face like a dried-up prune, dressed in a tweed skirt and a long-sleeved blouse. The name plate on the counter said she was Miss A. Tate. It seemed to Garnett that Dinkmeyer wasn't offering the Labour Exchange much competition. Dinkmeyer raised the counter flap and walked through. He nodded at Miss Tate and said, 'We're in conference; I don't want to be disturbed.' Miss Tate puckered up her lips, and the sour expression on her face indicated she'd taken an instant dislike to Garnett. The feeling was mutual.

Dinkmeyer's office was at the back, and was not much bigger than a priest's hole. There was just enough space for a desk to be slanted diagonally across the room and one upright chair for visitors. Dinkmeyer eased himself into the chair behind the desk and said ruefully, 'Now you see why I have to run a guest house on the side.' He opened a drawer, took out a packet of gum, and slipped a stick into his mouth. 'Okay,' he said, 'what do you want to know?'

'Is it safe to talk here?'

'Sure,' Dinkmeyer said amiably, 'I de-bugged the office myself and made it soundproof.'

Garnett said, 'I'm interested in you.'

Dinkmeyer stopped chewing. His pale blue eyes took on an innocent, surprised look. 'Well now, why should that be?'

'Because you're an American and you're still living in this country.'

'There's no accounting for taste.'

'That's no kind of an answer.'

'You want to know why I'm still walking around free, right? Well, I'll tell you—I'm respectable, that's why. You see, they have me marked down as an anti-Vietnam demonstrator, because, way back, I was mixed up in the Grosvenor Square riot. The fact is, they've got the story wrong. Sure I was there, but I was no demonstrator, believe you me. Fact is, I took a swing at one of the hippies and missed, and nailed one of your policemen instead. I was a crew chief in the USAF at the time, and Third Air Force at South Ruislip didn't go for my story. I drew a court-martial, and that made me as good as a pinko when Special Branch looked into my background. So they think I'm okay.'

'That's trusting of them.'

'Yeah, isn't it,' Dinkmeyer said in a flat voice.

'How well do you know the local business people?'

'Try me.'

'What do you know about Richard Olds?'

Dinkmeyer looked up at the ceiling as if seeking inspiration. 'Olds,' he said, 'is a small building-contractor; employs about fifteen people full time, and has his offices and yard in Gayton Street near the station. He's married, has three children, one boy, two girls, ages eleven, seven and six. His wife's name is Karen; she's around thirty, slim, dark, I guess you would call her attractive, although she dresses a bit like a suburban matron; she's active in the PTA and popular with her neighbours. They have a nice house called Greenacres in Chapperton Vale just off the Blandford Road. They do a fair bit of entertaining—bridge nights, that sort of thing. He is the head of Resistance Operations for the south-west. Plays it cool by keeping well in with the Russians. As a matter of fact, he landed the contract for the upkeep of their barracks at Wilton. A very smart boy.'

'You think so?'

'Sure. He's been in the Resistance for nearly five years without being rumbled. That makes him a smart boy in my book.'

Garnett lit a cigarette. 'On another tack,' he said, 'how do we explain my protracted stay in Salisbury to the police?'

'You've bought yourself a partnership in the business.'

'Have I?'

'You bet,' said Dinkmeyer, 'I've got the papers in my safe to prove it.'

The office was like an oven. The sweat streamed off Dinkmeyer's face, hung in the folds of his neck, and emerged in dark grey patches under his armpits. Garnett loosened his tie and undid the top button of his shirt. Under his jacket the nylon shirt clung to his back like a wet dishcloth. The cigarette between his damp fingers peeled apart, spilling hot ash and tobacco on to the worn linoleum. He leaned over the desk and stubbed out the remains of the cigarette in the ashtray.

Garnett said, 'How much longer do you plan to stay in this sweatbox?'

'Most of the afternoon, unless you have something else in mind.'

'I want to borrow your car.'

Dinkmeyer tossed the car keys across the desk. 'You going to be long?' he asked.

'A couple of hours, maybe three.'

Dinkmeyer sighed audibly, 'I guess I'll have to walk home. Don't burn up too many kilometres; I've only got twenty litres to see me through to the end of the month.'

'I'll give you some coupons.'

Dinkmeyer stopped chewing gum. 'No thanks,' he said, 'I play it straight.'

'I thought everyone dabbled on the black market.'

'Not me.'

'Suppose I need the car again before the end of the month?'

'I'll get you a bicycle.'

'Thanks,' said Garnett, 'you're a big help.' He walked out of the inner office, nodded at Miss Tate, and collected another sour look.

He got into the Volkswagen, drove up Castle Street, filtered off at the roundabout into St Paul's Road, and then turned into Fisherton Street. The police station was on the outskirts of the city. Before the war, it had been the headquarters of the Wiltshire Constabulary, but now there was a big sign in the middle of the lawn in front of the three-storeyed brick building which said: Sixth District, National Police Force. A steel-helmeted policeman with a Lee Enfield .38 pistol loitered inside the door.

Garnett left the car in the parking lot, showed his identity card to the sentry, and started to walk into the building. He was stopped by a second policeman, put up against the wall and searched. The searcher was cold, arrogant and hostile. On the pretext of making a thorough job of it, he roughed Garnett up in a mild way, seeking to bruise the spare flesh between his probing fingers.

'All right,' he said harshly, 'you're clean, what do you want?'

Garnett lowered his arms and turned round. He found himself looking into narrow unblinking hazel eyes, and he knew that given half a chance, he wouldn't find it difficult to kill this man. Garnett said, 'I want to register as a resident of this city.'

'Census Bureau is on the ground floor, end room on the left.' The policeman paused and then said, 'I've got a good memory for faces, so just watch your step.'

It was a meaningless threat, and Garnett knew it, but it did no harm to seem intimidated. He nodded gravely, hoping the expression on his face gave the impression that he had taken the warning to heart. He walked into the Census Bureau, smiled at the woman behind the counter, and took a copy of National Government Form C2 out of the holder on the wall, and completed the section dealing with a permanent change of residence. He checked the application through and then pushed it across the counter together with his Social Security Card. The woman picked up the card, nervously flicked a strand of hair out of her eyes, and then, looking up, compared the photograph on the card with the figure standing before her, and then began to go through the form in detail.

Behind her bent head, prominently displayed on the wall, was a list of wanted men. It was not entirely up to date, and it was far from accurate, but there was one new addition—an identikit portrait of a dark-haired man. The writing underneath was too small to read at that distance, but Garnett didn't need to see the legend. It was far from a good likeness, but it was still a shock to see himself on the wanted list.

The woman said, 'Mr Abel.'

Garnett said, 'Yes?'

'You've omitted to fill in your religious denomination —I presume it's Jewish?'

'No, as a matter of fact I'm C of E.'

The woman coloured slightly, scribbled his new address on the Social Security Card, franked it, and then pushed the card back under the grille without saying another word. Garnett picked it up and walked out of the police station. The sentry on the gate ignored him. He found that oddly reassuring.

He cleared the road block on the outskirts of Salisbury, and pointed the car in the direction of Warminster.

With an open road stretching before him, Garnett was tempted to put his foot down, but to have done so might have drawn unwelcome attention from a prowl car lying up in a side road. Safety these days depended on staying out of the limelight. Just about a kilometre beyond Heytesbury, he turned off the A 36 on to the minor road leading to Sutton Veny.

Brockenhurst Farm was on the outskirts of the village; the house, Georgian in character, looked neglected. Window frames had peeled down to the bare wood, a couple of displaced slate tiles lodged precariously in the guttering, and clumps of nettles choked the small front garden. Garnett swung the car into the yard, jolted over the rutted, hard baked earth, and pulled up in front of the barn. A woman, drying her hands on an apron, poked her head out of the kitchen.

Garnett opened the door of the Volkswagen and slid out. He smiled and said, 'My name is George Abel; I've come to see my cousin.'

The woman looked him up and down, and then jerked her head in the direction of the barn, 'In there,' she said.

He found Dane standing by a tractor, with the sleeves of her tartan shirt rolled up above the elbows; her head was bent forward, and he could see that she was engrossed in the task of sandpapering a row of sparking plugs. Her face, hands, and faded blue jeans were smeared with oil. Her blonde hair was short like a boy's.

'Hullo,' he said softly.

She looked up quickly and he was shaken by her appearance. Her cheeks were hollow, and there were deep purple shadows under her eyes.

'Well, well,' she said bitterly, 'look who's here. I didn't expect to see you again.'

'Nor I you,' Garnett said. 'Until the other day, I thought you were dead.'

'How convenient. I might have been better off dead at that.'

'Don't say that. I know it couldn't have been a picnic for you.'

'What do you know about it?' She ran a hand through her short fair hair. 'Look at me. You know what they did? They shaved my head until it was as bare as an eggshell, and then they jammed me in a cell with seven other women. Have you any idea what that was like?'

'I can guess.' Garnett moved closer to put his arm around her shoulders, but she stepped back out of his reach.

'Oh no you can't,' she said bitterly. 'Don't imagine we were all girls together—like hell we were. There were all sorts in that cell—shop-lifters, drug addicts, perverts —you name it. Only the collaborators had it made.'

Dane paused and took in a deep gulp of air. Her eyes glinted angrily because she could see that Garnett was struggling to find the right words.

Lamely, he repeated, 'I thought you were dead.'

'So you said before. And how was I supposed to have died?'

'Vickers told me you committed suicide when the police stopped you on Portsmouth Station.'

'And you believed that?'

'He made it sound convincing enough.'

'If you could believe that I would kill myself, then you don't really know me at all.' Her mouth set in a hard, straight line as she clenched her jaws and blinked her eyes repeatedly. 'All I needed was a message, something to hang on to. Was that too much to ask?'

'No, of course it wasn't,' said Garnett, 'but doesn't it occur to you that I was told you were dead so that I wouldn't try to make contact with you?'

'It occurs to me that you might have taken a bit more trouble to check that story instead of sitting back all these weeks doing nothing. To think I was anxious about you because you were wounded. I even worried in case you were picked up.' She laughed mirthlessly, 'I should have saved my sympathy for myself.'

Garnett moved forward again and stretched out a hand

35

to touch her, but she backed away spitting like a cat. 'Leave me alone. Since we have to work together again, we'll keep it on a business-like footing. We sell our farm produce in Salisbury Market every Tuesday and Saturday. If you've got anything for me, make a purchase from our stall, and I will meet you in the Wheatsheaf after the market closes.'

'It's too insecure.'

'Insecure or not,' she said with an edge to her voice, 'that's the way it's got to be. Now get the hell out of here.'

Garnett said, 'All right, I'll go along with you this once, but next time we'll make some other arrangement.'

Garnett knew that nothing he could say now would make the slightest difference. He could understand her antagonism and he just hoped she would get over it in time. He turned on his heel and walked out of the barn. He got into the Volkswagen, gunned the engine into life, made a U-turn, and swept out of the yard.

He motored back to Salisbury, idling along at 60kph, not really concentrating on the road, but thinking about Vickers and getting angrier by the minute. Next time they met, he promised himself, next time they came face to face, he'd make sure that Katz, or someone else like Katz, wasn't standing behind him when he got ready to throw a punch.

He first noticed the Vauxhall Victor in his rear view mirror after he had passed through Codford. The car had a beat-up look about it, and all that remained of the offside headlamp was the chrome reflector lying askew in the socket. The wing was crumpled and rust patches showed through the raised paintwork.

Two people sat up front. One, thick-set with close cropped black hair was obviously a man; the other, smaller, with a narrow fine-boned face and long brown hair could have been a woman. One other point interested Garnett; no matter how much he varied his speed, the Vauxhall remained a steady twenty metres behind him, as though the driver was taking part in a procession. He was beginning to get a fixation about it, until, coming up to Wilton, the Vauxhall suddenly picked up speed and went past the Volks like a thunderbolt, its holed exhaust giving a fair impersonation of a hot rod. The passenger with the shoulder-length hair turned to stare impassively at Garnett. He was wearing a lime-green shirt with mother of pearl buttons as big as golf balls down the front, and a yellow scarf at the neck. He turned right round in his seat and studied Garnett intently as the Vauxhall drew ahead, and then, quite deliberately, he poked out his tongue, threw back his head and laughed, and then turned once more to face the front.

A few minutes later the Vauxhall passed him again going in the opposite direction. Neither man looked at Garnett. They might have been yobos out on a joy ride on black market petrol, or they might just possibly be representative of something more sinister. Garnett wished he could remember just where they had picked him up.

4

THE SUN WAS up there blazing down from a cloudless sky, and it had been doing just that for the past seventy-one days without a break, and the farmers were grumbling because they wanted rain, and that at least was normal. Most other people were looking for rain too, because the English aren't used to a hot spell which goes on for more than a week, and they begin to miss the chill wind and rain.

The shirt was sticking to his back, and the sweat, running down his legs, collected in a reservoir above his ankle where the trouser leg was imprisoned by bicycle clips; but Garnett wasn't complaining about the weather; it was merely Dinkmeyer's idea of transport which got on his wick. The bike was an old Raleigh with bent pedals which knocked against the frame at each revolution, and the chain, the links of which could not have seen a drop of oil in years, screeched in protest every time he exerted a downward thrust with his foot.

He propped the bike against the kerb outside Dink-meyer's office in Castle Street, but didn't bother to chain the front wheel, because he saw no point in putting an obstacle in the way of anyone who felt like stealing it.

Garnett pushed open the door of the agency and went inside. Miss Tate looked up furtively, gave him a frosty smile, and then bent over her typewriter again. Dinkmeyer was in shirt sleeves, leaning back in the chair with his feet crossed on the desk, his jaw working overtime on a piece of gum. 'Any luck?' he said, his hand waving at the empty chair in front of the desk.

Garnett flopped down into the chair and lit a cigarette. 'I ran my eye over Olds' business premises.'

'So?'

'You could have saved me the journey; he's a small contractor, a glorified odd job man.'

'He employs fifteen men.'

'So you said. I don't see how he does it.'

'He has that repair contract with the Soviets,' said Dinkmeyer.

'I didn't see much evidence of building materials in his yard.'

'Maybe he has a store shed on site?'

Garnett drummed his fingers on the desk. Presently he said, 'Is Olds active?'

'He keeps in shape.'

'I didn't mean that—is his organisation active?'

'Everything they do is well planned and well executed. They take their time over setting up a job, but I guess you'd say they were pretty active.'

'Who do they hit most—the Soviets or the National Police Force?'

Dinkmeyer uncrossed his legs and swung them off the desk. 'I suppose it's about fifty-fifty.'

'You puzzle me,' said Garnett.

'Oh, yeah?'

'I don't see where you fit in.'

'I'm just a sympathetic observer, okay?'

'For whom?'

'Well, it sure as hell isn't the United States Government.'

'That leaves the field fairly open.'

'It certainly does,' Dinkmeyer agreed happily, 'and that's how it's going to stay.'

'Are you using the Volkswagen this afternoon?'

Dinkmeyer's smile faded. 'Aw, come on,' he said, 'I already told you I don't have the gas coupons for you to burn up.'

'I'll stay within the city limits.'

'What's wrong with the bike, or walking, come to that?'

'The bike is a heap of rust, and walking takes up too much time. It's Wednesday, early closing day, you won't be needing it.'

Dinkmeyer sighed. 'The trouble with you British,' he said, 'is that you are always looking for a hand-out.' He tossed the key across the desk. 'Are you coming back to the house for a bite, or are you going to eat here in town?'

'I thought I'd try the Red Lion.'

Dinkmeyer tossed another key across the desk. 'Okay,' he said, 'you lock up. You'll find the car in row N out back in the park, and the meter charge is about expired. Try not to get me a ticket.' He slid round the desk and walked out of the office.

A couple of minutes later Dinkmeyer re-appeared, red in the face. 'Hey,' he said, 'where did you leave the bike?'

'Right outside the office.'

'Well, I'll be goddamned, someone's stolen it.'

'The thief deserves a reward,' said Garnett.

'I paid two pounds for that bike.'

'You were robbed.'

'That I was,' Dinkmeyer said with feeling. He slammed the door behind him.

A little after two o'clock, Garnett drove out to Chapperton Vale and stalled the Volkswagen outside Olds' house. For the benefit of any onlooker, he repeatedly attempted to start the car, and then got out slamming the door behind him. He walked round to the back, raised the cowling, and pretended to poke around inside the engine.

Greenacres was not a small house. Pre-war it would have fetched around fifteen thousand, and at that price, a lot of people would have thought they had picked up a bargain. It was a rambling sort of place, partially screened by a tall cypress hedge, with a drive which curved up to the front door and then circled back round a small rock-garden. Behind the rock-garden and separate from the house, a double garage with tip-up doors yawned at him. Its sole occupant was a red Mini Cooper in almost show-room condition.

A woman in a short-sleeved, figure-hugging, dark blue dress tripped across the drive in high-heeled shoes, her black hair bobbing up and down on her shoulders. She almost ran into the garage, got into the Mini and fired the engine into life. She swept up to the main road, glanced left and right, and then turned right. The car was in top gear inside thirty metres. Garnett closed the engine cowling, got into the car and motored up the road. He made a series of right turns until he had doubled back on his tracks, when he then turned left.

It was almost 2:30 and the street was deserted. He wondered what most housewives would be doing at 2:30 in the afternoon; perhaps they did the ironing while they listened to the radio. On impulse he swung the car into the drive of Greenacres and parked it outside the front door. If you are going to break into a house, he told himself, be as bold as brass—make it look as if you are paying a social call. He got out and rang the front door bell. Nobody answered. Garnett walked round to the back of the house and tried the French windows of the lounge. Karen Olds was definitely a careless house-wife—the doors were unlocked.

The lounge was a page out of *Ideal Home*; wall-to-wall Wilton carpet and expensively upholstered furniture, and it occurred to him that pre-war Olds must have had a flourishing business. There was nothing pre-war about the well-stocked cocktail cabinet which contained bottles of gin, whisky and brandy labelled 'For Government Forces Only, Not For Re-Sale To The General Public'. He checked out the dining room, kitchen and study, getting the feel of the house and its occupants. He climbed the stairs, searched through three bedrooms belonging to the children and a guest room before he found the one he wanted. A glance through the built-in wardrobe showed him that all of Olds' suits had been made pre-war, whilst Karen Olds apparently made most of her own clothes, assuming the lengths of dress material were anything to go by. The drawers of the dressing table were stuffed with underwear and pack upon pack of tights. No matter how long the occupation lasted, it was going to be quite some time before Karen Olds began to feel the pinch.

Coleman, when he had been Head of Security, used to say you could tell a lot about people you hadn't met, just by giving their bedrooms the once over. The clothes would give you a line on their taste and might also indicate the nature of their sex life; untidy drawers and cupboards could point to an untidy, disorganised person; Coleman, of course, had been a disciple of Freud. Well, all right, Garnett thought, if we believe Coleman's theory, Karen Olds is a very uncomplicated woman with normal impulses, but she certainly doesn't fit Dinkmeyer's description of the earnest PTA type. He closed up the drawers, left the bedroom and went downstairs. He left by the front door, got into the Volkswagen and drove back to the city centre.

Garnett was just passing the Cathedral Close when it seemed that an invisible giant gave the car a shove, and he was forced to correct the steering. A split second later there was a loud thunder-clap, which momentarily led him to believe that a storm had suddenly built up, until he noticed a pall of grey-black smoke climbing leisurely into the azure sky. He turned the corner by the garage and followed the one way circuit past Woolworths, and made his way back to Castle Street via the Poultry Cross. He was stopped by a policeman at the junction of Blue Boar Row and Minster Street.

Sitting there in the silence of the car, he could hear the wail of fire engines and ambulance cars moving towards the pall of smoke, which appeared to be behind the Post Office on Castle Street. His eye lit on a bill-board standing outside the newsagent's across the road; bold orange letters on a yellow background said: '37th National Lottery. Results by closed-circuit TV today followed by Bingo. Big Cash Prizes. Short Talk by Representative Gibbs. All at Unity Theatre, Admission Free.'

And that, Garnett thought, was about the only way

the Government could get anyone to listen to a political speech these days. It suddenly struck him that the Unity Theatre was just behind the Post Office.

He sat there for the better part of two hours, smoking one cigarette after another, longing to ask the policeman what was going on but not daring to, because he knew from past experience that they were always out to make trouble after an incident, and he didn't want to be run in because a Bogie was feeling liverish.

Eventually he was allowed to move on, and Garnett drove up Castle Street and left the car in the car park, while he walked back to the scene of the incident. He found that Chipper Lane had been blocked off with a crush barrier, which kept most of the spectators at bay, but from his vantage-point, he could see two fire appliances at the bottom of the road, and he could smell the smouldering embers of charred wood and PVC.

A man at his elbow said, 'There must have been over two hundred women in there. What the hell did they want to blow that place up for? They weren't doing nobody any harm.' Perhaps unconsciously, the man had found the right words for their epitaph. Garnett moved away feeling sick and angry, and wondering what kind of man could believe that the death of one minor politician was worth the lives of a hundred or more innocent victims.

He got back to the house a little before six and went looking for Dinkmeyer. He found him in the greenhouse with a pencil-shaped cigar in his mouth. It was like being in a steam bath. Garnett removed his jacket and loosened his tie, and stuck a cigarette between his lips. Dinkmeyer said, 'Do you have to?'

'What?'

'Smoke.'

'Well, for God's sake, what are you doing then if you're not smoking?'

Dinkmeyer said, 'I haven't lit it boy, I'm just sucking on it. Tobacco smoke harms the plants.'

Garnett put the cigarette back in the packet. 'I've just

43

got back from the Unity Theatre,' he said.

Dinkmeyer removed the cigar from his mouth. 'I heard about it over the police waveband. They brought out fifty-three dead, mostly women.'

This morning you told me Olds believed in careful planning. Is this a typical example of his methods?'

'You figure Olds is responsible? I'd say that was a pretty big assumption to make.' He pointed the cigar at Garnett, 'Suppose you wanted to make a monkey out of the Resistance, wouldn't you dream up something like the Unity Theatre?'

Garnett shrugged his shoulders. 'I don't know,' he said. 'Has anything like that happened before?'

'No.'

'I'm finding it difficult to judge how reliable your information is.'

'Are you trying to pick a quarrel with me?' Dinkmeyer said mildly.

Garnett said, 'According to you, Karen Olds is a rather dowdy housewife, a good mother, and an earnest member of the PTA. I got the impression she was a demure, butter wouldn't melt in the mouth, type.'

'That's about the picture.'

'At a quarter past two this afternoon, Karen Olds almost ran out of her house, jumped into her car, and drove off in a hurry.'

'Maybe she was going to meet the kids from school, or was late for a hen party or something.'

'She wasn't dressed for an all girls together party, and school doesn't end until four.'

Dinkmeyer clamped the cigar back in his mouth. 'You think she was off to meet some man?'

'Now you're the one who's making a pretty big assumption. All I'm saying is that this afternoon Karen Olds behaved out of character, and anything which is out of character interests me.'

'So?'

'So I want to know if this is a regular occurrence, and if she is meeting a man, I want to know all about him.'

44

'That's logical.'

'I'm glad you think so, because you are the one who is doing the snooping.'

'I am?'

'You are. I'm going to be too busy. I have to see a friend of mine who is very good at figures. I mean to find out how much Olds is worth and where he gets his money.'

'You have a fixation about that guy.'

'Oh, I certainly have,' said Garnett, 'and I'm also curious about a man called McDonald.'

'You want to meet McDonald?'

'When I've found a way to make contact.'

'I'll fix it for you.'

Garnett fished a handkerchief out of his trouser pocket and mopped his face. 'Can you do that?' he said.

'Sure.' Dinkmeyer grinned. 'I wouldn't want you to get the idea I was unreliable.'

5

As the bus drew into Whiteparish, Garnett spotted the Ford Anglia parked outside the White Swan, with the burly figure of Katz sitting behind the wheel. It seemed to him to be about the most conspicuous meeting-place anyone could devise, but Katz had chosen it, and he assumed Katz knew what he was doing. He got off at the request stop, and hung about on the opposite side of the road to the pub until the bus was out of sight, and then he walked over to the Anglia and got in beside Katz. It was 10:30 in the morning and the pub wasn't open, and that didn't make Garnett any the happier. A car parked outside a pub which was closed excited curiosity.

Katz flashed him a broad smile, and the odour of peppermint toothpaste mingled with the perfume of after-shave lotion and deodorant. 'Where to?' he said cheerfully.

'Just drive around,' said Garnett, 'only don't follow the bus.'

'It will have to be Southampton or Salisbury then.'

'Not Salisbury, we shouldn't be seen together in Salisbury.' Katz backed out of the car park and headed out of Whiteparish in the direction of the A 36. He changed up through the gears with the finesse of a rally driver, and he gripped the steering wheel between his meaty hands as if determined to break it in half. The wheel bucked every time they hit a bump, and there were plenty of uneven spots on this particular stretch of road where the potholes had been cold-patched. Like a good many roads, it badly needed re-surfacing. 'I used to drive at Brands Hatch,' Katz said modestly.

'What else did you do pre-war?'

'I had a good time.'

'And since the war?'

'Oh, this and that.'

'What does that mean?'

'I started off as a very junior partner in Leak and Thorne, Chartered Accountants, but they didn't approve of my new methods. Privately, they thought I was a bit too smooth, only they were too polite to say so. We parted by mutual consent. My old man said it served me right for working for the Goys. I should worry what he thought. For years he's been knocking himself out, trying to make a go of his bespoke tailoring, and never had a pony to call his own.'

'Where did you learn to speak Russian?'

'I spent a year bumming around Paris before the war; lived with a white Russian. She taught me a number of things besides the language.' He grinned. 'Of course, that was before I was articled and had become respectable.'

Garnett said, 'And how long have you been with our firm?'

'A couple of years, but this is my first field job—that's the right expression, isn't it, a field job?'

'It's news to me.'

Katz looked disappointed. 'Vickers definitely said he was going to send me out into the field.'

'He has an odd sense of humour.'

'You don't think I'm equipped for the job, maybe?'

'I didn't say that.'

'So you were thinking it. Listen, I'm a good accountant, I'm telling you, and my Russian is good, and I can take care of myself.' He took one hand off the wheel and patted his stomach. 'Look, that's not fat down there, well, maybe a little fat, but mostly it's muscle. Look, I was born in Whitechapel—you think I don't know how to use my fists?'

'I already know, but there's just a bit more to it than being handy with your fists, if you want to survive.'

'Anything you want done, I can do.'

47

Garnett lit a cigarette. 'I want an accurate estimation of what Olds is worth, and how much money he is raking in, and where the money is coming from, and I want it done quickly and discreetly. His premises are in Gayton Road near Salisbury Station, and he has a large house called Greenacres in Chapperton Vale, which is just off the Blandford Road. If you have anything for me, call round to the Dinkmeyer Employment Agency in Castle Street between eleven and twelve. I don't expect to hear from you for a day or two. Don't telephone me and don't use the mail, all right?'

'Sure, I'll do a good job for you.'

'And don't take any risks.'

'Listen, for you, I'll be as discreet as the family doctor.'

'One more thing, don't commit any facts to paper, keep them in your head.'

Katz shook his head regretfully, 'You must take me for a mug.'

'I don't take you for anything,' said Garnett, 'I'm concerned with protecting my own skin.' He leaned forward and stubbed the cigarette out in the ashtray. 'Pull up here,' he said.

'You want to get out?'

'That's the general idea. There's a motel just up the road. You turn left there and head back to Romsey and pick up the A 27 for Salisbury. I'm going to catch the bus.'

He got out, closed the door behind him, and walked across the road to the bus stop. As Katz pulled away he stuck a hand out of the car window and gave Garnett a cheery salute. Garnett thought it a small miracle that Katz had managed to survive two years in the Resistance — perhaps luck favoured him.

The old man who was waiting at the bus stop seemed fascinated by the black cloud which was building up over Southampton. After a decent interval, he thought it well-mannered to open the conversation. He said he thought it looked like rain. He was quite right; the storm

48

broke fifteen minutes later, and the bus was, of course, running late.

Garnett arrived back at the employment agency just before three o'clock to find Miss Tate interviewing a girl who wanted a job as a secretary, and he could see from Miss Tate's expression that she didn't think much of her chances—perhaps because of the loud voice or the way the girl kept sniffing. Dinkmeyer wasn't in his office; he'd left a note pinned to the desk which said—'Lock up if I'm not back by five.' Garnett picked up the note to drop it into the wastepaper basket, and saw the crumpled up copy of the *Southern Daily News* was occupying most of the space. He rescued the paper and smoothed it out on the desk. A picture, taken inside the Unity Theatre, was splashed across the front page under a banner headline which said, 'Latest Terrorist Outrage'.

The photographer had done a good job because it was all there—the mangled bodies, the odd shoes, the abandoned handbags, shopping baskets and bingo cards amid the shattered tables, broken glass and plaster—the flotsam of pointless violence. The leader writer hadn't spared himself either, and it all added up to a damning piece of propaganda as far as the Resistance was concerned.

He remembered that Coleman had a study made some years back to determine the attitude of the Press towards the Resistance, and to see how closely individual editors toed the Government line, and he remembered that the *Southern Daily News* had been the least hostile paper, but now it seemed that the Resistance had fallen from favour.

Garnett tossed the paper back into the wastepaper basket, told Tate he was leaving, and asked her to lock up when she left. A light drizzle was falling as he tramped back to the house. He felt depressed and irritable, and if Vickers had been available, he would have given him a few home truths. In the past, he had often been obliged to work with some pretty amateurish people, but Katz was in a class of his own; Dane was brittle, and Dinkmeyer was very much an unknown quantity.

Garnett let himself into the house and went straight up to his room. He changed out of his damp suit, and towelled his hair until it was more or less dry, and then flopped down on to the bed. He tried to put Dane out of his mind but he kept remembering what she had been like before she went to prison, and he wondered how he was going to win back her trust; and, for the life of him, he couldn't find an answer to that problem. The curtains shifted in the gentle breeze and wafted a sweet, fresh smell of damp grass into the room, and presently he closed his eyes and drifted off to sleep.

Dinkmeyer woke him up as the light was beginning to fade. He looked distinctly pleased with himself. 'That Karen Olds has got hot pants, boy,' he said. 'Oh, she sure as hell has got hot pants.'

Garnett sat up on the bed and rubbed the sleep out of his eyes. 'Go on,' he said.

'Two thirty, right on the nail, she comes out of the drive in a bright red Mini and takes off as if she was late for a vital appointment. I followed her out to Amesbury, keeping well back in case she latches on to the fact that she is being followed. She parked the car in a side street and then went shopping. I figured that was odd—I mean, why go to Amesbury when she can get all the vegetables and canned foods she needs right here in Salisbury? About half an hour later she goes into a café, and presently this man joins her.'

'That's interesting.'

'Isn't it. He's a good-looking guy, about five ten, slim, I'd guess about one fifty pounds, short blond hair, and he looked a bit like Steve McQueen—if that means anything to you?'

'Oh, I've heard of Steve McQueen.'

'Well now, I was told you hadn't any interests outside this job. Anyway, they spend some time in earnest conversation and then they leave together. I thought she might go straight back to Salisbury because it was getting on for four o'clock, and she would want to be at home when the kids came out of school, but I guessed wrong. They drove out to Tidworth, went through the barrack area, and turned off the main road beyond the Ranges, and disappeared into a copse. I went on for three or four hundred metres and then pulled off on to the verge. I waited twenty minutes before I pulled on a plastic mac and walked back to the copse, and for a while, I thought I had boobed. I couldn't see any sign of them in the car because the front windscreen had misted over, and then she must have moved because I saw a knee in the side window, and I knew they had folded the front seats forward and were in the back. I lay up in the bushes, with the rain dripping down my neck, until they got out of the car. I got this shot with my Polaroid.'

He reached inside the breast pocket of his jacket and pressed a snapshot into Garnett's hand. Although the photograph had been taken at a distance of about thirty metres, they were sharply in focus. Karen Olds had her face averted from the camera, and was looking over her left shoulder at the man who was concentrating on zipping up her skirt. Garnett said, 'Do you know this man?'

Dinkmeyer shook his head. 'No, but I'll find him.'

'What makes you so sure?'

'She dropped the guy off in Tidworth.'

'So?'

'All right, it could be a blind, but the 248 Russian (Guards) Tank Division is quartered there.'

'You think this man is a soldier?'

'I've got a hunch he is.'

'You must have a reason.'

'I figure Karen Olds met this guy only recently, because otherwise word would have got around that she was having a hot affair, and this affair is hot because she's taking one hell of a risk in seeing him every afternoon. So I don't think he is a local man for that reason. I think she met him at a party, maybe one of those Anglo-Soviet get-togethers. It's a cinch Olds would be invited because he has that maintenance contract for the barracks at Wilton.'

'But you said she dropped the man off in Tidworth.'

'He could have been at the party. Anyway, it has to be somebody who can get time off every afternoon.'

'The Soviets work their soldiers from six in the morning to seven at night.'

'I figure this man to be an officer.'

'And just how are you going to find him?'

'I'll check out the newspaper offices and all the local photographers. The Russians love to publicise any Anglo-Soviet get-together. You never know, we might strike lucky and come up with something.'

He took the snapshot out of Garnett's hand and walked towards the door. He stopped abruptly and turned about snapping his fingers. 'Oh, one more thing,' he said, 'about McDonald. I've set it up for tomorrow night—The Go Go Go Club in Devizes. A guy named Harvey will pick you up from the club.'

'How will I recognise him?'

'He'll recognise you the moment you sign the membership book, so don't get smart and sign in as John Doe, okay?'

He didn't wait for a reply. He left the room and closed the door behind him.

6

THE GO GO GO Club lay between a fish and chip bar and an undertaker's parlour in Gordon Road, a quiet back street far removed from the main shopping centre. It was about the last place you would expect to find a strip club, but there it was, nestling coyly between two incongruous neighbours, its gaudy neon sign sticking out like a sore thumb. It was no bigger than a licensed betting shop and it did almost as much trade.

Garnett pushed aside the beaded curtain and stepped into the confessional box of an entrance, handed over a pound to the door-keeper, signed the membership book, and was then allowed to pass through the second door.

A cloud of stale tobacco smoke attacked his eyes and lungs, and deafening taped music reduced the babel of conversation to a low buzz. He fought his way to the bar, got a flat-looking lager, and then found himself a niche in the corner where the bar met the wall. The club tried hard to achieve the exotic. Japanese paper-lanterns hung from the walls and ceiling, and a tank full of lethargic goldfish balanced precariously on a rickety shelf facing the bar. Murals of over-developed girls with fixed smiles and G-strings were intended to divert attention from the cigarette burns on the gimcrack tables and chairs. The goldfish looked pretty miserable. Garnett didn't blame them.

A man in dark pants and ruffled silk shirt killed the tape music and stepped forward on to the floor, clutching a mike in one hand. In a nasal voice he said, 'Friends, for your entertainment tonight, we have two artistes— Bunny Meares, who is new to the club, and our old

friend Lorraine Odell. Let's give a big hand for Lorraine.'
He stepped back off the floor, waved a hand towards the
staircase at the back of the room, and turned on the tape,
almost drowning the handclaps, stamping feet and
chorus of whistles.

A strawberry blonde in a white strapless sheath dress
came down the staircase and stepped on to the floor, and,
quite suddenly, the talking stopped, and those in the front
leaned forward in their seats to get a better look. The
girl was well schooled in bumps and grinds, and her
smile promised a lot. Jinking her hips, she peeled off
elbow-length white satin gloves and threw them at the
audience. She undid the hook at the back of her dress
and allowed a fat, balding man in the front row to
unzip it all the way down to her hips. The dress fell in
a hoop about her feet, and she stepped out of it and kicked
it to one side. The audience roared its approval.

An aggressive voice in Garnett's ear said, 'Getting a
cheap thrill, are we?'

The man was like a bantam cock looking for a fight.
Shorter than Garnett, he obviously wasn't intimidated by
their discrepancy in height. His brown eyes reflected
contempt and anger; the lean, tanned face was hard and
vicious. Alert, watchful, he was as friendly and about as
harmless as a puff adder. Brown hair brushed forward
in a cow lick above the left eyebrow did nothing to soften
the thin cruel mouth. Two large blackheads in the left
nostril only served to increase Garnett's immediate dislike of the man.

Garnett said pleasantly, 'Why don't you be a nice little
man and shove off?'

He turned his back on the man, and saw that Lorraine
was now down to her panties and bra. The bra stayed on
while she twice circled the floor, and then it too joined
the pile of discarded clothing. She posed in the centre
of the floor and pushed both naked breasts up with her
hands, pouted demurely, and then flounced off on
another circuit of the floor, gradually rolling the panties
down over her hips. The man tapped Garnett on the

shoulder and said, 'Nobody tells me to shove off.'

Garnett said, 'Go and pick on someone your own size.'

There was now only a G-string between the girl and obscenity, not that obscenity worried anyone any more. She stood legs apart, thumbs hooked into the G-string, a quizzical expression on her face, mutely asking the audience whether she should remove it; and the crowd shouted Yes, Yes.

The insistent voice said, 'You crummy bastard, you're like the rest of them, you want to screw her. Come on outside.'

'What does it matter to you what I think?'

'It matters a lot, she's my wife.'

A great roar went up as the G-string was flung into the air, and the girl arched her back and thrust her pelvis forward.

The voice said, 'Come outside and be a man, that is if you are able to.'

The pun registered on Garnett, and as the house lights went down, he grabbed the man's arm and said, 'Okay, if that's the way you want it, let's go.'

Outside in the fresh night air the man was almost friendly.

'The name's Harvey,' he said, 'you were slow on the uptake.'

'You're too subtle for me.'

'I thought you people from London were supposed to be sharp.'

'Some of us are more than others.'

Harvey said, 'Right, if we're all through with social pleasantries, the van is parked further down the street.' He walked off abruptly without waiting for Garnett.

The van was an old Morris ten hundredweight with balding tyres and a body eaten through with rust. Harvey opened the rear doors and removed the sacking from the steel floor.

'You got a handkerchief?' he asked.

Garnett pulled one out of his jacket pocket, 'Here,' he said, 'you keep it.'

'I don't want it. Just blindfold yourself, lie down on the floor, and I'll cover you with this piece of sacking. You take the sacking off your head or remove the blindfold before I tell you to do so, and I'll put a bullet through your head, and that's a promise.'

'All right,' said Garnett, 'don't let's make a drama out of it.' He tied the handkerchief around his eyes, crawled into the van on all fours and allowed Harvey to cover him with the sacking. The doors slammed behind him; he heard footsteps on the pavement outside; another door opened, Harvey grunted, the engine spluttered into life, and then the van lurched away from the kerb.

He tried to work out the route by committing the twists and turns to memory, but as with Katz in London, he got the feeling they were moving in circles, and after several minutes of futile effort, he gave it up as a bad job. They rode around for about half an hour, and then Harvey opened the van doors and led him up a short flight of steps, along a passage and into a room, where he sat Garnett down in an upright chair before removing the blindfold. The bright light had him blinking rapidly.

As he became accustomed to the glare, the man sitting across the table from him gradually came into focus. 'I'm McDonald,' he said, 'you wanted to have a talk with me.' He was softly spoken. A serious-minded man with thin black hair, a Clement Attlee moustache and thick pebble-lensed glasses, he was wearing a dark grey suit which had gone shiny at the knees and elbows. He was the picture the NUT liked to paint every time they put in a pay claim. Garnett didn't know it but McDonald had been a school teacher. Garnett looked round the room, his eyes taking in the worn carpet, the bookcase and the Peter Scott print on the distempered wall. 'This could be a headmaster's study,' he said.

'It could be but it isn't. Now what did you want to see me about?'

'What about Harvey?'

'What about him? Don't you trust Harvey? I do,

56

Harvey is my right hand, you don't have to worry about Frank Harvey.'

Garnett shrugged his shoulders. 'So Harvey stays.'

McDonald smiled, 'We're agreed on that,' he said. 'Now what does London want with me?'

'Let's say we want to hear why you broke with Olds.'

'There were a number of reasons.'

'One will do.'

McDonald removed his glasses and leaned forward across the table. Garnett knew he was about to deliver a lecture, and he wasn't far wrong. McDonald said, 'A Resistance Group needs three things—personnel, weapons and money. You need the money to buy arms, right?' He paused to light a cigarette. 'Money isn't easy to come by, sometimes you have to steal it. We stole it, a lot of it, getting on for half a million in a score of bank and post office raids, and Olds was the banker—you follow me?'

'I think I'm ahead of you.'

'Three years ago we were an effective force, and an active one, and I would have followed Olds anywhere, and then things gradually began to go sour on us. The police started to find our arms caches, our casualty rate climbed, and replacements slowed down to a mere trickle. Olds said we should re-build and concentrate our activities against soft targets until we were strong again. You know what soft targets are, Mr Abel?' The cigarette wagged up and down in his lips spilling ash into his lap.

'I've heard a lot of definitions,' said Garnett, 'suppose you give me yours.'

'Collaborators, policemen, informers to start with; then we changed direction, started to hit the supermarkets and warehouses.' McDonald took the cigarette out of his mouth and squashed it in the ashtray. 'It wasn't long before I realised we were up to our ears in the black market. Olds had turned us into a bunch of crooks masquerading as patriots. I had it out with him, I asked him why, and do you know what he said to me? He said we needed the money to buy guns from the militia.' McDonald slowly shook his head. 'Of course, there was an element of truth in what he said; we did buy arms from the militia, but not at the prices he quoted —five hundred pounds for a Sterling sub-machine-gun. He was lining his own pocket.'

Garnett said, 'London has a different picture of Olds. According to us, he is supposed to be a fire-eating Resistance leader.'

'Olds can pull the wool over the eyes of most people. We know him better.'

'So you broke with him?'

'I wasn't the only one.'

'Oh yes,' said Garnett, 'I keep forgetting about friend Harvey here.'

Harvey said, 'A hell of a lot more than just me came across.'

'Sykes?'

'That's right, and Olds had him knocked off with a 12 bore, and he hung the Cromptons.'

'And as a reprisal you blew up the house in Amesbury, killing five of Olds' people?'

'We did nothing of the kind,' said McDonald.

'He'd probably say the same thing about Sykes and the Cromptons and those men who were killed with a hand grenade in that café in Trowbridge. I mean, all you're going on is mere supposition. What proof have you got that Olds is behind it?'

'There was an eye witness at Trowbridge.'

'Who?'

'Me,' said Harvey, 'I was inside the café when the grenade was rolled in. The man who did it was Lee, Amos Lee, nicknamed "The Weasel". Wears his hair right down to his shoulders.'

'All right,' said Garnett, 'you've made your point.'

McDonald smiled thinly. 'I find that a small consolation,' he said. 'Now, if you have no further questions, I'll get Frank to run you back.'

It was getting on for midnight by the time Garnett arrived back, and there wasn't a light showing anywhere in the house. He let himself in with a latch key and quietly walked upstairs in the dark. This absurd business of relying on public transport whenever Dinkmeyer wanted the Volkswagen was beginning to get on his nerves, and he decided that something would have to be done about it. He remembered seeing a Norton 500 going cheap in the garage just up the road from the agency, and he resolved to buy it. Anything was better than the present set-up. He opened the door to his room, half turned to face the wall, and finding the switch, put on the light.

Dinkmeyer said, 'Welcome back, son.'

Garnett jumped. As he whirled round his right hand flew instinctively to his hip, and then he felt foolish because he wasn't armed. 'Christ,' he said, 'don't ever do that again. What do you want to lie there in the dark for?'

Dinkmeyer swung his feet off the bed and sat up. 'I can't sleep with the light on,' he said. He yawned and stretched his arms above his head. 'Did you meet McDonald?'

'Yes.'

'What do you think of him?'

'I suppose he's okay. He made a good case against Olds—said he was a crook.'

'Aren't we all.'

'According to McDonald,' Garnett said patiently, 'Olds has given up fighting and gone in for organised crime.'

'Can he prove it?'

'No.' Garnett paused and then said, 'Have you heard of Amos Lee, a weasel-faced man with long hair?'

'No, I can't say I have.'

'Lee is supposed to have killed three of McDonald's men in Trowbridge.'

Dinkmeyer scratched his head. 'What are you driving at.'

'Amos Lee followed me back from near Sutton Veny the other night. Funny, it's almost as if he had been waiting for me to show up at the farm. I mean, apart from you, who else knew I was coming to Salisbury?'

Dinkmeyer stood up. 'You have the nicest way of voicing your suspicions. While we are at it, here's something else to think about. I ran Karen Olds' boy friend to earth, found a picture of him in the *Salisbury Express and Times*. He's Captain Feodor Ilyushin, an interpreter with Headquarters 64th Mechanised Army. In case you don't know, Headquarters 64th Mechanised Army is stationed at Wilton. Maybe you think that's goddamned funny too.'

7

RAIN, SLOSHING DOWN from a lead-coloured sky, bounced off shop awnings and formed large puddles on the uneven pavement. Thunder rumbled in the distance like a giant with an upset stomach. Sitting there at a corner table near the window, with a litre of mild and bitter in front of him, Garnett could see Dane standing behind one of the stalls. She was wearing a soiled trench mac and a red scarf hid her short hair. Even at that distance, she looked tired and drawn. Her hands moved fretfully over a pyramid of apples, moving first one apple and then another, and achieving nothing in the process, except that perhaps it helped to steady her frayed nerves. He noticed that she was continually looking about her as if expecting to find a Special Branch man watching her from amongst the small crowd of shoppers remaining in the market. He saw her speak to the man standing beside her and then she left the stall, and hands thrust deep into the pockets of her raincoat, walked towards the pub, her eyes downcast.

She saw him as soon as she came into the bar and made straight for his table. Dane sat down opposite him, eyed the glass of sherry in front of her and said, 'Is this for me?' He nodded, and she picked up the glass and drained it in one go. She pulled a face and then said, 'Hell, that tasted awful.'

'I'm sorry, can I get you something else?'

'No, thank you.' She looked around her. 'What happens now?'

'I thought we would go for a stroll as soon as the rain eases off.'

61

'It's not raining much now. Come on, let's go, I want to get back.'

'Are you in a hurry or something?'

'I can get a lift on the farm truck if I'm ready to go in the next ten minutes or so.'

'Why not take a bus?'

'It costs too much.'

'I'll pay your fare.'

Her lips curled, 'How generous,' she said.

'Forget the truck, you're not going back on it.'

Two spots of anger showed on her high cheekbones, and for a moment it seemed she might lose her temper, but she clenched her teeth and calmed down. 'What's a little rain between friends?' She stood up. 'Come on, it won't hurt you.'

He caught her up at the door and took hold of her arm. He led her towards the Avon, through New Street and Crane Street, and the rain, which had driven most people indoors, was falling lightly now. A police prowl car cruised slowly down the street, its occupants turning to stare at them, and Garnett slipped his arm round her waist and hugged her close, because only lovers would be abroad in such weather.

'There's no need to overdo it,' she said, 'surely they are out of sight by now?'

'No,' he lied, 'they've stopped at the lights.'

He hung on to her until they turned into the parkland and then he no longer had any excuse to hold her close, and she removed his arm. 'Well?' she said quietly.

'In a nutshell, it doesn't look too good where Olds is concerned. At best, he is a security risk; his wife is sleeping with a Russian officer. On that score alone he should be replaced, and of course that means his organisation will have to be re-built from the bottom up. There's also good reason to suppose that his Resistance activities are merely a front for large scale black market operations. I also think there may be some truth to McDonald's accusations. Tell Vickers I'll give him a more detailed report when Katz has completed his investigation into the financial structure of Olds' business company. Have you got all that?'

'Yes, I presume you want me to paraphrase it?'

'If you would, and I would also like to see a copy of the signal after you have sent it.'

'That's it then,' she said, 'I'll say goodbye.'

'Not so fast.'

She raised one eyebrow. 'What now?'

'Is anything worrying you?'

'Yes. You are.'

He smiled and then said gently, 'You look ill, your face is drawn, you've lost weight and your nerves are on edge.'

'For God's sake,' she said irritably, 'can't I menstruate without you making a national issue out of it?'

'Are you sure it's only that?'

'I've just said so, haven't I? Now if you haven't got anything else for me I'm going.'

He caught hold of her arm and pulled her back. 'This present arrangement,' he said, 'it's no good. If I have anything I want sent over the radio, it has to wait for either Tuesday or Saturday when you're in the market, and any message for me is going to be at least a day old and maybe as much as four. From now on I'm calling at the farm every night of the week.'

'That's far too dangerous.'

He shook his head. 'People will take us for lovers. I'll be there every night at eight.'

'You'd better make it six, they've changed the schedule and frequencies.'

'When did this happen?'

'The other day.'

'Nobody told me.'

She shrugged her shoulders, 'Perhaps they didn't think it was necessary.'

'All right, I'll be there by six.' He drew her close and kissed her. Her body was as hard and as unyielding as a plank, and her eyes were cold and distant. He pushed her away and said, 'Christ, what's got into you?'

63

Her expression didn't change. 'I thought I had made that abundantly clear at the farm.'

'You can't still be brooding about that.'

'Can't I? Well, you had better understand this much — the only thing that is holding us together is this job.'

She turned and walked away, her stride shortening and becoming quicker and more urgent until she was almost running, and he stood there in the fine drizzle wishing like hell he could find a way to pick up the threads again. And then he thought about Vickers and Endicott, and he felt a surge of anger because of what they had done to her.

'Wait until next time we meet,' he whispered to himself, 'you bastards have got a surprise coming to you.'

Katz was in another part of the city, in a room which looked out over the Close at the Cathedral spire. There was a girl with him. She was sitting on the edge of the bed, carefully rolling on her stockings, whilst he sprawled in the chair watching her through sleep-laden eyes. She was Sandra Watson, a pert, dark-haired nineteen-year-old, who for the past four years had been employed as a clerk by Olds. Getting close to Sandra Watson was, Katz considered, a master stroke. Not that it had been difficult. For some reason, despite the fact that he was far from good looking, women were attracted to Katz.

He had discovered this for himself at the tender age of fourteen in the back stalls of the Essoldo Cinema one Saturday afternoon, when, bored by the slow moving Western on the screen, he had transferred his attention to a girl sitting next to him. He had been mildly surprised at her lack of objection, and when she left the cinema, had followed her. Their relationship had been brief, but illuminating to Katz, and the beginning of a series of sexual adventures from normal to bizarre.

Sandra Watson finished dressing and looked at her tiny, cheap rolled-gold wristwatch and said, 'I must be going.'

Katz made no move to get up. 'Will I see you again?'

64

'Sure, how about tomorrow?' She shook her head. 'Monday? Tuesday?'

'I'm free Wednesday afternoon.'

'Okay, Wednesday it is,' he said affably.

'Aren't you going to see me out?'

'You know the way.'

She tossed her head angrily. 'Well really,' she said, 'some people have no manners. At least Ken treats me like a lady.' She intended to flounce out of the room, but Katz gave her a slap on the buttocks as she went by, and the effect was ruined.

'The trouble with your fiancé,' said Katz, 'is that he doesn't know how to handle a woman like you.'

'And I suppose you do?' she said, but there was no anger left in her voice.

Katz winked. 'You know I do.'

She rubbed her behind. 'The trouble with you,' she said, 'is that you don't know your own strength. 'Bye love, see you Wednesday.'

She closed the door of the room behind her and ran quickly downstairs. Katz listened to the sound of her heels clacking on the pavement outside until they faded out of earshot, and then he got up from the chair and lay down on the crumpled bed, crossing one leg over the other and folding his arms behind his head.

The Sandra Watsons in his life were becoming fewer and farther between these days. He would have to find a number of convincing reasons why Garnett should be persuaded to let him stay in Salisbury, when, so far, for all his digging, he had not come up with anything significant.

8

THE WEATHER HAD turned again, and the temperature in Dinkmeyer's office had climbed up to eighty degrees fahrenheit once more. Dinkmeyer, in a blue short-sleeved cotton shirt, was suitably dressed, but Garnett in nylon shirt and heavy cavalry twill trousers was sweltering. The sweat rolled off him.

Garnett said, 'I think Katz is stringing me along.'

Dinkmeyer removed the dead cigar from his mouth and looked up from the newspaper which was spread out over the desk. 'Okay,' he said, 'I'll buy it. Why do you think Katz is stringing you along?'

'Because he hasn't told me anything which I haven't already found out for myself.'

'That doesn't necessarily prove he is stringing you along.'

'Look, he told me the house is worth at least fifteen thousand; I already know that. He tells me Olds employs only a dozen or so men full time, therefore he is a small business man; I already know that too. Does he know Olds' bank balance? No, because he can't walk into the bank and ask to see Olds' account.'

Dinkmeyer said, 'Be reasonable. Give him time, he's working on Sandra Watson.'

'And I know the kind of work he's been putting in,' Garnett said grimly.

'Okay, if that's the way you feel, what are you going to do about it?'

Garnett pointed a finger at the door. 'Next time that stallion comes in here,' he said, 'I'm going to tell him to pack up and go back to where he came from.'

'Will that make you feel good?'

'It'll do more than that. I shall sleep better at nights, because I shan't have to worry about Katz. While he is around there is a chance he will lead them to us.'

'A question,' said Dinkmeyer.

'Yes?'

'Who is them?'

'I wish to God I knew.'

Dinkmeyer stuck the dead cigar back in his mouth. 'Riddles,' he said, shaking his head sadly, 'you're always talking in riddles.'

'I'm thinking.'

'You must have a twisted mind.'

'McDonald and Olds broke apart a year and a half ago, and yet Olds doesn't do anything about it for fourteen months. Why?'

Dinkmeyer grunted. 'Maybe he didn't think McDonald would prove to be such a drawing power. As soon as he started to lose support, he decided to do something about it.'

'Do you believe that?'

Dinkmeyer looked up at the ceiling. 'No, I don't,' he said slowly. 'It's too easy to lay everything at Olds' door. I'd like to be convinced that Olds was personally acquainted with the men he's supposed to have killed.'

'McDonald seemed to think so.'

Dinkmeyer took the dead cigar out of his mouth and threw it into the wastepaper basket. 'Hell,' he said, 'McDonald is a bigot, he'll believe what he wants to believe. He's a bender, he bends the facts to suit his own convictions. Karen Olds may sleep with a Russian officer, but that doesn't automatically make her husband a traitor. Sure, he's a risk and I agree we should get rid of him, but if I were in your shoes, I'd try to figure out the connection between Sykes and the Cromptons and all those other people who've been killed recently. I mean, how come no one in McDonald's organisation has run Amos Lee to ground? He isn't hiding his face, is he? You've seen him, why hasn't anyone else?' Dinkmeyer picked up the newspaper, 'And another thing, here's the Chief Constable of Wiltshire going on record that the Resistance are at each others' throats. How come he is so certain of his facts?' Dinkmeyer paused and then said, 'I have a feeling we are being got at. One of these days I am going to get into my car and find the ignition has been wired up to a stick of gelignite, or else I am going to end up in a dark alley with the back of my head shot off. And then a police spokesman is going to say it was just the Resistance settling an old score.'

'Yes?' Garnett said vaguely.

Dinkmeyer sighed. 'You haven't been listening.'

'You've given me an idea.'

'I'll bet.'

'No, really. I think I'll join Katz in the skin game.'

Dinkmeyer scratched his head. 'Seventeen years I've been in this country and still I can't speak the language.'

'I want to see a strip show.'

'In the middle of the afternoon?'

'Why not?'

'No reason I guess, except that I think people who catch a peep show in the middle of the afternoon must be sick.'

'But it's okay if they go to a late show, is that what you're saying?'

'I don't know what I'm saying. I must be old-fashioned, peep shows bore me.'

Garnett got up and walked to the door. He glanced back over his shoulder. 'You know what,' he said, 'they bore me too.'

'Then why go?'

'Because, on my way to the office this morning, I passed the Kit Kat Club in Bowlalley Lane, and there on a bill-board right next to the sign which puts the club off limits to all Soviet personnel, was a picture of the star attraction of today's show; and you know who she is?'

Dinkmeyer shook his head.

'Lorraine Odell, the stripper from the Go Go Go Club.'

'Are you going to walk there, or do I lose the use of

my car again?'

Garnett said, 'Didn't you know, this morning I bought myself a Norton 500 cc. The tyres are nearly bald, the saddle is bone hard, and the engine couldn't pull the skin off a rice pudding, but it's better than pushing a rusty bicycle.' The door closed behind him. Dinkmeyer went back to his paper.

The Kit Kat Club was just a white-washed cellar lit by ultra-violet, with beer-barrel tables and chairs. There were perhaps a dozen or so shadowy figures sitting around the room listening to the juke box. Lorraine Odell was sitting with a small, dark-haired girl in a blue lurex sleeveless dress. Odell wore calf-length boots, black leather skirt and bolero jacket over a white nylon blouse. The ultra-violet light picked out the white bra under her blouse. Both girls looked bored.

Garnett went up to the bar, got himself a small whisky, and drifted over to their table. Odell looked up, stared at him contemptuously, and said, 'Who asked you to join us?' Her voice was a nasal, jarring whine.

'I'm not trying to make a pick-up.'

'Oh no? I've heard that one before.'

'It's business. Can I get you a drink?'

'No thanks. We never take a drink off a stranger.'

'I'm not exactly a stranger. I know your husband, Frank Harvey.'

She raised her eyebrows, almost cracking the pancake mask on her face. 'So what?'

'So we're almost acquainted. I've got a proposition to put to you.'

The girl at Odell's side laughed mirthlessly. 'How many does that make now, Lorrie?'

'Too many.' Odell opened her handbag and took out a packet of ten cigarettes. She put the filter tip between her lips and fumbled with a book of matches. Garnett leaned across the table and lit it for her with a Ronson lighter.

'Thanks,' she said.

'About my proposition.'

'What about it?'

'A friend of mine is giving a party.'

'No.'

'No what?'

'No, I'm not interested in private parties.' She tapped the cigarette against the ashtray. A circle of strawberry-pink lipstick encircled the filter tip like a plimsoll line. 'You can stuff private parties, I don't need the money.'

'I've yet to meet anyone who couldn't use a little extra.'

'You've met one now. I've got all the work I can handle.'

'Oh yes?'

'Oh yes,' she snapped, 'I work the clubs in Devizes, Swindon, Amesbury, Andover, Salisbury and Winchester. I don't need your help, Mr—?'

'Abel, George Abel,' Garnett said affably. 'Here's my card; my partner and I run an employment agency in Castle Street.'

She picked up his card and fingered it doubtfully. 'You're not having me on?' she said.

'This is a serious business proposition.'

'How much?'

'Seventy-five pounds for a one hour show.'

Her eyes widened. 'Seventy-five pounds,' she breathed. 'What do I have to do to earn that?'

'Your usual show.'

'Like hell, the last time I was offered that kind of money for a private party, the host wanted me to join him in a spot of discipline.'

Garnett said, 'This is on the level, no funny stuff. The host is a well-known business man. His name is Richard Olds; he's an acquaintance of your husband.' Garnett leaned forward. 'Look, if you're not sure about it, why not talk it over with Frank and see what he thinks of the idea?'

Odell looked at her wrist watch. 'It's almost time for our number, are you staying for the show?'

'I don't think so.'

'Suppose I decide to take you up on the offer, how do I get in touch with you?'

'Dinkmeyer's Employment Agency—we're listed in the yellow pages.'

She got up and eased her way round the table. 'I'll call you if I decide to take up the offer,' she said.

'Do that,' said Garnett. He watched her disappear backstage and smiled to himself. The bait had been laid; the question was, would anyone come sniffing round.

Katz lay on his back staring up at the ceiling, while with his left hand he absent-mindedly scratched the hairs on his stomach. Sandra Watson, he decided, was beginning to bore him. She was a puppet, with a mechanical performance in bed, which at first he had mistaken for genuine emotion, until it became evident that the moans and groans were contrived. A sharp fingernail ran down his rib cage and made him jump. Turning to face her, Katz said, 'What was that in aid of?'

'I'm hungry.'

'So you're hungry.'

'I didn't have any lunch.'

'You want to eat?'

She pouted. 'You're very ungallant.'

'You want to eat, yes or no?'

'Yes.'

'All right,' said Katz, 'we'll get dressed, and I'll run you home.'

'You're mean and horrid.'

Katz smiled. 'It was a joke—not a good one,' he spread his hands, 'but a joke all the same.' He touched her thigh gently. 'Come on,' he said, 'we'll go and fill your empty stomach.'

Katz rolled off the bed and started dressing. The girl had been an interesting diversion for a few days, but she was of no help where Olds was concerned, and it was best to quietly drop her. He would just stop seeing her, and if she persisted in running after him, he would somehow find the necessary excuses to put her off. If Olds was lining his pockets, then he was a very clever man, because he couldn't find any indication of it. Katz finished dressing and sat down on the edge of the bed while he waited for Sandra Watson to finish brushing her hair. Finally, he said, 'You look wonderful, come on, let's go.'

He was very, very gallant in those last few minutes. He helped her into the car, said again how marvellous she looked, and resisted the temptation to fondle the acres of thigh exposed by the brief mini-skirt. He said, 'Where shall we go?' and she said, 'The Cadena in Blue Boar Row,' and he turned the ignition key, and that was the last thing he ever did. Blast is a curious and unpredictable phenomenon, and its effect on the human frame is equally incalculable. It is unusual for anyone to be killed by the direct effects of over pressure since the body is remarkably resilient—it can stand up to one hundred and fifty pounds per square inch before serious damage occurs, whereas the average building will collapse under the overall pressure of five pounds per square inch. When the ten pound charge connected to the ignition circuit was triggered, the force of the explosion blew Katz through the roof of the Anglia and removed every stitch of Watson's clothing before she was thrown out of the car, a split second after the side door had been wrenched off. Apart from a large number of needle-fine puncture marks from waist to neck, the police surgeon could find no obvious cause of death. With Katz it was different; the roof had pulped his head like an over-ripe water melon.

He rode almost upright pushing the battered Norton to its absolute limit when he passed through the quiet villages. An artist might have appreciated the countryside on a warm summer's evening, but Garnett had a different image on his mind. He saw a pulped figure lying in the road, and uppermost in his mind was the thought that perhaps Katz had been killed because he had stumbled on to something.

He had a bare thirty minutes to reach Brockenhurst

Farm and catch the evening schedule, and he cursed whoever it was who had been responsible for changing the time. Before he reached the farm, Garnett had mentally drafted four signals and rejected every one because they were too wordy. The message had to be detailed yet concise, because if it lasted more than a minute or so, it might be intercepted, and the location of the transmitter fixed by DF. He turned into the farmyard and cut the engine, leaned the Norton against the wall of the house, and knocked on the kitchen door. Dane opened it. She didn't smile, nor did she speak to Garnett, but avoiding his eyes, she slipped by and walked towards the barn.

There was a rickety ladder which afforded access to the loft, and since it would not bear their combined weight, Garnett let her go ahead. The rungs were rotten, and he tested each one before putting his full weight upon it. The loft was dirty, and he could hear the rats scuttling about in the eaves, and he was surprised that they didn't seem to bother Dane. He sat down on a pile of empty sacks and watched her drag the attaché case out of its hiding place, snap the locks open, and extend the aerial rod up through the roof between a gap in the slates. The man who had built the wireless set into the leather attaché case could be justly proud of his craftsmanship; the only trouble was that the case was too heavy for the average person to carry around for any length of time.

Dane set the frequency, checked the aerial and said, 'All right, what's the message?'

'Tell them Katz murdered 1600 hours today; Olds believed implicated; advise. You know the nicknames for Katz and Olds?'

'Katz is Victor, Olds is Henry, right?'

'Correct. Encode their nicknames as well as the rest of the text.'

'I know my job,' she said quietly.

She worked quickly, encoding the message and then ripping it out on the morse key at forty words a minute.

She got a routine acknowledgement, took off the earphones and switched the set to another frequency.

'What happens now?' said Garnett.

'We wait ten minutes or so, and then we may or may not get our instructions.'

Garnett sat back and eyed Dane reflectively. He wished he could reach her somehow, but one glance at that stiff back and the haughty way she held her head, convinced him he had no hope. Their call sign bleeped, and Dane hastily shoved the headset back on over her ears. Her pencil raced across a scratch pad as the message came through as fast, if not faster, than her own transmission. There were no corrupt groups, and consequently she broke the code quickly, and handed the transcript to Garnett.

The message read: 'Contact and inform Olds he is relieved pending court-martial. Appoint suitable deputy. Further instructions follow tomorrow. Acknowledge.'

'Okay?' said Dane.

'Sure, acknowledge it.'

She flicked on to yet a third frequency, further safeguarding the possibility of intercept.

Garnett got to his feet. 'See you tomorrow then,' he said. Dane didn't answer him.

He started down the ladder without thinking and the fifth rung gave way as soon as he put his full weight on it. His forehead cracked against the ladder, and dazed, he failed to get a hand hold. Unable to check the fall, he hit the floor awkwardly, lost his balance, and fell sideways, striking his head against a post and cutting his forehead open above the right eyebrow.

The barn began to spin and he groaned aloud.

Dimly he was aware of Dane scrambling down the rotten ladder. Some instinct warned him to keep still as Dane bent over him. Slowly he opened his eyes and looked into a face softened with concern. As she bent to wipe the blood off his face, he stretched up an arm and put it around her neck. He felt her stiffen and pull back slightly, but Garnett tightened his grip and pulled her

74

face down to his. Gently he kissed her face, her eyes and her lips, and gradually the tension left her body and relaxed against his. And her mouth opened under his darting tongue, and he forgot about the blood on his face and the throbbing pain in his head. She raised her head, and there were tears in her eyes, and she said, 'Oh God, don't you ever leave me again.' And they were together again because he had fallen off a ladder and cut his head open; and as his hand moved up her bare golden-brown thigh, he thought the goddamned war could wait for ten minutes.

9

DINKMEYER WAS WORRIED and he had cause to be. Not
for the first time, he regretted opting to take his discharge in England; but ten years ago there seemed to
be any number of very good reasons for doing so. His
wife's parents weren't young, and as neither of them was
particularly mobile, Julie virtually ran their small hotel
in Thetford for them. As Julie pointed out, her parents
couldn't afford to retire just yet and so the question of
leaving them didn't arise; and, besides, there was Sue
to consider, and Sue was a problem. She wasn't mentally
handicapped, but her IQ was low enough to warrant
sending her to a special school, and as she was making
such good progress there, even Dinkmeyer was forced
to concede that it would be a shame to take her away.
He was fond of Sue, and perhaps if she had been his
own daughter he would never have experienced any
regrets, but in fact Sue was the product of Julie's first
marriage, and her father had not been in touch with her
for years.

None of this bothered him at the time, and he had
happily taken his discharge and gone to work in the
hotel; and that was how he came to meet Vickers. Vickers
was then working in Manpower Planning at the Ministry of Defence, and used to spend most week-ends in
Thetford, where he had a small cottage. Their friendship
was something which Dinkmeyer now regarded as a
mixed blessing.

The war had caught Dinkmeyer in the wrong place at
the wrong time. As a former pilot, he had expected to
be recalled to active duty, but when no summons came,

he assumed there had been a foul up in records, and so he made the first of two visits to the United States Embassy in Grosvenor Square. They were very polite at the Embassy that first time; they took his name, address and service details and thanked him for calling, and said the best thing he could do was to return to Thetford and wait for instructions to come through in the normal way. And so he drove back home to find what was left of the hotel still smouldering.

There was still one fire tender on the scene, and the crew chief told him that a MIG 21 had apparently jettisoned its napalm bombs over the town whilst trying to evade a couple of RAF Phantoms; but if he wanted further details, he suggested Dinkmeyer tried the police. They were very sympathetic at the police station, and he knew his worst fears were confirmed when they diffidently asked him to go with them to the local school, which had been commandeered for use as a temporary mortuary. He was shown three unidentified bodies, two of which were so badly burned as to make them unrecognisable, but Julie at least he was able to identify. There was no sign of Sue, and it was another thirty-six hours before the police found her wandering in a daze near the Stanford Training Area twelve kilometres away. Piece by piece, Dinkmeyer learned that Sue had returned home on the school bus at four o'clock, and found the hotel blazing. She said she had asked one of the firemen where her mother was, but he had been too busy fighting the fire to pay much attention to her; and after that she was a little vague about her movements.

There was no reason to stay in Thetford now, and Dinkmeyer thought it best to get the child to a safer place, and so, for the second time he made a visit to the Embassy. He couldn't have chosen a worse time. Soviet parachute and airborne forces had been reported landing in East Anglia, and just about every ex-patriate in Britain was on the doorstep. Sue of course was the problem—she was not an American citizen—and even in a time of crisis, there is always someone who believes in doing things by the book.

He found rooms in Bayswater while he continued to haunt the Embassy in those last few days before the Armistice was arranged. He remembered he was walking with Sue down Whitehall, past Horse Guards Parade, when the news was given out that it was all over. He had spent another fruitless morning at the Embassy, only to be told that Pan Am and TWA were now operating out of Shannon, and if he wanted to get home, he had better get himself to Eire, and even then nothing could be guaranteed. And then, right outside the front entrance of the War Office, he bumped into Vickers.

Vickers was in civilian clothes; not the dark lounge suit, bowler hat and briefcase which identifies a man as much as a uniform does, but hatless in a blue pin-stripe and checked shirt. Dinkmeyer noticed with a shock that he had shaved off his moustache and had parted his hair differently. Vickers was equally surprised to see him. Dinkmeyer never could fathom why Vickers should have bothered with him at that particular moment, when his country was about to be occupied, and the United States had accepted the Armistice conditions; but the fact remained that Vickers did find the time to listen to his story. He took Dinkmeyer to a Lyons Café, and they sat there drinking tea and Sue tackling a sticky bun; and after he had finished telling him about Julie, Vickers had asked him if he wanted to even things up, and he had said yes without really knowing what he was letting himself in for.

Now, when he came to look back on that chance meeting, Dinkmeyer realised that Vickers hadn't allowed him time to think things over. In a few swift hours, he had got him a new passport and a new identity. He became ex-Master Sergeant Walter S. Dinkmeyer, and perhaps the hardest part was training Sue to forget that her stepfather had once been known as Captain Paul Keith, USAF.

In the course of the next few weeks, his background was carefully manufactured, and before Russian Military

Government had time to organise National Registration, Dinkmeyer was given enough money to start up in business, and was sent to Salisbury to operate a dead letter-box system for Vickers. For four and a half years there had been no hitch, but now there was every chance that this man Garnett, sitting opposite him in the kitchen with a piece of sticking plaster over his right eyebrow, was going to blow his cover.

Dinkmeyer said, 'You're set on seeing Olds tonight?'

'It was implicit in the signal.'

'But it didn't say so in so many words?'

'No, of course it didn't. It said, "Contact and inform Olds he is relieved pending court martial, appoint suitable deputy; further instructions follow tomorrow." That seems to indicate a sense of urgency to me.'

'Do you think that Olds is going to believe you have had instructions from London to that effect?'

'No, I don't; that's why I need your help.'

Dinkmeyer lit one of his long thin cigars. 'I don't think you understand my position,' he said slowly, 'and I don't think Vickers would like me to get too involved.'

Garnett snorted. 'How much longer do you think you can stay in this country and still be a neutral observer?'

Dinkmeyer sighed. 'Listen,' he said patiently, 'I'm the cut-out between Vickers and the south-west. I run the DLB, and we've got a good set-up here, and I won't see it ruined just because you've got your balls on fire.'

'And who do you think is going to be dropping any messages in on you if this goes sour?'

Dinkmeyer ignored him. 'It has taken years to set this up right, you should know that. Look, if you're going to be any good as a spy, you also have to be a successful businessman. Lonsdale knew that and so did Abel. I run a reputable guest house, and I've got a legitimate business employment agency, and both places are a perfect cover for a DLB. And you want to bust it wide open.'

'We are still going to call on Olds.'

'It's nearly ten o'clock, why don't we leave this until morning when you've had time to think on it?'

'We go tonight,' Garnett said evenly.

Dinkmeyer hurled his cigar into the kitchen grate. 'This is one time,' he said angrily, 'when I wish there was a curfew in force.'

All the way out to Greenacres, Dinkmeyer nursed the hope that perhaps Olds would have company, and then even Garnett wouldn't be pigheaded enough to force the issue, but when they pulled into the empty drive that hope disappeared, and he swore under his breath.

Garnett read his mind. 'Bad luck,' he said softly. 'If there had been another car outside the house, you would have won yourself a reprieve.' He got out of the car and rang the front door bell. After a moment's hesitation, Dinkmeyer reluctantly followed him.

The door was opened by Karen Olds—not the Karen Olds he had seen on film, but more like the picture Dinkmeyer had originally painted of her. She was wearing a fawn-coloured trouser suit and gold open-toed sandals; black-framed glasses gave her a demure but earnest look. She brushed a wisp of hair back off her forehead. 'Can I help you?' she said vaguely.

Garnett said, 'We're from Head Office, Mrs Olds, we'd like to see your husband, please.' She looked puzzled and he added, 'It's a business matter and I'm afraid it's urgent.'

She opened the door a fraction and Garnett stepped inside the hall before she had a chance to change her mind. She glanced nervously over her shoulder and said, 'Richard?' There was no reply, and her voice rose an octave. 'Richard,' she said, 'there are two men here to see you.'

The door of the lounge opened slowly and Olds appeared, dressed in a white open-necked shirt, green twill trousers and carpet slippers. He was a small man, not much bigger than his wife, and he looked insignificant. It was hard to imagine that this slight, worried-looking figure with his few strands of hair carefully brushed back to cover the bald patch on his crown, was the head of operations for the south-west.

Olds said, 'Who are you, and what do you want?'

'We haven't met,' said Garnett, 'I'm from Head Office. I believe you already know Mr Dinkmeyer, or at least have done business with his employment agency.' He walked towards Olds. 'May we use your study? This is a confidential matter.'

Olds looked at his wife, saw from her expression that she was apprehensive, and said, 'It's all right darling, you go back to the television. I won't be long.' He glanced sideways at Garnett. 'You'd better follow me,' he said tersely.

The study was opposite the lounge, and Garnett almost made the mistake of leading the way. Olds closed the study door behind them and sat down at the roll-top desk. 'Is this going to take long?' he said. 'I've had a very busy day, and I'm tired, and I would like to get to bed.'

Garnett said, 'Show him the photograph.'

Dinkmeyer reached inside his jacket pocket and gave Olds the snapshot. Olds studied it carefully. It didn't seem to surprise him that another man was zipping up his wife's skirt.

'How much?' he said.

'What?'

'How much for the negative?'

'Is that all you can say?' said Garnett.

Olds rubbed his eyes, pinching the bridge of his nose between finger and thumb. He looked very tired. 'It's happened once before, a long time ago, pre-war in fact. I had to pay a hundred and fifty for that negative; this one isn't worth ten. Of course, there have been other men between times,' he said wearily, 'but I've always turned a blind eye because she can't help it you see, and she is usually very discreet.'

'She wasn't very discreet this time,' Garnett said harshly, 'her latest lover happens to be Captain Feodor Illyushin of the Soviet Army. Maybe you can shrug that one off but we can't. The message from London is that you are relieved of command pending court-martial. You're too big a security risk to be left in charge.'

Olds searched through his pockets and brought out a packet of cigarettes. His hands were shaking so much that he had difficulty in opening the flip top. 'What do I do now?' he said hoarsely.

'You do nothing, you sit tight and wait for further orders. What I want from you are the names of the two men you think would make the most suitable replacements.'

'How do I know you're not from Special Branch?'

'Why don't you ask Dinkmeyer?'

'You may be forcing him to co-operate.'

'I don't have to convince you,' said Garnett. 'If I was from Special Branch, I'd come round with a hell of a lot more than a snapshot to put the pressure on you. If I was from Special Branch, I'd take you down to headquarters and roast the information out of you.'

Olds moistened his lips. In an almost inaudible voice he said, 'You could try either Lewis Campion or Mervyn Stockbridge—either one would make a suitable deputy.'

'And the addresses?'

'Campion lives at 39, Albemarle Gardens, Andover; you'll find Stockbridge at 107, Torrington Drive, Frome.'

'Thank you,' Garnett said dryly, 'London will be pleased to hear you have been so co-operative. Incidentally, a word of advice—I meant what I said about sitting tight. You try to run away, or go to the police, and we'll find ways to reach you, friend, you may rely on that.' He walked out of the room followed by Dinkmeyer. Neither Karen nor Richard Olds bothered to see them out of the house.

As they drove off, Garnett said, 'I'll need to use your car tomorrow.' Dinkmeyer whistled tunelessly through his teeth. 'I'll have to visit Frome and Andover.' He waited, but Dinkmeyer refused to nibble. 'After all, what would you do if you were running things in London? You'd want to restore morale, right? And the only thing that would really raise morale is to pull off something big. Anyway,' he finished lamely, 'we have to be ready for such a possibility, don't you think so?'

'Well, I'll tell you,' Dinkmeyer said slowly, 'if I was running things in London, I'd fire you. I don't like you, Mr Abel, or whatever your name is. You're too clever to be let loose on your own. You took out a piece of insurance tonight, and I don't like being your collateral. You think I'm dumb or something? I know the way your mind clicks. You figured if Olds was really bent, he might send someone after you. You didn't need my help to pressure him. I was just brought along to let him know you weren't alone, and there was more than one target to shoot at.'

'Are you finished?'

'Yes,' said Dinkmeyer.

Garnett said, 'Well, I'll tell you, Mr Dinkmeyer, or whatever your name is, from now on you're responsible for Mr Olds. He doesn't break wind but what I want to know about it.'

10

HE COULD REMEMBER every word of the message, and the short, terse, military phraseology kept repeating itself in his mind like a TV commercial, and like a jingle, it went straight to the point. It said: 'First stop Make Initial Contact Funland Bournemouth Tomorrow 1200 And Advise Courier Olds Replacement stop Second stop Courier Will Advise RV With Planner stop Target Is Big Repeat Big stop Although Essential Morale Raised You Have Discretion Time/Place Of Attack Within Limits stop Fourth stop Recognition Indicator Keep Smiling Message Ends.'

He walked down the West Undercliff Promenade, threading his way through the crowds of holidays makers, his eyes on the look out for the Funland Amusement Arcade. In a changing world there were some things which were constant; come mid-June, the British started to gather at the seaside resorts like flocks of migratory birds, arriving in a trickle at first and then becoming a flood in late July, when there was hardly room to move on the beach. It was the season of concert parties, coach trips, crazy golf, ice cream, wasps, litter and wet bathing suits and beach towels hanging out to dry from hotel bedrooms; and the ozone, which everybody came to breathe, was frequently spiced with the smell of fish and chips and warm beer. You could buy winkles, shrimps, popcorn, candy floss, and bric-à-brac souvenirs from a hundred casual traders only too pleased to separate you from your money, but nobody cared too much about that, because they were on holiday, and you are supposed to enjoy yourself at the seaside.

Funland offered Bingo, one-armed bandits, fruit machines, pin tables, mechanical grabs, hoop-la, and a battery of shooting galleries. Garnett changed a pound note with the attendant for a handful of loose change and played the fruit machine, losing steadily, until bored with trying to get three lemons up in a row, he moved on to the shooting gallery. He watched a couple of youngsters splatter the outer and magpie rings of the target and then tried his luck. He didn't do any better —the ·177 BSA air rifle had a floating foresight and a hair trigger. A voice at his elbow said, 'You're not having much luck.'

Garnett turned his head. The man grinned at him. 'Cop this,' he said. He fired six pellets, reeled in his target on the pulley, and studied the results. A puzzled look replaced the confident expression on his face. He ran his fingers through short brown hair. 'I couldn't have done worse if I'd kept my eyes closed. You staying in digs in Bournemouth or down for the day?'

'Day trip.'

'I came down on a coach trip last year, liked the look of the place and the birds, and decided to spend my next summer holiday here. I made a mistake.'

'You did?'

'Yeah. I picked a lousy boarding house near the station—makes me wish I'd stopped up in the Smoke. Still, you can't grumble, the weather isn't bad and, like my old man used to say, you've got to look on the bright side of life and keep smiling.' He laid the target on the counter, winked at Garnett and said, 'I think I'll go and spend my money somewhere else.' He walked away and didn't look back.

Garnett lit a cigarette and strolled casually after him. He caught up with the stranger on the pavement outside the arcade.

The man said, 'Let's stroll along the promenade towards the lift. It's better if we stick to first names—I'm called Alan.'

'I'm George,' said Garnett.

'Do you like popcorn, George?'

'No.'

'I've got a yen for some—won't be a minute, cock.' Moving off at a tangent, he drifted over to a stall and bought a bag. He came back, the wide grin on his face almost stretching to meet the sideburns below his ears. He poked the bag under Garnett's nose. 'You're sure you won't have a handful, George?'

'No thanks.'

He shrugged his shoulders. Between mouthfuls of popcorn, he said, 'We hear you've been pretty busy, George.'

'I've seen a bit of the countryside.'

'I bet you have. The point is, have you found a suitable replacement for Henry?'

'I've settled for Lewis Campion.'

'Did you have much choice?'

'There was one other starter.'

'But he wasn't good enough?'

'No.'

'Where does Campion live?'

'In Andover, 39, Albemarle Gardens.'

'And is his cover good enough?'

'I think so.'

'All right, I expect the man will be satisfied with your choice.'

'He will have to be, won't he,' Garnett said dryly.

'Well, okay, keep your hair on, George, we've all got our jobs to do. I'll leave you at the lift. You go back to the railway station. You go to the taxi rank and keep your eyes open for a Vauxhall, licence number NVY 502F. Now, it's a pirate, so don't wait in the queue—he'll be cruising round looking in at the station now and then. When you see the cab, signal the driver with a V-sign, and he'll come over. Tell the driver you want to go to Poole. He'll tell you what we have in mind.' He screwed up the empty popcorn bag and tossed it into a litter bin. Wiping his hands on a white handkerchief, he said,

'This is where we part company, George. Enjoy yourself.'

Garnett said, 'You must be joking.'

He caught a bus to the Wimbourne Road, alighting just short of the county cricket ground to walk the rest of the way to the station. He had chosen the longest possible route, and he stopped frequently, using shop windows as a mirror to see if he was being followed. The checks proved negative. The rest was as easy as falling off a log. Minutes later he arrived at the station, the pirate cab showed up, the driver recognised Garnett's signal and pulled up alongside him. There was a brief swearing match with the drivers of the Fleetway Cabs, who were plying for trade from the official rank, but it didn't amount to much.

As they rolled out of town on the A35 to Poole, the driver pushed his peaked cap to the back of his head, scratched his hair and then said, 'What we have in mind, George, could be difficult, but it is still a very tempting target. You know what happens in late September early October every year?'

'The leaves begin to turn.'

The man shook his head. 'I should have guessed,' he said. 'Vickers told me you were a comedian. Autumn is the manoeuvre season; one year it's held in the north, the next in southern England. This year the soldiers are going to play games in the south. These manoeuvres are stage-managed for the benefit of the Press and TV people. Things have to go off without a hitch because the Soviets don't like to lose face. So, about a couple of months beforehand, the Exercise Director gets his Army Commanders together and they work out all the moves like it was a chess match. That's why Marshal Andreyev is spending this week in Warminster.'

'And Andreyev is the target?'

'Yes.'

'Warminster is stiff with soldiers.'

'We weren't thinking of pulling it off in Warminster.

You see, the Marshal left his wife in Kiev.'

'What's the matter, don't they trust him?'

'She has a face like a currant bun.'

'All right, so the separation isn't any hardship.'

'Of course it isn't, especially when he has a mistress like Jean Adams.'

'Is the name supposed to mean something to me?' said Garnett.

'It shouldn't. Andreyev likes to keep his paramours out of the public eye, but where he goes, she goes.'

'And she is with him now?'

'Right. She's installed in a private house in Great Cheverell; North Brook Manor, and he pays her a visit every night.'

'But he doesn't stay the night?'

The taxi driver blasted the horn angrily as he swerved to avoid two cyclists. He kept up a steady stream of obscenities for a couple of minutes before he calmed down.

'What did you say, George?' he said.

'I asked if Andreyev stayed the night with her.'

'Not as far as we know. The conference is now in its third day, and our informant says Andreyev visited her on the two previous evenings at differing times, but only stayed an hour on each occasion.'

'Anything else?'

'He uses a black Zephyr—one of the second grade staff-cars from the motor pool. No star plate or pennant is displayed. He just takes his driver, orderly and Major Zhukov along with him.'

Garnett said, 'Who's Zhukov?'

'His aide. We think he doubles up as a second body-guard.'

They were moving through an endless strip of suburban houses. It was a fact that wherever you went in England you saw the same type of house on the outskirts of any town. Sometimes Garnett thought that there could only have been one architect in the whole country. People used to sneer at the ribbon developments which had sprung up in the thirties, but three decades later they were still building identical shoe-box houses. It had got so that in the south of England one town merged into another and even the people had begun to look alike.

The man said, 'What do you think?'

Garnett dragged his eyes away from the window. 'It's a possibility. I'd need to know a lot more, meet the informant, look the place over for myself and then set it up.'

'We haven't got too much time. He'll leave on the seventh day, which gives us tonight and two more nights.'

Garnett said, 'Then the sooner I meet the informant the better.'

The man took one hand off the wheel and scratched his head again. 'Well now, George,' he said, 'that's going to be difficult. He's gone back to London.'

'How inconvenient. You are sure this man exists?'

'You don't think we would send you off on a wild-goose chase, do you? Look, for weeks now we have had a man watching Adams and noting every move she makes. He followed her down here, hung around long enough to establish the pattern, and then went back to London. Vickers has been after Andreyev for months and this is the best chance we've had to nail him.'

Garnett said, 'All right, you tell Vickers you've made the sale.' He lit a cigarette. Out of the corner of his eye he saw a sign which said, 'Poole Welcomes Safe Drivers'. 'Are you going to drop me off here?' he said.

'Anywhere you say.'

'Make it the town centre then.'

'There is just one more thing, George.' The man cleared his throat. 'How do I get in touch with you again?'

'You don't.'

'I have to be there when you pull it off—Vickers was very clear about that.'

'What's the matter, doesn't he trust me?'

'Let's say he hasn't got much faith in the people you will have to work with. He figures that with me around the odds are not stacked so heavily against you, see?'

'No, I don't.'

'I'm a marksman, that's why.'

'Well, well. In that case you'd better stay at Brocken-hurst Farm in Sutton Veny until I decide the how, when and where of the assassination. Ask to see a girl called Dane, she'll look after you.' Garnett leaned forward in his seat and tapped the man on the shoulder. 'Pull into the kerb,' he said, 'I'll pay you off here.'

The man did as he was told. Garnett opened his door, got out, and opened the near side front door. He tossed a couple of pound notes on to the front seat while he studied the sad, thin face closely, so that he would be able to describe it in detail to Dane. 'Have you got a name?' he said.

'Lenny.'

'You Welsh?'

'On my mother's side.'

'What was her name?'

'Dilys. What is this all about? How will it help me to recognise Dane when I see her?'

Garnett said, 'You don't have to recognise her, she'll know you on sight.' He slammed the door and walked away.

Garnett wanted a cigarette. He wanted one badly, and it was sheer torture to know that there was a packet and a lighter in his jacket pocket; but he couldn't use them because of the risk of showing a light in the gathering dusk. He rested his back against a fir tree, picked a blade of grass and chewed it. From his position on the hillside he had a good view of the house, which stood back from the minor road leading to Market Lavington. North Brook Manor didn't live up to its name. It was an ordinary, stone-built house, with maybe four or five bedrooms. There was a pretentious gravel drive leading up to the front porch, but that was the only touch of grandeur about the place. He thought it more than likely that an estate agent was responsible for adding the word **Manor** after North Brook.

He glanced at his luminous wrist watch and saw the minute hand coming up to four minutes past ten, and he wondered what Dane was doing at that precise moment in time. Was she lying in her narrow bed in that cramped attic room with the sloping ceiling, or was she down-stairs watching television with the rest of the Brocken-hurst family? Thinking about Dane was the most pleasant way he knew of passing the time. He could escape the present by building a dream of their future together, however remote and uncertain that might be. It was hard to visualise an end to the Soviet occupation and there were times, when feeling depressed, he doubted whether he would be alive to see it.

Headlights appeared in the distance on his left, and presently he could distinguish the hum of the car engine. The beam cut across the meadow land below the wood, and a rabbit froze in its tracks transfixed by the sudden glare. The fringe of the pine wood where Garnett was lying remained in darkness. The car, a dark-coloured Zephyr, swung into the drive of North Brook Manor, made a right-handed U-turn, and stopped opposite the front door. A light came on in the hall, the door opened, spilling a yellow shaft on to the gravel, and three men got out of the car. The driver remained behind the wheel. The time was 10 : 19. Minutes later the light in the room above the porch went out. Garnett hadn't caught a glimpse of Adams from first to last.

The man sitting inside the car made the business of approaching the Manor a very risky proposition. If they were to nail Andreyev while he was visiting his mistress, they would have to be waiting for him inside the house before he arrived, in which case they would need to know how many people lived at North Brook Manor. On balance, he favoured the idea of ambushing Andreyev somewhere on the road between Westbury and Great Cheverell, but as Campion would be doing the job, his would have to be the final decision. Tomorrow he would drive Campion along the route and let him see the lie of the land for himself. They needed time to brief the men and obtain the arms and ammunition. No matter which way he looked at it, it seemed virtually certain that the job would have to be scheduled to coincide with Andreyev's final visit to the Manor in forty-eight hours' time. It was going to be a close run thing.

At 11:34 the Marshal departed as quietly as he had arrived. Ten minutes later, when the house was in darkness, Garnett left his cover and walked back to the lane behind the hillcrest where he had hidden the motor cycle in an overgrown ditch. He wheeled the Norton a full kilometre before he kicked the engine into life.

11

THE BLUEBOTTLE SETTLED on the DDT fly card long enough to become contaminated. It took off leisurely and flew at the window in Dinkmeyer's office seeking a way out. It behaved normally until the poison started to take effect, and then began to execute a series of wild aerobatic manoeuvres. Losing control, the fly landed on its back on the window sill, whirred its wings frantically making a loud buzzing noise, and then, after a final spasm of twitching legs, it died. It reminded Garnett of the effect nerve gas had on humans.

Dinkmeyer said, 'Campion is happy about the job?'

'Yes.'

'And you, and he, and this Lenny are all going along?'

'That's right,' said Garnett.

Dinkmeyer shook his head. 'You've got too much brass for one job.'

Garnett lit a cigarette. 'You know what it's like. These things have a way of snowballing. Head Office takes a personal interest in the show, and before you know it, every sub-chief with an axe to grind is hanging around to see that nothing goes wrong.'

'With one notable exception.'

'Right; you're not involved.'

'Why?'

'Because if anything goes wrong, you'll have to make a full report to London next time a courier comes through. Any report is going to be too long and detailed to send over the air, so Dane is out.'

Dinkmeyer said, 'If the worst does happen, what do I tell them?'

'You tell them we didn't like the idea of taking Andreyev at North Brook Manor because there were too many unknown factors, and the number of withdrawal routes was very limited, so Campion settled for an ambush on the road. The site he selected is on the far side of Eddington in an isolated house. We've got a clear field over a good killing zone and a diverse number of escape outlets. Security has been good; only Campion and I know the plan. The rest of the group—with the exception of Lenny—have no idea what the target is yet. Campion won't brief them until the last minute.'

'And tonight is the big night?'

Garnett stubbed his cigarette out in the ashtray. 'It is,' he said. 'With luck I'll see you tomorrow.'

Dinkmeyer said, 'Watch out for yourself.'

'I will,' said Garnett. 'You make sure you keep watching Olds; it's time London did something about him.' He walked out of the office, closing the door behind him.

The Norton was in the car park where he had left it immobilised. Garnett replaced the rotor arm, kicked the engine into life and engaged first gear. The grating noise confirmed his suspicion that the clutch was wearing out. At least the Norton had one redeeming feature; there was no danger of the countryside flashing by unseen, for even with the throttle wide open, the bike was good for 80 kph and no more. At that speed you had time to admire the scenery. He weaved his way towards Sutton Veny, wondering if he would be alive to retrace his steps this time tomorrow. The plan was sound enough, but he would be working with men who were strangers, and that made the issue uncertain.

He arrived at Brockenhurst Farm just before five o'clock, and ran the motor cycle into the barn. Dane emerged from the farmhouse carrying a bundle of clothing and walked across the yard to join him. Garnett propped the Norton against the supporting beam and turned to face her. 'Hullo,' he said, 'where's Lenny?'

'In the house.' She handed Garnett the bundle of clothing.

'He's already changed.'

Garnett removed his jacket and draped it over the pillion seat, kicked off his elastic-sided boots and dropped his pants.

Dane said, 'It's a good thing I'm not easily embarrassed.'

He smiled. 'Come on, admit it hon, you haven't blushed in years.'

Her eyes crinkled. She shoved a pair of faded blue denims at him and said, 'Here, put these on and stop acting like a sex symbol.'

The denims were a tight fit round the waist, and he had trouble tucking the checked shirt inside the pants.

'You're putting on weight,' Dane said with a grin.

'You've shrunk the pants.'

'Nonsense.'

Garnett bent down and laced up the hobnailed boots. He kicked the toecaps against the stone floor to take the shine off them, and then crammed his fingernails with dirt. 'A leaf out of Buchan,' he said.

'What?'

'*The Thirty-Nine Steps*. Hannay said you should look the part, no false beards, just look the part.' He rolled up his clothes into an untidy bundle and gave them to Dane. 'I'll pick them up later tonight or early tomorrow morning.'

'You don't take care of your clothes,' she said.

'It's a failing of mine. I think we had better go and get hold of Lenny.'

Garnett draped the denim jacket over one arm and slipped his other arm around her waist and led her out into the yard. He whistled a couple of times and Lenny came out of the house like a well-trained gun-dog, and they stood by the roadside, awkward and ill at ease while they waited for the truck to come by.

Ten minutes later, a four-ton tipper with the letters WCC painted on the body, drew up outside the farm.

Garnett ignored Campion, who was sitting in the cab with the driver, and walked round to the back. He flung his jacket over the tailboard and climbed inside. Lenny followed him.

There were four other men sitting inside a metal tank, which had been tipped on its side to make a crude shelter. One of the men gave Garnett a gap-toothed smile and said, 'How do you like working for the Wiltshire County Council then, mate?'

Garnett didn't answer him; he squatted down resting his back against the side of the truck and lit a cigarette. When he glanced back down the road, Dane was just a speck in the distance. Garnett looked at the four men and said, 'Have you been told what to do?'

Gap-tooth glanced at his companions, saw they weren't going to answer, and appointed himself as their spokesman. 'Don't you fret,' he said, 'we've been told what's expected of we.'

The cigarette suddenly tasted foul and he flipped it over the side. 'What about the hardware?' said Garnett.

The man patted the box between his legs. 'We're sitting on it.'

Lenny said, 'I wish to hell someone would tell me what is going on.'

'The house is out,' Garnett said tersely. 'We're going for an ambush, and you don't need to know any more than that, because you're just coming along as an observer.'

Lenny shrugged his shoulders. He was an even-tempered man, who was not easily riled, and he had no intention of becoming ruffled by a display of irritation. He turned a friendly smile on Garnett and said, 'Okay, you're the boss.'

Garnett jerked his thumb at the cab, 'You're wrong there,' he said, 'the boss is riding up front.'

They hit the Boreham Road and turned left along the approach road to Warminster, which, it seemed to Garnett, was more impressive than the town itself; one moment you were riding along a broad avenue, and the next you had passed through the town, almost before you were aware of it. He had read in a guide book that Warminster had once been the centre of the wool trade in the early Middle Ages, and he was inclined to believe that the town had scarcely grown in size since those days. They were, however, in the midst of history — Roman soldiers had passed this way as the legions pulled out from the North and retired on Bath. One day, he hoped the Soviet occupation forces would also come to the conclusion that Britain was a barren and unfriendly land. If they didn't, it wouldn't be for want of trying on his part.

Garnett raised his eyes and studied the other men. They were a silent, moody group; there was none of the traditional coarse banter, but in his experience, this was not so very unusual. Only the very brave, or those with no imagination, could joke at a time when the average man was convinced that his bowels had turned to water.

The vibration of the steel floor set up an unpleasant tingling sensation in his buttocks and in the soles of his feet. Garnett shifted to a more comfortable position, and caught a glimpse of the White Horse of Westbury cut into the hill above them on the right hand side of the road. He calculated there was another five minutes to go. He tapped Gap-tooth on the leg to indicate he wanted to get at the box.

Dragging the box close to him, Garnett raised the lid and sorted through the collection of arms. He chose a ·38 Smith and Wesson, checked the cartridges in the cylinder, and then stuck the pistol into the waistband of his trousers.

Lenny said, 'Don't I get anything?'

'Help yourself,' said Garnett. 'Take what you like, only leave the Stoner alone.'

Lenny grubbed around inside the box and brought out a 9mm Stechkin. 'I'll take this,' he said. 'It's the best machine-pistol I've handled. She's got a twenty-round magazine, you've got the capacity to fire semi or full automatic, and the Soviets have made a wooden holster for it which can be slotted into the pistol grip to make an extended butt. You hold it like a rifle, see, and she's accurate up to 200 metres. You tell me another hand gun that's got that performance.'

It was an unnatural outburst brought on by the prevailing mood of tension in the group, a mood, which as the hour of crisis approaches makes voluble men silent, and introverts, like Lenny, garrulous.

'You must have read the brochure,' Garnett said dryly.

Bratton and Eddington were behind them now, and they were moving along a sunken, narrow, tree-lined road. The sun filtered through the overhanging branches and cast a dappled pattern on the tarmac. The road climbed out of the cutting and went into a slow gentle curve. Coming out of the curve, the truck driver changed into third and began to slow up. As they rolled to a stop, Garnett grabbed his jacket and vaulted over the tailboard. Two men followed him. Someone tossed a couple of signboards on to the grass verge. One read 'Slow Down', the other—'Road Works Ahead'. The men picked up the signboards and walked back down the road.

Opposite the truck and lying back from the road was a small, isolated, white-washed cottage. Garnett pushed open the gate and walked up the front path. He carried the jacket draped over one arm to conceal the ·38 tucked in the waistband of his denims. He pounded an insistent tattoo on the door with the brass knocker and waited.

The door was opened by a small, brown-haired woman with an apron tied round her waist and traces of flour on her hands. A baby was crying somewhere in the house. Garnett jerked his thumb in the direction of the truck. 'Can we use your phone?' he said. 'We've broken down.'

The woman looked past him and saw the driver tinkering with the engine. She pushed a wisp of hair out of her eyes. 'Ours is out of order,' she said, 'but there's a call box not far down the road.'

She started to close the door but Garnett shoved his foot in the crack. 'We'll pay for the call, lady.'

'The phone is out of order; are you deaf or something?'

He had the pistol out of the slacks and pointing at her stomach before she finished speaking. He mouth opened, the colour drained from her face, and she looked as if she was going to scream.

As Garnett moved into the hall, she found her tongue. 'What the bloody hell do you think you are doing?'

The phone was standing on a small table just inside the door. Garnett changed the pistol over to the other hand, side-stepped one pace to his right, and ripped the wires out.

The woman struck him across the face. 'I told you that bloody phone was out of order,' she shouted.

She raised her arm to strike again, but he grabbed hold of her wrist and twisted it up behind her back. 'Now, you listen to me,' he said fiercely, 'we've come here to kill a man. If you don't want to get hurt in the process, you'd better do exactly as I say. The people with me can be a mean lot when they want to be.'

'You're hurting my arm.'

'You just walk ahead of me and be a good girl, and then maybe I'll let go of your arm.' He pushed her down the hall into the tiny square-shaped kitchen at the back of the house.

There was a mixing bowl put to soak in the sink, a slab of raw pastry lay on the formica-topped working space, and a saucepan of milk simmered on the electric stove. The pram was outside the back door, which was ajar. The baby was still mewling fitfully.

The woman said, 'He knows it's time for his feed.'

Garnett released her arm and stood back. The woman rubbed her wrist, shot him a venomous look, thought about giving him another piece of her mind, and then decided there were more pressing things to be seen to. She lifted the saucepan of milk off the stove and carefully poured it into the feed bottle.

Garnett said, 'Your husband gets home just after six, doesn't he?'

The woman ignored him. She pulled the teat on over the neck of the bottle, put it against her face and then, deciding that it was too hot, cooled it off under the cold-water tap. She placed the bottle on the kitchen table, lifted the baby out of the pram, and sat down. She reached out for the bottle and met Garnett's gaze. 'Haven't you got anything better to do than stand around watching me feed the baby?' she snapped.

'I'll second that,' said Lenny.

Garnett said, 'About ten minutes from now her husband will open the front gate, wheel his bicycle up the path, walk it round the house, and prop it against the wall. When he walks through that door I'll be waiting for him.'

'Anything else you'd like to tell me, or am I still to be kept in the dark?'

'Right now,' said Garnett, 'the others should be placing a Mk VII anti-tank mine in the culvert which runs underneath the surface of the road. We plan to electrically detonate the mine from this house. Either the mine will blow the car to bits, or if it is fired too soon, it will make a big enough crater to stop the Zephyr. If it's the latter, we finish Andreyev off with the Stoner machine-gun.'

Lenny said, 'If we had a rocket launcher we could be sure of stopping the car.'

'Unfortunately, one isn't available.'

Lenny put the Stechkin down, leaned back against the dresser and crossed his ankles. 'The road signs are intended to slow the car down so that we can identify it before we spring the ambush?'

Garnett said, 'Correct. We have one man there with a mitre radio set to tip us off. He'll be poking around inside a manhole. If Andreyev doesn't show up before dusk, he will put out red warning-lights and conceal himself behind the hedgerow bordering the road. We also have an image intensification sight on the Stoner machine-gun to improve our night vision.'

'The truck worries me.'

'What about it?'

'It's no longer there, that's what worries me.'

Garnett lit a cigarette. 'We no longer need it. The driver has taken it on to Devizes. He's been told to ditch it somewhere. When it's time for us to go we shall move out on foot, cross a couple of fields at the bottom of the garden, and make for the lane this side of the railway embankment. Two cars will be waiting for us in the lane.' He paused, and then said, 'Are you happy now, or is there anything else you want to know?'

'Just one thing, I'm dying for a leak.'

'Try the lavatory upstairs,' said Garnett.

'Oh no you don't. I'm not having you walking all over the house in your dirty boots. If you want to go to the lavatory, you use the outside privy.'

Lenny walked out of the back door; he looked back at Garnett and gave him a lopsided smile. 'Isn't that just like a woman,' he said.

The woman finished feeding the baby, burped him, and then started to walk out of the room. Garnett put out an arm and barred her way.

'Where do you think you're going?' he said.

Her eyes narrowed and her lips flattened out into a thin, straight line. 'I'm going to put him in his cot. I don't know who you think you are, but I can tell you I've just about had a bellyful of you and your lot.'

From the back step Lenny said, 'Still giving you the benefit of her tongue then, is she? You want to let her feel the back of your hand, that'll shut her up soon enough.'

'All right,' Garnett said quietly, 'I've heard enough from both of you to last me a long time.'

'You've heard nothing yet, I can tell you.'

Garnett rounded on the woman. 'I'm going to say this just the once; shut your bloody trap.'

The woman stared at him pop-eyed, her mouth opening and closing like a stranded goldfish.

'That's more like it,' he said quietly. 'All right, Lenny, take her into the other room and don't let her out of your sight. She wants to put the baby in the cot, well, that's too bad, she'll have to nurse him a bit longer because she can't go upstairs. Understand?'

'Yes.'

'And tell Campion I want to see him.'

Lenny arched an eyebrow. 'There's leadership for you,' he said. 'See, we're all running to do your bidding.' He turned on his heel and followed the woman out of the kitchen.

Lenny was trying to needle him and he wondered why. Perhaps it was his way of masking the tension he felt. There was no accounting for the way people reacted under pressure; he could remember one sergeant-major who, in the heat of close-quarter combat, had reversed the accepted drill for throwing a hand grenade. He had somehow managed to lob the pin at the enemy whilst dropping the live grenade behind him.

He heard footsteps behind him, and turning, Garnett came face to face with Campion. There was a glint of anger in the hazel eyes and the lean face was set in a hard expression.

Campion said, 'What do you want now?'

Footsteps crunched on the path outside and a man whistled tunelessly through his teeth. Garnett placed a finger to his lips and stepped behind the kitchen door. He signalled Campion to get out of sight, and eased the Smith and Wesson out of the waistband of his trousers. He heard the man lean the bicycle against the wall, move the pram to one side, and kick his boots against the scraper. He stepped inside, wiped his boots on the mat, and said in a loud voice, 'Ellen, it's me, I'm home, girl. Are you upstairs?'

He walked forward into the kitchen, and Garnett kicked the back door shut. The man jumped, spun round and, seeing the pistol in Garnett's hand, his eyes widened in surprise. A red tongue appeared to lick his lips, and

Garnett smelled the beer on his breath. 'What the hell's going on?' he said huskily.

'There's nothing to get worried about. As long as you do as I say, you'll not come to any harm.'

'Where's Ellen?'

'In the other room with the baby.'

'What do you want with us? You'll find nothing worth stealing in this house.'

'We are not here to steal anything, Mr—?'

'Wheeler.'

'We are just going to use your house for an hour or so, Mr Wheeler.'

A voice from the other room said faintly, 'Is that you Bernard?'

Wheeler raised his voice. 'Don't you fret, it's me.'

'Tell these men to clear out and leave us alone.'

Wheeler eyed the pistol in Garnett's hand. 'I don't think they will take much notice of what I say, Ellen.'

'Now that's what I call a sensible attitude.' Garnett looked at Campion and said, 'Take him into the other room and have Lenny stand guard over the pair of them. I'm going to run a check on the set-up.'

Campion said, and there was a note of hostility in his voice, 'What's the matter, can't you trust us not to make a balls-up?'

'I want to satisfy myself that everything is all right. Those are my instructions; if you don't like it, complain to London next time a courier comes through.' Garnett tucked the gun back into the waistband of his slacks and walked upstairs.

The Stoner had been set up in the front bedroom, and Garnett didn't like the way they had done it one little bit. The windows were still closed, and the machine-gun should have been placed further back in the room to minimise the muzzle flash. He made them open the windows, because it was going to be a hairy enough business anyway when the Mk VII was detonated, without the increased hazard of flying glass. He showed them how to keep the net curtains in place with thumbtacks for, as Garnett pointed out, if later on a breeze got up, the flapping curtains might attract someone's attention. He had the Stoner mounted on a small chest of drawers and lashed the bipod legs in place. He could find no fault with the way they had assembled the gun, and that at least was reassuring. He looked at the two men who were going to man it and said, 'How much do you know about this weapon?'

One of them, a short stocky man with beetle-black eyebrows which joined across the bridge of his nose, said, 'It's a 5·56mm calibre weapons system; like a Johnny Seven toy; with the box of parts that goes with it, you can have a rifle, carbine, a magazine-fed or belt-fed machine-gun. Anything else you want to know?'

Garnett said, 'No, you've said it all.' He stubbed out his cigarette in a china ashtray.

He went downstairs again and found Campion in the front room checking the initiation circuit. Leaning over Campion's shoulder, he said, 'Have you concealed the cable leading to the mine?'

'For Christ's sake,' said Campion, 'do you think we are completely green? Why don't you sit down and stop flapping. You're beginning to get on my nerves.'

Garnett lit two cigarettes and gave one to Campion. 'All right,' he said, 'from now on I'll keep quiet.'

Campion sighed. 'I know you are only doing your job, but we've got too many chiefs and not enough Indians. Look, if it makes you any the happier, we've emplaced the mine and put a man on the road signs who is in radio touch. I've got two men upstairs with the Stoner, and a fourth with a Sterling acting as a longstop down the road. As soon as I get word that the car is on the way, I'll detonate the mine. There's no point trying to set it off under the Zephyr—I've seen too many ambushes go off at half-cock to know that aiming for the jackpot is too chancy a business. Besides, if the first circuit fails, I have got time to switch to the back-up. Given average luck, the car will be severely damaged by the blast, and even if it does escape scot free, the driver won't be able to avoid ploughing into the crater. All right?'

'Sure. Where's Lenny?'

'Where you left him, keeping an eye on the Wheelers.'

Garnett hooked a chair up to the window and sat down. A Post Office van moved up the road, and five minutes later a woman passed by with a black Labrador on a lead. He could hear the rooks cawing in the trees; and then he heard a faint puttering noise which gradually got louder, and presently, a HOUND helicopter appeared over the rim of the hill in front of him. It dipped down and flew overhead, and then, to judge from the sound, it seemed to bank away before recrossing the house and disappearing from sight behind the trees further down the road.

Campion said, 'What the hell do you make of that? Do you think he is coming by air?'

Garnett stubbed out his cigarette in a potted plant. A distant fluttering noise caught his attention and he cocked his head on one side. It sounded like a swarm of angry bees at first—and then the penny dropped.

'For God's sake,' he said hoarsely, 'let's get the hell out of it. There's a lot more than just one HOUND up there; the bastards are throwing a cordon around us.'

Campion smashed a clenched fist against the window sill. 'How?' he shouted, 'how did they know?'

Garnett said, 'I don't know, but I'm not staying here to find out.' He kicked the chair to one side, ran out into the hall, and, pausing briefly at the foot of the stairs, shouted to the men above to get out. He ran towards the kitchen, bumped into Lenny, and grabbing him by the arm, hustled him out of the house. Ellen Wheeler followed them jeering and shouting.

Garnett raced down the narrow cinder path which divided the vegetable garden in two, and hurdled the low wooden fence at the bottom. He pounded across the open field spattered with cow pats, and burst through the hedgerow into the second field. He heard the cars moving off in the lane, and there was nothing, absolutely nothing he could do about it. His heart was thumping against his ribs and his legs were leaden stumps beneath him, and the distant hedgerow swam before his eyes, but he gritted his teeth and ploughed on.

The hedge was fronted by a barbed-wire fence, and he saw it too late to set himself up for a good take off. He took off on the left foot, and knew immediately that he couldn't lift the right leg high enough. The toe cap caught the top strand and flipped him head first through the hedge, and instinctively he threw up his free arm to shield his face. He hit the uneven ground awkwardly and winded himself. He rose to his feet shakily and nursed his bruised rib cage.

Garnett could see the lane clearly, but of course there was no sign of the cars now. He had no idea where the HOUNDS had off-loaded, no idea how many troops might be holding the cordon, and no idea where his companions were. He told himself there was no point in running blindly forward; he must start using his brains to think of a way out, and that was easier said than done. The railway embankment sliced across the landscape as far as the eye could see in either direction, and although he could see nothing beyond it, he was prepared to bet the cordon was out there somewhere.

The puttering noise was there again, and this acted as a spur as he ran towards the narrow line of trees stretching away on his right, seeking to put some cover between himself and the command ship circling above. As he reached the tree line he heard a short crackle of gunfire, which sounded some distance behind him, and there were voices shouting in anger or fear; and then there was another short burst of gunfire, staccato and final, and then there was no more shouting, and the damned HOUND came skipping in low towards the wooded strip where he was hiding, like a hungry gannet after another fish. It was low, too low for his liking, and the wash from the rotor blades flattened the tree tops and whipped up the loose top soil and flung it in his face. He knew that if he looked up he would see them scanning the area with their binoculars, and it seemed an eternity before the HOUND turned away and disappeared from sight behind the embankment. He took a deep breath and let it out slowly and wiped the sweat from his forehead.

A voice said, 'That was too close for my liking.'

Garnett spun round, the pistol in his hand pointing at Lenny's stomach. Lenny smiled uneasily. 'Don't point that thing at me,' he said, 'it makes me nervous.'

'How did you get here?'

'I followed you, see, like your shadow I was.'

'I didn't hear you.'

'Perhaps you weren't listening very hard.' He moved a pace closer. 'Did you hear the shooting just now?'

'I heard it.'

'Where do you think the bastards are then?'

'Behind the embankment.'

'We can't stay here for ever, can we. I mean, the cordon may start to close in and they'll flush us out.'

'This line of trees stops just short of the embankment and from there on it's pretty bare-arsed, but you are all right once you've got across the railway line.'

'You know this part of the world?' said Lenny.

'I've studied a map of the area.'

'That's nice.'

There was another burst of firing way over on their left. Garnett said, 'About six hundred metres away—that was a Sterling answering the AK 47.'

'Fascinating,' said Lenny. 'Don't you think we ought to move?'

Garnett shrugged his shoulders. 'Let's hope they're looking in the direction where those shots came from. Anyway, there is only one way to find out.'

'Okay, you go ahead then,' said Lenny.

It seemed a long way from the end of the tree line to the top of the embankment and he felt naked all the way, and somewhere in the distance, but out of sight, the damned command ship was still hovering around the area. He crawled the last few metres, and even then when he peeped over the top, he felt sure that his head stood out like a football on a billiard table. He saw the two sentries one hundred metres away on his left, and ducked behind the embankment.

Behind him Lenny whispered, 'What's the matter?'

'There are two sentries to our left—they'll nail us as soon as we come over the top.'

'We can't have that, can we. Tell you what, I'll attract their attention like, while you make a run for it.' He smiled slowly. 'London said to take good care of you, see. No sense in arguing about it, is there?'

He backed off and moved a hundred metres or so down the line. He smiled back at Garnett, and then started up the embankment, moving hunched up with his head down like an ostrich, the butt of the Stechkin in his shoulder. He showed himself above the skyline, shouted to the soldiers and fired a burst before disappearing behind the cover of the embankment. He ran further to his left and repeated the performance.

Garnett threw himself over the top of the embankment and rolled down the far side. He was on his feet inside a second and running flat out for the next hedgerow. Behind him, Lenny kept up a running battle with the soldiers. He went through the hedge like a knife through butter and fell into a steep drainage ditch full of stinging nettles. The barrel of the Smith and Wesson went into the bank, and when he pulled it out, he found it was plugged with soft earth. If he had to use it in that condition, the barrel would either bulge or peel open like a banana skin. He hoped like hell it wouldn't be necessary to use it.

Keeping low in the ditch and scuttling forward like a cossack dancer, Garnett made slow progress. The nettles whipped against his face and hands, raising painful white lumps, and he cursed and blinded under his breath and the sweat ran down into his eyes and made them smart. Moving forward in that cramped position taxed his strength, and after he had covered a bare three hundred metres, he was almost in a state of collapse. He stopped to rest, his chest heaving, the bile in the back of his throat threatening to spew out. And now that the shouting and the staccato bark of the Kalashnikovs and the menacing puttering of the command ship had died away to nothing, the countryside seemed unnaturally quiet, and yet the very stillness was oddly hostile. Gradually his heart stopped its wild beating and the feeling of sickness passed.

Garnett moved on, and the ditch got more and more shallow with each step, and he wondered if it would peter out altogether before he succeeded in infiltrating through the cordon. A series of faint but urgent whistle-blasts reached his alert ears. He wasn't sure whether to put it down to imagination or not, but he thought he also heard the excited baying of dogs on a scent. He climbed out of the ditch and started to move at a jog trot. Five minutes later he was convinced the dogs were rapidly closing the gap between them, and he supposed the helicopter must have refuelled because the damn thing was puttering around again, only this time it was carrying out a systematic map-square by map-square search.

He came upon the abandoned mill quite suddenly, just when he had reached the conclusion that he had drifted too far to the north to hit it. It was, he thought, the only reasonable hiding place in the whole area, but now that he had stumbled across it, the dilapidated shell, which was all that remained of the building, didn't seem such a good bolt-hole after all. The mill was in ruins, the wheel was rotten and encrusted with moss; the stream, blocked with rubble, had overflowed into a natural hollow to form a deep, stagnant pond choked with rushes. An unbroken yellow scum covered the entire surface except for a patch of dark water near the wheel. He was not a strong swimmer, and the idea of entering that dank pond and swimming in its murky depths to avoid disturbing the scum while he made for the rushes in the centre, appalled him. It appalled him until he caught a glimpse of the helicopter moving on a parallel course not five hundred metres away.

He walked quickly around the edge of the pond and

lowered himself into the patch of dark water. He filled his lungs with air and sank beneath the surface, and swam slowly along the bottom. It was a dark, slimy and silent world. His lungs felt as though they would burst, but reaching those rushes meant everything to him, so he forced himself to go slowly because one break in the yellow scum would betray his position. He forced his way into the thickest part of the rushes and then slowly surfaced with the blood pounding in his ears. The air never smelt so fresh or so sweet.

The dogs tracked him to the mill and he was forced to submerge again. It occurred to him, that if he had been really clever he would have rigged himself up with a snorkel made of reeds, but the idea came too late to be of practical value, and so he was obliged to surface periodically, but the curious thing was that, quite suddenly, and for no apparent reason, the Russians called off the search.

He stayed in the pool until it was quite dark, and then he swam ashore and collapsed on to the grass shivering with cold. He had, of course, lost the ·38 Smith and Wesson. It was somewhere at the bottom of the pond and he had no intention of looking for it.

He started walking, hoping that the movement would take the chill off his body, but caution made him move slowly. He made a wide detour around Westbury and Warminster, and after a couple of hours his clothing had almost dried out, but he could not stop his hands shaking. He saw no signs of patrol activity, and he reached Brockenhurst Farm just as dawn was breaking. He knew that he was exceptionally lucky to have survived the fiasco and he wondered what the hell London would make of it all, and then he decided he didn't give a bugger what London thought. He found himself under Dane's bedroom, and picking up a handful of loose earth, he tossed it up at her window.

12

DANE WAS IN the middle of a nightmare. She dreamt she
was inside Holloway again in solitary confinement.

There was this narrow, small room with grey walls
and no window and the all-seeing eye of the television
camera in the ceiling. And there was this harsh light, and
the letter box, and the loudspeaker, and the child's chair,
and the hot air blower, and of course, the sprinkler. The
light was in the ceiling, and although it was out of her
reach, it was nevertheless protected by steel battens. This
light was an instrument of refined torture, for at the
trip of a switch the cell could be plunged into total darkness or else lit by a glare which seared the eyeballs. And
hand in hand with the light was the loudspeaker, which,
at any time of the day or night, would emit inhuman
nerve-shattering screams, or else, as a variation, the shriek
of jet engines pitched high up in the decibel range to
cause a violent pain in the ear drums. The chair was
small even for a child, but she had to sit on it rigidly
to attention for most of her waking hours. Failure to do
so meant that the temperature of the cell would be
lowered to sub zero, or raised to such a degree that she
would gasp for breath, or perhaps the sprinklers would
soak her right through to the skin. And so she did as
she was told, suffered agonies from cramped muscles,
knew what it was like to be hungry, to go without sleep,
to lose track of time, and perhaps the most demoralising
thing of all, the knowledge that these indignities were
inflicted upon her not by the Russians but by English
women. And for what? For brawling in the exercise
yard because an inmate had propositioned her. Well all
right, she had thought, the next time I am propositioned

I won't knock the woman down.

The soft pattering sound woke her up with a start, and for a moment she thought she was still in solitary confinement and they had turned the sprinklers on, and then she realised that someone was throwing something at her window. She got out of bed, pushed her feet into a pair of worn slippers, and shuffled over to the window. In the half light of dawn she failed at first to recognise the bedraggled, dirty figure standing in the yard below, until he spoke, and then she knew it was Garnett. She placed a finger to her lips as a sign he should make less noise, and then slipping a dressing gown over her gold-coloured pyjamas, she tip-toed down the creaking staircase and opened the back door. She made him take off his boots in the kitchen before she led him up to her room. He looked tired and done in and his clothes smelt foul.

Garnett said, 'Why all the secrecy?'

'The Brockenhursts are getting jumpy.'

'Oh?'

'They didn't like the idea of Lenny staying here, and they think you are seeing too much of me too regularly.'

'That's too bad,' he said wearily, 'they can just stop moaning; they are paid to take risks.' He sank down into a chair.

'Have you got a cigarette?' He snapped his fingers. 'I forgot, of course, you don't smoke.'

Dane sat down on the edge of her bed and crossed one shapely leg over the other. Tired as he was, it was still a distraction. He rubbed a thumb over the stubble on his jaw. 'Aren't you going to ask me how we got on?' he said.

'You'll tell me in your own good time,' she said.

'It was a fiasco—they got wind of the job.'

'How?'

'I wish I knew; maybe they monitored your transmission.'

Dane frowned. 'That's unlikely. I encode every message and change frequency every fifty seconds when I'm sending. They would need a minute to locate me on the waveband.'

Garnett said, 'I thought one minute was the time they needed to get a positional fix.'

'You may be right,' she said vaguely, 'I suppose to be really safe from intercept, I should have been given the means to squirt.'

'What?'

'You pre-record the message and then push it through in a second, before they have a chance to find your frequency. Still,' she said thoughtfully, 'it's a pretty complicated piece of equipment and there are snags.'

Garnett said, 'I wonder how they knew where to find us.'

'You haven't been listening.'

He was on a separate train of thought and nothing was going to distract him. 'You didn't know, so even if they did intercept the message to London, they wouldn't have got much. They put the cordon in close because they knew exactly where to find us. Lenny couldn't have told them because he wasn't briefed until the last minute. Dinkmeyer knew most of the details but not enough to pin-point the house. Only one man knew everything and that was the truck driver. He dropped us outside the cottage and then went on to Devizes. He could have tipped them off.'

'You think you were betrayed?'

'I have a hunch we were. If we weren't betrayed, the Russians were enjoying a giant-sized piece of luck.' He paused and then said, 'If I am right about the truck driver, he will know about this place. I think you had better shift the radio out of the barn. Can you ride a motor cycle?' She nodded. 'How are you off for money? If you need any, take it from the wallet in the hip pocket of my spare slacks.'

'I'm all right.'

'Okay. You get dressed, take the Norton and get that transmitter out of here. I want you to hide it; find some place where you can get at it unobstrusively if we have to use it again. Then I want you to stay away from the farm for the next few hours until we are satisfied that the law is not going to turn the place over. Fix up some sort of coding arrangement with Brockenhurst and then periodically call his number. Use a different public call box each time.'

'Wouldn't they have raided the farm by now if the truck driver had tipped them off?'

'I don't know, maybe, maybe not, but we are not going to take any chances.'

'Supposing they do turn the place over, and I have to stay in hiding, how will you get in touch with me?'

Garnett said, 'There is a newsagent in town who handles personal adverts. You can put a card in their window. We need to think of some job which isn't too far out, and which isn't going to attract too much demand.'

'I can play the piano,' she said.

'Fine,' said Garnett, 'there isn't much demand for piano lessons. Use the name Valerie Ross and leave your address. Okay?'

'I understand,' she said quietly. 'What are you going to do?'

'I'm going to bath, shave and change my clothes, and then get a bus into Salisbury. I have to find out if Dinkmeyer is still in circulation. If you get the chance, pass a message to London—tell them the job was a fiasco, say I suspect there was a leak and am investigating.'

It took him under twenty minutes to bath, shave and change, and he need not have hurried. Nobody dropped in on them, neither the police, nor the Special Branch, nor Soviet counter-intelligence appeared to be interested in the farm. Their indifference was almost uncanny, and Garnett could think of no logical explanation for their failure to follow up a lead. There was, it seemed, no need to panic, and so he decided they wouldn't move out until the normal traffic flow got underway.

He sent Dane off around eight o'clock, and then walked down to the request stop on the Boreham Road and caught a bus into Salisbury shortly after 8 : 30. The journey was uneventful. It was, for August, a chilly overcast day, and after his immersion in the pond, he felt the cold. He thought it would be just his luck to go down with flu. He got off the bus in Fisherton Street, bought a local newspaper, and went into a coffee bar on Butcher Row.

Garnett found what he was looking for in the stop press. Bald, accurate and to the point, it merely said that, acting on information, the security forces had killed six terrorists near Eddington. They had had enough time to catch the paper before it went to press and they could have given the news a spread if they had so chosen. They had, instead, played it down and he wondered why. He finished his coffee and left. He strolled up to an empty call box at the junction of Minster Street and Blue Boar Row and called Dinkmeyer.

He said brightly, 'How is everything?'

'Fine, just fine,' said Dinkmeyer. 'Where are you?'

Garnett said, 'Not far away, I'll be with you in five minutes.' He hung up and left the call box.

He walked up Castle Street and everything seemed normal enough. Miss Tate behaved in her normal fashion—she shot him a filthy look and went back to her typewriter, and there was nothing unusual about that. He pushed open the door of Dinkmeyer's office and went inside, and then everything stopped being normal.

The man lurking behind the door was small, slim, fair-haired and very, very young. He was also frightened; he kept licking his lips, and the .38 Webley in his hand was shaking, and that made him dangerous, because if Garnett made one false move, he was going to pull the trigger and nobody would pay much attention since the revolver sported a bulbous silencer.

The boy said, 'Close the door.' His voice was cracked and on edge.

Garnett said, 'All right, what's it all about?'

The boy ignored him. 'Is this the man?' he said to Dinkmeyer.

Dinkmeyer nodded. 'Okay, pick up the phone and call them.'

'Are you from the police?' said Garnett.

'Do I look like a policeman?'

'No, I suppose not, you're too young. How old are you —seventeen, eighteen?'

'Have you got a thing about age, dad?'

There was a yellow fuzz on the cheeks, spiky bristles on the chin where he hadn't stood up close enough to the razor, and an angry red spot with a white head at the corner of his mouth. The eyes were pale blue and devoid of expression. He was about as safe as a booby trap. There was a faint tinkle as Dinkmeyer put the phone back on the cradle, but the pale blue eyes didn't leave Garnett for a second. Scarcely moving his lips, the boy said, 'How long?'

Dinkmeyer cleared his throat. 'About a couple of minutes.'

'You bastard,' Garnett said softly, 'you pig sick bastard.'

'You think I like doing this?' Dinkmeyer shouted. 'Listen, right now they have a man sitting next to Sue. If I fail to co-operate they'll take care of her. You know what Sue is like; do you think I could let anything happen to her?'

'No, of course you couldn't.'

'Why don't you two kiss and make up?' the boy said.

Garnett said, 'For the second time of asking, suppose you tell me what this is all about?'

'It's about grassing, it's about the six men you set up for the Ivans. It's about your funeral.'

His breath was so bad that garlic in comparison would have smelt as sweet as a rose. The upper incisors in his mouth were black stumps which fed poison into his stomach. Garnett thought he was lucky to have only one pimple on his face.

The boy said, 'It's time to go, dad. You be good now. Just walk out into the street and slide into the back seat of the Cortina parked by the kerb. I'll be a pace behind you.'

'And then what happens?'

'We go somewhere quiet and we get the shovel out of the boot and you start digging.' He giggled mirthlessly. 'You'll find the exercise good for your health.'

The boy had seen too many Westerns on TV. The elbow of the gun hand was tucked against the ribs with the forearm parallel to the floor. He was careful not to stand too close because he knew just how much damage a Karate chop could do to the wrist. Someone should have told him just how much damage a wooden door can do to an arm.

He made Garnett walk in front of him, but he failed to remember that the door to Dinkmeyer's office opened outwards. He also made the mistake of allowing Garnett to be just that one pace or two too far ahead. One moment Garnett was nicely in view, the next he had side-stepped to his right and was out of sight behind the partially opened door. There followed a combination of increasing errors. The boy should have hit the door with his right shoulder but instead he tried to squeeze through the gap, and he was still holding the Webley revolver in that ridiculous cowboy posture when the door caught his right arm and moved it through an arc of sixty degrees, trapping it against the frame. There was a thrust of one hundred and seventy-five pounds behind the door and the force of the impact broke his arm as easily as if it had been a matchstick. By pure reflex action, his finger jerked on the trigger before the pistol fell out of his hand, and a bullet slammed into the wall behind Miss Tate, ricocheted off at a tangent, and almost spent, hit the opposite wall. The Webley made a dull plopping noise; not so the boy, his agonised cry hit the high decibel range.

Garnett jerked the door open, sank his right fist into the boy's stomach and, as he doubled up, chopped him down with a rabbit punch. The boy hit the floor and lay still. Garnett scooped up the Webley, glanced at Dinkmeyer and said, 'Get him out of here.'

'They may get funny with Sue.'

Garnett frowned and then said, 'They can't blame you because I escaped. You could tell them you tried to stop me.'

'Hit me,' said Dinkmeyer.

'What?'

'Hit me, I want it to look right.' He saw Garnett hesitate and said, 'Come on, what's holding you back?'

Garnett hit him.

He turned and walked away. Agatha Tate was sitting bolt upright in her chair, a glazed expression in her eyes, her body from the waist up trembling like a jelly. The .38 had missed her skull by a fraction of a centimetre. Garnett said, 'Cheer up, it may never happen.'

He walked out of the front door holding his right arm loosely across his stomach so that the Webley was tucked out of sight inside his jacket. Four quick strides took him across the pavement. He wrenched open the rear door of the mink-coloured Cortina and slid inside, holding the Webley on the man who was sitting behind the driver. 'All right,' he said, 'let's move out of here before we have any more trouble.' The driver hesitated long enough to convince Garnett that he was going to be difficult. 'I said move out. There is a uniformed policeman just up the road who is watching us. This is a No Parking area, do you want him sticking his oar in?'

The gears grated as the driver shifted into first, and his foot slipped off the clutch as he accelerated. The Cortina made a series of kangaroo hops before getting underway. The plump man on the back seat said nervously, 'What happens now?'

'You have a nickname?'

Brown eyes goggled at him from behind tortoise-shell rimmed glasses. 'Felix,' the man said huskily.

'Felix,' said Garnett, rolling the name round his tongue. 'Well, Felix, we are going to drive out of Salisbury on the A 30, talk things over, and then I'll drop you both off at intervals.'

Felix blinked his eyes rapidly. 'I don't understand.'

'Neither do I,' said Garnett, 'at least, not fully. What

were you trying to do?'

'Larkin said you had sold us out.'

'Larkin? Is he the man who drove us out to the ambush site?'

'I wouldn't know what part he played.'

'He's around five ten, about one sixty pounds, has a prominent beaky nose.'

'That's Larkin,' said Felix.

'So he got in touch with you, said I had sold out, and you called round to settle the account. Isn't that about right?'

'Yes.'

'Didn't it occur to you that Larkin might have been covering his tracks, that maybe he was the one who tipped off the Russians?'

'We did plan to hold an enquiry,' Felix said defensively.

Garnett said, 'Like hell you did, you had a firing squad in mind. When you get back to Salisbury, you had better see the man who gave you the errand, and tell him he had the wrong end of the stick.'

Felix had an unhappy hang-dog expression on his face. A worried frown appeared on his brow, and he shifted in his seat. 'I wish you would come with us,' he said plaintively, 'my control isn't going to like the way things have turned out one little bit.' He turned a round, podgy face on Garnett. 'Don't you think it would be more convincing coming from you?' he said.

'Somehow,' said Garnett dryly, 'I don't feel up to it.'

They had left the outskirts of Salisbury behind them now, and were moving along a dead straight road flanked by a trim, low-lying hedge. Some four hundred metres ahead, a ten ton diesel truck lumbered along at a steady sixty kilometres an hour belching a trail of black smoke. Four ZIL 157 cargo trucks passed them going in the opposite direction. A fleeting glimpse of a white sign-post told Garnett that they were four kilometres from Stockbridge.

Garnett said, 'I presume you have a gun, Felix.'

'I have a .38 Police Positive,' Felix said grimly.

'Hip or shoulder?'

'Hip, left side.'

'Dear me,' said Garnett, 'how funny. You'll have to unbutton your jacket, Felix old boy, and turn over on your right side facing the window.'

Felix turned a delicate shade of pink. He unbuttoned his jacket and rolled over on to his right hip. His fat buttocks filled and strained the seat of the shiny blue serge slacks to bursting point. Garnett reached across and deftly plucked the .38 Police Positive out of the holster.

Garnett said, 'You needn't bother to overtake the diesel. Just pull into the next lay-by you come to.'

The driver spoke for the first time. He was commendably brief and to the point. 'Get fucked,' he said.

Felix sighed. 'For God's sake, save the heroics and do as the man says.'

The sign said—Lay-by one kilometre ahead. They overtook the diesel doing ninety-five, and the driver gave no sign of slowing up, but at the last minute he swung into the lay-by and braked fiercely. The diesel truck gave an angry blast as it went by.

'You're a crud, Felix,' the driver said wearily, 'all you needed was an ounce of guts and we could have taken him as easily as falling off a log.'

Garnett said, 'Out you get, Felix.'

'I can't, the car is fitted with child-proof locks. I can't open the door from the inside.'

'I'll let him out,' said the driver.

'The hell you will,' said Garnett, 'you stay where you are. All right, Felix, I suggest you wind the window down as far as it will go, slip your arm through and open the door from the outside. Now that shouldn't be too difficult for an athletically minded man like you, should it.'

Felix succeeded in opening the door after a bit of a struggle. He stepped out into the road, banging his head against the door sill as he did so, and swearing under his breath. Garnett slammed the door shut and told the driver to move out. He caught one final glimpse of the pear-shaped figure gazing sadly after them in the rear view mirror, and then the road went into a sharp curve, and Felix disappeared from view.

Garnett sensed he was going to have trouble with the driver. He wasn't going to be a push-over like Felix, and he was young and cocky enough to try his luck. Dark, tinted sunglasses hid the expression in his eyes, blue-black hair almost covered his ears and curled up over his shirt collar, and a Zapata moustache and olive skin gave him a Mexican appearance. There was a lot of flesh on his frame, and it wasn't flabby. There was no question of him rolling tamely over on his side like some overgrown, over-friendly spaniel while Garnett picked him clean. The moment he leaned over to reach the shoulder holster, trouble would start. Perhaps, thought Garnett, he was just waiting for the opportunity to grab hold of his arm and batter his head against the windscreen.

The driver said, 'We are no distance from Sutton Scotney. How far are you planning to go?'

'Pull over.'

'There is no lay-by around here.'

'Pull on to the verge.'

'Okay, if that's the way you want it.'

He made no effort to slow down as he swung the car off the road and mounted the grass verge. Garnett was bounced up and down and then flung forward as the driver hit the brakes hard. There was no point in waiting to see what he had in mind—Garnett believed in acting first. He cracked the barrel over the driver's skull. He grunted once, and then fell over the wheel. Garnett climbed over the seat, opened the nearside door and got out. He glanced left and right, satisfied himself that the road was clear, and then grabbed hold of the driver by his shoulders, dragged him across the seat and rolled him into the ditch. He got back into the car, revved up the engine, and swung back on to the road.

The driver was still a problem. He might just be mad enough to go to the police, and the police might just take notice of him, and they might just set up a road block at the wrong place and the wrong time as far as Garnett was concerned, and they would catch him in a car which didn't belong to him, and they would find one .38 Webley and one .38 Police Positive on the front seat, and that carried a mandatory death sentence. It was important to get to London in one piece and the fastest way was not always the safest.

Garnett peeled off the A 30 and headed towards Winchester. Some three kilometres beyond Sutton Scotney, he stopped the car and dumped both pistols down a drain, and then drove on. He parked the Cortina in a multi-storey car park, made his way to Winchester Station and caught a stopping train to Waterloo.

He did not know how he was going to get in touch with Vickers, but he still remembered the fail safe telephone number, and he decided to put it to use once more. He went through the barrier at Waterloo, found an empty call box and rang the number. He said, 'I'm up in Town for the day. I'd like to see the chairman about a managerial problem we've come up against in the provinces.'

The voice said, 'I'm not sure he is available. Can you call back in an hour?'

Garnett said he could. He hung up and left the booth. One hour later he called back. They gave him the run around pushing him from one RV to another while they checked to see if he had a tail. He met no one, but spent a small fortune on telephoning in for further instructions. Around 2:30, the voice at the other end of the line told him to look inside his left pocket. He did so and found a business card. On the card was printed Hawes Antiques, North Street, Harrow on the Hill. On the reverse was written, 'Ask for a Congreve clock'. For the life of him, Garnett could not figure out when or where the card had been planted on him.

13

GARNETT WALKED UP the steep, curving hill feeling that he was stepping back in time. Below him, and as far as the eye could see, lay the unplanned, concrete urban jungle. Only the hill was a reminder that once this town had had a separate identity before it was engulfed and finally became as much a part of London as Balham, Whitechapel or West Ham. Somehow the Hill had survived and remained much as it had been at the turn of the century. They were still there, solid reminders of a past civilisation—the church, the Round Speech Room, the antique shops, the King's Head, the tall houses, and that last anachronism, Harrow School. The inmates might not wear straw boaters in the summer any longer, but that was the only significant change, apart from the fact that the annual intake primarily came from the sons of Party members. Harrow was still out to create an elite—which must have seared the souls of quite a few revisionists. There was, Garnett thought, no such animal as a classless society. He walked past the school houses, silent and empty now because of the long summer break.

The antique shop at the top of North Street had bow-fronted mullioned windows reaching almost to ground level, and the thick glass made it difficult to see into the interior. Gilt letters on a white background said, 'Hawes, established 1869'. He pushed open the white door and a bell tinkled in the back of the shop. The trouble with antique shops nowadays, thought Garnett, was that the chances of picking up a bargain had gone for ever. Too many people knew the value of silver and porcelain. Hideous pieces of pottery, which Garnett was certain had once been offered as prizes in a fun fair before World War One, were now fetching absurdly high prices.

A well-corseted woman with greying hair appeared from the back room. Her face was youthful, and only the fleshiness of her arms and the beginnings of a dowager's hump, betrayed the fact that she was closer to fifty than forty. She was neat and smart looking in a navy-blue dress which had been fashionable a decade back. The legs beneath the hem-line demurely covering the knees, were as slim and shapely as any teenager's. Pale green eyes glinted behind rimless glasses. In a voice which was at once business-like, friendly and yet authoritative she said, 'Can I help you?' There was only a ghost of a smile on her lips, but it was genuine.

Garnett said, 'I wondered if you happened to have a Congreve clock.'

The faint smile froze but didn't leave her lips. She walked past him, locked the door, and reversed the sign in the window to read 'Closed'.

'Isn't that going to seem odd to some people?' said Garnett.

'Oh, no,' she said, 'you see, I suffer from migraine a bit and I often close the shop early; besides, trade is slack at this time of year.' She motioned him to follow her into the back room. 'We've been expecting you for the past hour; what delayed you?'

'The trains on the Underground,' he said tersely. 'At this time of day they are few and far between. It doesn't help when you're sent on a grand tour of the London public transport system either.'

The back room looked out over the school playing-fields which sloped down to the Roxeth Road. If the shop had been on the other side of the street, they might have had a commanding view of the gasometer in South Harrow, a sight calculated to lower anyone's spirits.

Vickers was sprawled in an armchair by the window, a glass ashtray full of cigarette butts at his elbow. He waved a hand at Garnett indicating the empty chair opposite him. Ejecting the still smouldering ember of yet another cigarette into the ashtray, he bestowed a wintery smile on Garnett and said, 'Now tell me what all the fuss is about.'

Garnett glanced sideways at the woman who made no sign of leaving the room, and then looked questioningly at Vickers. Vickers said, 'Miss Seagrave is one of our brightest intelligence officers.'

Garnett said, 'I'm afraid we didn't pull it off.'

Vickers looked puzzled. 'Pull what off?'

'The job.'

'What job?' Vickers said with a note of irritation in his voice.

'The assassination of Andreyev. Don't tell me you didn't know anything about it.'

Vickers crossed one elegant leg over the other. He remained cool and detached, but it must have been an effort. 'I know Katz was murdered; I know you nominated Campion to replace Olds; but I know absolutely nothing about the Andreyev affair.'

Garnet turned red. 'Don't tell me,' he said angrily, 'that the orders were given without your knowledge or consent.'

'No such orders were given.'

'Now look here, General,' said Garnett, 'don't try that line with me. I was there when Dane got the message.'

'Oh, when was this?'

'Five days ago at 6:20 pm.'

Vickers said, 'You must be imagining things. Dane is scheduled from 2200 to 2300 hours.'

'That was the old schedule before it was changed to 1800 to 1900. You really ought to get yourself up to date, General.'

A spot of anger showed in Vickers' face. 'Dane is still maintaining the original schedule.'

'You must be mistaken.'

'There is no mistake,' Vickers said, raising his voice, 'each operator has his or her own distinctive fist on the morse key. Beyond any shadow of a doubt, Dane is still transmitting to us at 2200. If you have seen her communicating at any other time, you can be sure she was not in contact with us.'

In a low voice, Garnett said, 'You didn't order Andreyev's execution?'

'No, I did not.'

Garnett licked his lips. 'But I met two agents in Bournemouth. One of them was called Lenny—if he was a Russian agent, he was very convincing. He knew a hell of a lot about you, General.'

Vickers said, 'What's your opinion, Charlotte?'

Seagrave cleared her throat. 'I think we have another cat on our hands.'

'A what?' said Garnett.

'Mathilde Carré.'

'Who is she?'

'It's too long a story.'

'Give him a run down,' said Vickers, 'because I am inclined to agree with you.'

Seagrave looked up at the ceiling as if seeking inspiration. 'When France capitulated in 1940,' she recited, 'the first major Resistance organisation was built up by a number of ex-Polish Army officers who had gone to ground. Prominent among these officers was Captain Roman Czerniawski who met Mathilde Carré by chance and recruited her into his organisation because she appeared to be trustworthy and hated the Germans. In a relatively short space of time, Czerniawski's organisation covered all of German occupied France, and Mathilde, nicknamed "the Cat" because she moved so quietly, became his most valuable and hard-working aide. The Germans, of course, tried to locate the Resistance radio posts with their radio direction finding service, but they did not have much joy.'

Seagrave paused and lit a cigarette. 'And then,' she said, 'the Germans had a stroke of luck, because down in the Cherbourg area, a Luftwaffe corporal became suspicious of a Frenchwoman who was questioning workers at a fuel depot. He reported the matter to the Field Police, where it was dealt with by a Sergeant Hugo Bleicher. To cut a long story short, Bleicher managed to arrest one of Czerniawski's cell leaders, who agreed to co-operate. As a result of the information he gave them, the Abwehr were able to arrest Czerniawski and Carré. They got nothing out of Czerniawski, but Bleicher told Carré that he had enough evidence to send her and all her associates to the firing squad. He said that if she agreed to help him, her friends would be treated as prisoners of war, and would be safe from the Gestapo. In consideration of this, plus the sum of sixty thousand francs a month, "the Cat" went to work for Bleicher, and in three days Czerniawski's organisation was completely broken up.'

Seagrave stubbed out her cigarette. 'Unfortunately,' she said, 'it did not end there. "The Cat" also knew the codes, pre-arranged security checks, and the schedule of transmissions to London. With the help of a radio operator who had also been turned, the Germans were able to feed London with false information, and in return, were given details of the agents who were to be parachuted into France. It was some considerable time before this ploy was detected by us.'

Garnett said, 'What you're saying is that Dane has been turned?'

'I think that is a reasonable assumption to make,' said Vickers.

'Well, I bloody well don't,' Garnett said loudly.

In a gentle voice, Seagrave said, 'Perhaps we are rushing to a premature conclusion. I would like to know if Mr Garnett was aware of being followed at any time. I understand he met two agents in Bournemouth, who must have known him by sight, unless of course a pre-arranged visual signal had been made.'

A nagging doubt began to fester in Garnett's mind. Reluctantly he said, 'I think I was followed by a long-haired man calling himself Amos Lee. I've been told he belongs to Olds' group.'

'When did this happen?' Vickers asked.

'I believe they picked me up somewhere outside Sutton Veny the first time I went to see Dane.'

'Well now,' Vickers said in a silky voice, 'it seems he knew where and when to find you.'

And then they started on him, Seagrave and Vickers in turn, surgically dissecting everything he said, probing for a nerve end here, and then uncovering some new aspect of damning evidence there. Did he ever see either of the men he met in Bournemouth again? Yes. Who? A man called Lenny. Where? He took part in the ambush. How did he arrange a further RV with this Lenny? He stayed at Brockenhurst Farm until we left for the ambush site. Was the farm raided immediately after the ambush miscarried? No. On reflection, didn't he find that rather odd? Yes, perhaps, I really don't know what to think. What do you make of Olds now? I think he is a security risk. But not a traitor? He might be. But you said Amos Lee was one of his men and he followed you. Might he not be the man who gave your description to Lenny? It's possible. But we know Lenny is a double agent, and so therefore there is a connection between Olds and Dane and Lee; wouldn't you agree?

Garnett chose not to answer. In the silence which followed this last unanswered question, Seagrave cleared her throat and said, 'Personally, I am satisfied that Dane has been turned. She has been clever enough to pass certain of Mr Garnett's messages to us in their original form, but I have no doubt she was instructed to do so by her control.'

'Balls,' said Garnett.

Vickers said, 'Miss Seagrave is a very intelligent woman, she's a PhD, and I value her opinions.'

'General, I don't care if she got a first in fornication, I know Dane, and I know she has not and never could be turned.'

'She was in prison, Garnett, we don't know what kind of pressure was put upon her. Perhaps when they found out she was involved in the Parkhurst affair, they offered her much the same proposition as Bleicher offered Mathilde Carré. I know Endicott screened Dane before we sent her down to Sutton Veny, and of course I have a great deal of faith in Endicott's methods, but no one is infallible and mistakes can be made. I am satisfied in my own mind that, unfortunately, Dane is now a double agent. Obviously, we now have to determine how much damage has been done, and then take appropriate measures.'

'What does that mean?'

Vickers fitted a cigarette into the long black filter. He took his time quite deliberately, and Garnett knew he was thinking out an oblique answer.

'You know,' he said uneasily.

Garnett said, 'Let's not be coy, General, she is going to be killed if you have your way.'

Vickers' facial expression didn't change. He was ice-cold.

He said, 'I know you are emotionally involved, but you must realise we have no alternative.'

Garnett leaned forward in his chair and thrust his face close. 'You must also realise, General,' he said slowly, 'that if a decision is made to terminate Dane, I'll kill you.'

It was a bluff and they both knew it, but it still riled Vickers. 'I don't like threats,' he said.

'I don't like making them.'

Vickers sighed. 'This is getting us nowhere, David. We should save our anger for the Russians, God knows they've earned it. If Dane is in the clear, I'd like to know how they got on to you.'

Garnett said, 'There were seven of us in the ambush party, and officially I was the only one to escape through the cordon, but I couldn't have done it without Lenny's help, and we know he is bogus. They knew exactly where to find us, and Dane couldn't have told them because she didn't know, and come to that, neither did Lenny until the last minute, and I had my eye on him all the time.' He stopped, snapped his fingers and said, 'No, I bloody well didn't. The bastard went to the lavatory. He could have put a beacon out for them. There was a single HOUND moving ahead of the main lift, and it flew over the house a couple of times. Maybe it was pin-pointing the audio signal from the beacon.'

'Impressive,' said Vickers, 'but it doesn't clear Dane. It merely indicates they had a fail safe plan.'

It was going to take a lot to make Vickers change his mind about Dane and Garnett badly needed some facts, and then he remembered what Dane had said about the technique of squirting.

'General,' he said quietly, 'correct me if I'm wrong, but you believe Dane has been turned because she is still sticking to the original schedules and is sending you corrupted signals?'

'I told you before, no one can disguise their touch.'

'All right, I accept that. Now, I understand the technique for squirting is to pre-record your message. Now, what is to prevent the Russians tape-recording Dane, and then cutting up the tape to suit their own purposes?'

Vickers opened his mouth, closed it hurriedly, and raised one eyebrow instead.

Seagrave said, 'Technically, it is quite feasible.'

Garnett rammed the point home. 'McDonald and Olds split up eighteen months ago, but the shooting didn't start until fifteen months later, long before Dane arrived on the scene.'

'What are you getting at?'

'I think we ought to find out who Dane is transmitting to, and then deal with them, because amongst other things, I have an idea Lenny is a Russian, and I think we've got a bogus Resistance group on our hands which is out to wreck us.'

'In Wiltshire, Garnett,' Vickers said sarcastically, 'only in Wiltshire and a bit of Hampshire, not in the rest of the country.'

'It has to start somewhere, General, and you were worried enough about a split between McDonald and Olds to send me down there.'

Vickers ejected the stub of his cigarette into the ash-tray. A haze of blue smoke hung in the room and Garnett felt his eyes smarting. In the silence, the noise of the clock ticking away on the mantelpiece above the fireplace, sounded unnaturally loud.

Vickers said, 'What do you think, Charlotte?'

The PhD brain came into play again. 'There is no doubt,' she said, 'no doubt at all, that Mr Garnett has been compromised. The question is, how much information has he unwittingly given to the other side?'

'I gave them Campion, and, if he wasn't already working for them, maybe Olds, provided they did a clever enough tailing job. And they must know about Dinkmeyer, but otherwise they are at a dead end. All right, so my cover is broken, but it doesn't matter.'

Vickers raised both eyebrows this time. 'My dear Garnett, you must be mad.'

Garnett ignored him. 'I was allowed to escape because they wanted the game to go on.'

A smile slowly spread across Vickers' face—it wasn't a warm one, but it was definitely a satisfied one. 'So they do,' he said, 'so they do. I think you had better go back to Salisbury before they miss you, dear boy.'

'I'm going to need some help.'

'We shall have to warn Campion's people off somehow. We've got enough problems already without them trying to give you the chop. You'll need a secure link to us of course, and a wireless intercept detachment to locate the ghost station. Two men should be enough for that job.'

'I'm going to need more than a couple of helpers.'

Vickers sighed. 'I'm merely thinking aloud, David. Perhaps you had better tell me how many men you have in mind, and we'll talk about it.'

Garnett told him. Two hours later they were still haggling.

14

THE RIGHT LEG had gone to sleep, which wasn't surprising, because Garnett was curled up in the front seat of the Mini-van trying unsuccessfully to doze. He shifted to a more comfortable position and felt the tingling sensation of pins and needles in his dead limb. He opened one eye and looked at Norris, and was happy to see that he was concentrating on the road. He gave no sign of wanting to start a conversation and Garnett was happy about that too, because if there was one thing he couldn't stand it was riding beside a chatty driver. Norris was part of the help that Garnett had squeezed out of Vickers after a wrangle lasting well over two hours. It had been a hard sell, not only to convince Vickers that it made sense to keep the game going, but also to positively back the enterprise. He had marshalled some pretty flimsy arguments and made them sound authoritative, and now, as they rolled through Hartley Wintney caught up in the stream of early-morning traffic, he went over them again in his mind in an effort to convince himself this time.

His safety depended upon the basic assumption that the Russians were greedy. He knew that if he had been in their place, he would have ended the play with Campion and tried a new tack. He would have concentrated on discrediting the Resistance by mounting a series of outrages designed to alienate the public, and would have abandoned the concept of penetrating the Resistance organisation. He believed that the Russians wanted to have their cake and eat it too. If Campion had been killed in the ambush, and it was reasonable to assume that this was the case, then the Russians had lost a profitable source of information, and therefore they must be hoping he would give them another lead. It was, of course, a comforting illusion, just as long as the Russians didn't know much about Olds—if they could lay their hands on him, they had access to all the information they wanted and they would no longer need Garnett. The first thing he had to do, therefore, was to remove Olds from the scene in such a way that the other side would be convinced that he had been liquidated by the Resistance. This would be in keeping with the signals which the Russians had passed on to Vickers, and it would also help to create the impression that the Resistance was not aware that it was being manipulated. If he could pull it off, Garnett considered that the odds against him would be considerably reduced.

Garnett sat up straight, massaged his cramped leg, and then lit a cigarette. Norris didn't take his eyes off the road for a second. He was twenty-three but he had an absurdly young face which made him look nearer sixteen. Straw-coloured hair, freckles, an upturned button nose, and a gangling loose-limbed frame added to the illusion of schoolboy adolescence. He was an ex-boy soldier who had purchased his discharge shortly before the war, and was reputed to be a king among communicators and well able to take care of himself, whatever that was supposed to mean. Garnett just hoped Vickers hadn't sold him a pup.

Garnett said, 'Do you have any worries before we part company?'

Norris shook his head, and then said, 'You'll call me channel echo on the mitre, and if you say "pick up the windfalls", I pass the word along. Otherwise I do nothing. Red One means I meet you at the first RV one hour later. I don't acknowledge any message; I am to listen out for one minute on the hour every hour from 0600 until 2200 every day for the next three days. Anything you have for London will be passed verbally to me at the RV. I'll pre-record any such messages and then squirt them through. Okay?'

'I hope it is,' said Garnett. 'We'll take a time check.'

'I'll pull into the side of the road.'

'Not now. Take a time check from the BBC after you have dumped me off in Andover.'

Garnett stubbed out the cigarette and sank down in the seat again. 'Wake me up when we get there,' he said.

He was, however, far too keyed up to sleep. He knew Dinkmeyer would be surprised to see him again, and perhaps even Tate would throw away her sour expression for minute or two. They were like a talisman, a sort of rabbit's foot; as long as they were still at large, it was a sign that the other side had no intention of winding up the game just yet. And of course Vickers had checked up on that very point before he decided to back Garnett; although, even then, he had not exactly pushed the boat out for him. All the resources he needed for three days and then—nothing. Garnett wondered what was so bloody significant about three days. It was just one man's opinion that they could run the bluff for three days before the Ivans rumbled it, and it wasn't as if this opinion was based on fact; for his money, it had been motivated by a second-hand knowledge of certain OSS operations in World War Two.

Garnett checked his wristwatch, lit another cigarette, and then stubbed it out almost immediately. He was impatient, and the journey seemed to be taking an intolerably long time. Norris dropped him off in the centre of Andover just before 9 am. Ten minutes later he caught a train to Salisbury.

There was an air of tension in the employment agency. Agatha Tate had taken up knitting, but she wasn't getting much therapeutic value out of it—she was dropping stitches left and right. She looked up as he entered, and for once there wasn't a sour expression on her face. On the other hand, there wasn't a warm look of welcome there either—she just looked plain frightened. Garnett gave her a reassuring smile. It wasn't intended to mean anything, but she took it as an invitation to follow him into Dinkmeyer's office.

Dinkmeyer was sitting hunched up in his chair with his elbows resting on the desk and his hands pressed together as if in supplication.

'Praying?' said Garnett.

Dinkmeyer turned a bloodshot eye on him. 'I thought I had seen the last of you,' he said wearily.

'Is Sue all right?'

'I wonder you care.'

'Is she or isn't she?'

'She was half-scared to death but otherwise she didn't come to any harm.'

'I'm glad to hear it. What about the boy?'

'What boy?'

'The one with the broken arm.'

'Oh, him.' Dinkmeyer found one of his slim cigars and struck a match against the wall. He cupped the flame with the palm of his left hand as if shielding it against a high wind. He blew out the match and contemplated the tip of his cigar. 'Oh, him,' he said for the second time, 'I guess he's okay. I gave him a shot of whisky, he made a telephone call to his friend who was minding Sue, and then he walked out of here, and thank Christ I haven't seen him again.'

Tate said, 'Would you mind telling us what is going on, Mr Abel. I had a strange call from London last night, and it would seem we are in some kind of trouble.'

'You are in trouble,' said Garnett, 'the Ivans probably have this place under surveillance right now.'

'What are we going to do?'

'We carry on as though nothing had happened.'

Dinkmeyer said, 'Now I know you're nuts.'

'They think they are toying with us, so we play them along. We act as though we don't know we are being watched, while we try to run to ground this bogus Resistance cell which the Russians have set up.'

'Listen,' said Dinkmeyer, 'we run a DLB, right? Any time London wants us to be a target they can go find someone else. I won't have any part of it.'

'I don't think you've got much option,' Garnett said coldly.

'The hell I have.'

'I'm not going to argue with you. If you both do as I tell you, we may be able to swing it, but if either of you thinks that running away will solve everything, then you're the one who's nuts.'

'How long do we play this cat and mouse game?'

'Three days.'

'And then what?'

'We get out to a safer place.'

'Three days,' Dinkmeyer said to himself, 'hell, it's going to seem like three years.' He looked up at Garnett again. 'Okay,' he said quietly, 'what do you want us to do?'

'Nothing, absolutely nothing, for the time being. You don't alter the pattern of your behaviour, that's all.'

Dinkmeyer said, 'You've been adrift for nearly twenty-four hours, don't kid yourself that it has passed unnoticed.'

'They would expect me to lie low after the ambush. Of course, they may or may not be interested in knowing how I dealt with our callers yesterday, but I'm betting that, in the hope of getting another lead from me, they will curb their curiosity for a while.'

'Let's hope their minds are working along the same line as yours,' Tate said dryly.

Garnett said, 'Is the Volkswagen in its usual parking place?'

Dinkmeyer groped inside his jacket pocket, brought out the keys, and tossed them to Garnett. 'One of these days,' he growled, 'you may get around to providing your own transport.'

The sky blue Volkswagen was parked in row L next to a black Austin Cambridge. Garnett unlocked the door and got inside. The engine fired into life at the first touch on the button and it still sounded like a sewing machine. He drove out through West Harnham on the road to Netherhampton looking for a garage with a hydraulic lift. He found one with a ramp three kilometres out of West Harnham and pulled into the forecourt.

A short plump man in grease-covered overalls sauntered out of the repair shop wiping his hands on a piece of cotton waste.

'How many?' he said gruffly.

'None.'

'None?'

'I want to check my sump. I'm using a lot of oil. I could be burning it, on the other hand maybe I've got a cracked sump.'

'Can you bring it in tomorrow?'

'I'd like to check on it now.'

'Can't, I've got too much work on hand as it is. Nothing but patching up these days, it's the shortage of spares you see.' He stopped short and stared at the pound note which Garnett had pressed into his hand. 'Well, I suppose I could take a quick look,' he said. 'Tell you what, you put her up on the ramp while I get the inspection lamp.'

Garnett said, 'I'm very grateful.'

He got back into the Volkswagen and drove it up on to the ramp. He was standing in the well of the inspection pit when the mechanic returned with the lamp.

The man said, 'You want to watch it, you'll get muck all over your jacket.' He pointed the flash up at the sump and poked around with a screwdriver. 'Looks as though you could do with a new gasket,' he said, 'but I can't see any crack.'

Garnett wasn't listening. He was looking for a sign of bare metal showing through the mud encrusted chassis. Like most people, Dinkmeyer never bothered to clean the underneath of the car, and it looked as if it had been driven across a newly ploughed field in the wet. He figured that, if they had fixed a homing device on the Volkswagen, they would have ensured that the magnetised clamps had a good surface on which to anchor. There was no getting round the fact that they had had plenty of opportunity to fix such a device when the Volkswagen was stuck in the car park, and they wouldn't be stupid enough to risk its detection by leaving it in place for ever; but, as far as he could see, they had never emplaced a homing device, and he was now certain that he had not led them to Olds.

Garnett said, 'What do you suggest?'

'I haven't got a gasket to fit this job. I would have to make one. I wouldn't want to touch it before the end of the week. Like I said, I've got a lot of work on hand.'

'I'll give you a call around Saturday,' said Garnett. He gave the man another pound and backed the car off the ramp.

Garnett back-tracked, drove through the city, and made his way to Bemerton by way of Churchfields Road and Lower Road. As soon as he was clear of the city, he pulled into the verge and got out of the car. There was not a pedestrian or a cyclist or another car in sight. He reached inside his breast pocket and brought out the flat, compact mitre radio set. Smaller in size and hardly thicker than the average wallet, it had a range of five kilometres. He extended the rod aerial and flicked the set on to channel echo. The time was exactly eleven o'clock. Holding the set close, he spoke into the mouthpiece. 'Pick up the windfalls,' he said. He then pushed the aerial back into its housing, got into the Volkswagen, and drove on.

Two hours later, having taken a roundabout route, he parked the car in a clearing in the woods overlooking the village of Hinton. At 1:32 a green Rover 90 also pulled into the clearing and parked some twenty metres away. Garnett got out of the car, lit a cigarette, and strolled across to the Rover.

The man sitting behind the wheel was wearing a light grey suit. The curly blond hair and side-boards made his strong, square-shaped face look hard. Garnett was prepared to bet that, but for the war, he would have drifted into crime and would have been much sought after as a heavy. He had all the necessary qualities of brute strength and ruthlessness. As Garnett came closer, he wound the window down and a thin-lipped smile appeared on his face.

Garnett said, 'Are you the doctor?'

'Right in one.'

'That's about the most inappropriate nickname I've heard to date.'

The man shrugged his shoulders. 'I did three years as a medical student.'

'Is everything set up?'

'Of course.'

'Brief me,' said Garnett.

'It's your plan, you ought to know the details better than anyone else.'

'I'd still like to hear it.' Garnett smiled. 'Just to make sure everything is as I said it should be.'

The man sighed. 'About half an hour ago, a mutual friend of ours called on Olds in his office. Our friend is carrying a brief case, an unusual one. You remember that toy which fascinated all the kids before the war—Secret Sam—you pressed a button and a plastic bullet shot out of the attaché case? Our man has a Secret Sam device fitted with a silencer. It's a beautiful job. He's going to invite Olds to drive him out here.'

'And if Olds refuses?'

'He'll kill him. Don't look so shocked—we are going to enormous lengths to rig a killing, why not leave them a real corpse? Much more convincing.'

'I want Olds de-briefed by an expert, not laid to rest in a box,' Garnett said angrily.

The man smiled again. 'Don't worry,' he said, 'our man will only kill him in the last resort.'

Garnett dropped the cigarette butt on to the grass and trod it into the earth. 'He would be well advised not to exceed his instructions,' he said. Garnett turned away and walked back to the Volkswagen. The doctor was not his favourite character, and given the choice, he preferred to wait alone. The doctor didn't seem in the least put out.

Garnett sat in the Volkswagen chain-smoking. In what seemed a long time while he waited for the other car to show up, he had much, almost too much, on his mind. He was not a good chess player, and this game called for someone with the ability to play three-dimensional chess against a Grand Master. Put simply, he had to figure their moves in advance, give the appearance of conforming with them while making a covert counter-attack. Perhaps Vickers was right to insist on a time limit of three days, because suddenly he doubted whether he had the ability to keep it going longer than that.

He checked his wristwatch yet again and saw it was 1:45, and began to wonder what was delaying them. He needn't have worried, a bare three minutes later a white Zephyr rolled into the clearing and pulled up behind him. In his rear view mirror he could see Olds behind the wheel and another man sitting beside him. Garnett opened the door, got out and walked back to the Zephyr. The man sitting with Olds slid out and Garnett took his place.

Olds was the colour of putty, tiny beads of sweat collected above his lip and ran down his chin. A pink tongue flicked out and moistened his lips. In a small voice he said, 'I might have guessed you would be in at the kill.'

'There isn't going to be any killing.'

'No?'

'No, but we are going to make a whole lot of people think there has been one.'

'That Italian-looking man who made me come out here, he said if I didn't comply, he would kill me.'

'Oh he would, he would have killed you without a second thought and he would have got away with it. He had a friend waiting outside your yard with another car in case he had to make a run for it. We're very thorough people.'

Olds removed his glasses and rubbed his eyes. 'What happens now?'

Garnett ignored the question. 'How long have you been wearing glasses?' he asked.

'I wear a pair solely for driving.'

Garnett said, 'All right, now I'll tell you what we have in mind. You are going to remove your jacket, and then I'm going to summon the doctor over, and he is going to cut your wrist because we have to have some blood in this car, and it has to be your blood because the other side has some very smart forensic men, and then we are going to spirit you away, and then later, when we think it is safe to do so, we'll get your wife and children out.'

'Will Karen know my death is a hoax?'

'No.'

'She will be worried sick, I wouldn't like that.'

Garnett said, 'That's too bad, you will just have to lump it.' He signalled the doctor to come over and got out of the car.

They were quick and they were meticulous. Working in concert, they cut Olds' wrist and allowed the blood to spurt over the seat and the panel of the offside door. They arranged his jacket and then used a .38 Webley with silencer to pump three bullets from the passenger seat at an oblique downward angle, so that the bullets passed through the jacket and the driver's seat into the chassis. If the bullets were ever recovered, there was a chance that tests would show the presence of man-made fibres on the flattened shells. They took off one of his elastic-sided shoes and left it inside the car to give the impression that the door sill had ripped it off his foot when they dragged him clear. They dropped his glasses on to the grass and crushed them, and then they removed his jacket from the front seat. Finally, they left a trail of blood leading to the Rover 90. In all, it look them less than five minutes, and when they were gone, there was enough evidence left behind in the clearing to suggest Olds had put up a struggle and had been shot. They hoped the blood stains and the number of bullet holes might lead the police to assume that the wounds had been fatal, an assumption they intended to reinforce later that day with documentary evidence.

Garnett remained in the clearing after the Rover had

gone. He remained, not from any desire to admire his handiwork, but because the time was fast approaching when Norris would be listening out on his mitre radio set, and if he missed the schedule he would lose an hour, and time was now a precious commodity. It was risky to hang around, but he was not likely to find another secluded spot within the next five minutes. He brought out the mitre, erected the rod, and at two o'clock passed the codeword Red One to Norris. He then telescoped the aerial, got into the Volkswagen, and drove away. He had less than sixty minutes in which to locate Dane and make the RV.

Garnett debated whether or not to check out the newsagents in Warminster to see if Dane had left a veiled forwarding address, and then decided he wouldn't, because everything seemed to point to the fact that the Russians were content to play a cat and mouse game. Whether Dane was bent or straight, he was sure she was at Brockenhurst Farm. If Dane was straight her telephone would be tapped; if she was bent she would report their conversation anyway. It made sense to telephone her because the Soviets would know, by one means or another, that he had re-established contact, and if he was fairly open about doing it, they would assume he was unaware of their counter-intelligence cell.

As he was passing through Wylye, he spotted a call box and pulled into the side of the road. He got out, walked back to the call box, and rang up the farm. Garnett didn't recognise the voice on the other end of the line. He said, 'It's George Abel, may I speak to Valerie, please?'

The voice was still unintelligible, but about a minute later, Dane came on the line. 'Hullo, George,' she said in a cool voice, 'this is a surprise.'

He made his tone sound apologetic. 'I had to call you up after the row we had last night, to see if you were still speaking to me.'

'I'm glad you called. I felt awful about the row after you had gone.'

'Yes, well, let's call it so much water under the bridge. I'll see you this evening, same time as usual, okay?'

'Fine. Take care of yourself. darling.'

He heard a smacking noise as she blew him a kiss just before she hung up. She had been very cool and quick to follow his cue lines. Either she had expected him to call or she was a hell of a sight quicker on the uptake than he would ever have credited. For a sickening moment, he wondered whether she might not be on the wrong side of the fence after all. He left the call box and went back to the car in a troubled frame of mind.

Garnett cut across the A36, went through Deptford and Winterbourne Stoke, and then turned sharp left at the junction of the A303 and the A360 for Stonehenge. He found a slot in the official car park, paid his admission fee, walked through the tunnel under the road, and joined the dozens of tourists milling around the circle of stones. You needed a 20NP guide book to appreciate the wonder of Stonehenge, because the Ministry of Public Works and Buildings didn't hand out information for free—the only signs they put up in the area told you not to deface the stones.

He found Norris leaning back against one of the fallen stones photographing the section which was still intact. He drifted over, stood next to Norris and lit a cigarette. He waited until there was no one within earshot and then said, 'We're going to set up the intercept for tonight. I'll give you Dane's frequencies if you call me before 6 pm, and that will save you the trouble of searching through the waveband to pick up the ghost station. After Dane has finished transmitting, meet me in the George at Norton St Philip and let me know how you got on. Understand?'

'Yes.'

Garnett paused and then said, 'You'd better tell London that we removed Olds without a hitch.'

'Anything else?' said Norris.

'No.'

Norris smiled. 'Given the frequencies, I'll guarantee

to locate that ghost station for you.' He moved away and started filming another vista.

Garnett wandered around, spoke to three other people, all of whom were perfect strangers, and then left. He figured that if by chance he had been shadowed since he left Hinton, they wouldn't have the resources immediately available to follow four different suspects simultaneously.

15

DINKMEYER LOOKED UP as Garnett strolled through the door, and a sour expression registered on his face. He stared at his wristwatch pointedly and tapped the glass.

Garnett said, 'It hasn't stopped, and you've made your point, it is nearly four o'clock.'

Dinkmeyer lit a slim cigar. 'Make me an offer,' he said.

'What?'

'You can have the car for two hundred plus the Norton. It would save us both a lot of grief.'

'For a moment I thought you were concerned with the way time is running out on us.'

'Not me,' said Dinkmeyer, 'the sooner the next seventy-two hours passes, the better.'

'I see.'

'And you can cut that crap out. I don't need you looking down your goddamned nose at me. I'll do what I have to do, but I don't aim to be an enthusiast. I don't want to be a hero, I just want to survive. I don't see much percentage in keeping a stiff upper lip—if I'm on edge I show it, and I am on edge. You try sitting in this office knowing there is a good chance they're watching every move you make. If I was doing something it might be different.'

Garnett said, 'Well, now's your chance. Go take a walk through the Market Place, and let me know what happens.'

'Are you on the level?'

'If you hurry, you'll be there in time to see it happen.'

Dinkmeyer mashed the butt of his cigar in the ashtray.

'If this is some kind of a joke,' he said, 'I'm going to be pretty sore at you when I return.'

'You won't be sore.'

Dinkmeyer got up and walked towards the door. 'Watch the office for me while I'm away,' he said, 'you never know, we might have a customer.'

The street door banged closed behind him. Garnett lit a cigarette and then just as quickly snuffed it out. On an empty stomach, the smell alone was enough to make him feel queasy. He strolled into the outer office and stopped behind Tate, who was sitting bolt upright at the desk with a book propped against the Imperial typewriter. The knitting had been shoved away somewhere out of sight.

He cleared his throat and said, 'You wouldn't have anything to eat, I suppose?'

Tate bent down and opened the bottom right-hand drawer of the desk and brought out a small tin of biscuits, which she passed back over her shoulder. 'Ginger nuts,' she said, 'don't hog the lot.'

He wasn't going to get fat on the contents of the tin. There were just seven biscuits and a few broken bits. He ate five. She didn't say so, but the look on her face plainly showed she thought he had taken advantage of her generosity. He wondered if he should press his luck and ask her to make him a cup of tea, and then he thought, why the hell not. He opened his mouth to put the idea into words. Tate chose that very second to voice her own thoughts.

Scarcely above a whisper, she said, 'What is going to happen to us. Mr Abel?'

'I honestly don't know. Oh, we'll get out of this mess all right, but what happens after that ...' he shrugged his shoulders, 'well, who the hell knows what they have in mind for us.'

There was a brief pause, and he was just about to ask for that cup of tea when she was off again.

'I've been thinking about what you said this morning, and I wondered if they might not be watching us from one of those shops across the street.' She hesitated, and then went on, 'I'm probably being silly.'

'No you're not. If you have seen something which strikes you as being odd, I want to hear about it.'

'You have probably noticed there are sites for five shops in the block opposite. There is a tobacconist, a chemist, a hairdressing salon and two premises which have been empty for some months. All the flats above these shops are occupied, except one. The one which isn't let is above what used to be a draper's. Well, this morning I noticed something rather odd. The sun was shining directly into the flats and I could see the net curtains in all the windows, and in some cases there were ornaments and vases of flowers on the window sills, but I could not see into that empty flat. It was just as if the sun bounced off the glass. Do you know what I think, Mr Abel?' He opened his mouth to reply, but Tate didn't give him a chance. 'I think there is something peculiar about the glass in the window,' she said. 'I don't believe you can see through it.'

Garnett lit a cigarette. His stomach was too busy digesting the ginger nuts to complain. He mulled over what Tate had said about the window, and the more he thought about it, the more he was convinced there was something in what she said. If they had put a surveillance detail into the flat, it would certainly explain how they got on to Katz, and they would have had no difficulty, no difficulty at all, in following poor old Katz. And what had Katz said?—'This is my first field job'—and, by God, he'd been pretty shitty with Katz, laying down the rules, telling him not to use the telephone or the post, be smart, call in at the office. And Katz had followed that advice to the letter and got himself blown to pieces.

Tate said, 'Well, what do you think, Mr Abel?'

'What?'

'About the window.'

'Oh that,' he said, 'I think you could be right.'

Garnett drifted back into Dinkmeyer's office and slumped down on to the hard-backed chair. He let the cigarette fall on to the floor and then crushed it under the heel of his shoe. And now the picture was so much clearer. He remembered that first bloody message to Vickers, the one where he said Katz was looking into the financial set-up. Okay, so they knew someone by the name of Victor was examining the books of someone called Henry, so if, by watching the office, they discovered Katz was Victor, why didn't they get on to the fact that Henry was Olds? 'Unless,' he said to himself aloud, 'unless they already had a description of Katz.'

'They say that talking to yourself is the first sign of madness.'

He looked up and saw Dinkmeyer standing in the doorway holding a piece of paper in his hand. 'You're back,' he said vaguely.

'It certainly isn't my shadow,' said Dinkmeyer. He thrust the piece of paper into Garnett's hand. 'Not five minutes ago, a guy went through the market place on a motor cycle like a bat out of hell. He had a girl riding pillion, and she was tossing these leaflets out of a saddle bag like confetti. What the hell is it supposed to mean?'

Garnett read the leaflet. It was direct and unambiguous. It said—'Pursuant to the Order of the Central Committee, A Field General Court Martial was convened on 15 August to try Richard Olds in absentia on charges of treason. Evidence was produced proving that for the past four months, Olds, alias Henry, actively collaborated with the enemy, and was directly implicated in the murder of Daniel Sykes and others. The accused was found guilty and sentenced to death. Sentence was promulgated and executed this day.'

Garnett put the leaflet to one side. He felt pleased with himself. It had been his idea to supply corroborating evidence that a murder had been committed, but he had to know if it had sounded convincing to an outsider. 'Not bad,' he said with studied indifference.

'Not bad? Is that all you can say? A man has been murdered on the strength of some pretty flimsy evidence which you dug up. What kind of man are you?'

'Olds isn't dead.'

'He isn't?'

Garnett stood up. 'You were meant to think that. It only took a leaflet to convince you; you wait until the Soviets find the rest of the evidence.' He gently pushed a dumbfounded Dinkmeyer to one side and walked out of the office into the street.

He walked up to the terminus and caught the bus to Warminster with less than a couple of minutes to spare. He sat on the top deck, smoking one cigarette after another, while he waited impatiently for the journey to end. The distance from Salisbury to the outskirts of Warminster was thirty-eight kilometres—the bus journey made it seem more like three hundred and eighty. He left the bus at the Boreham Road stop, and set off for Sutton Veny at a brisk walk. He found himself blowing a bit, and for the hundredth time he vowed to give up smoking. He knew the vow wouldn't last.

Dane was waiting for him. She was leaning against the yard gate, her chin resting on her folded arms. She was wearing a sleeveless white blouse, faded blue linen skirt, white ankle socks and sneakers. As soon as she caught sight of him coming up the road, a wide smile appeared on her face and she waved an arm to greet him. There was no doubting her spontaneous pleasure, but all the same, Garnett wished she hadn't sounded quite so calm when he had spoken to her on the telephone earlier in the day. In her place he would have been a little apprehensive. That tiny seed of doubt which Charlotte Seagrave had planted in his mind was still there.

As he pushed open the gate, she put her arms around his neck and kissed him. 'My God, I'm glad you're safe,' she said.

He slipped an arm around her waist and walked her across the yard. 'It's good to see you,' he said lamely. 'Is everything all right? I mean, have you got the transmitter here?' He could feel her drawing away from him, and he knew that his cold, business-like approach had hurt her. Well, so what, he thought, in this sort of war you cannot afford the luxury of trusting anyone until their loyalty is proved beyond doubt. And he wanted, more than anything else in the world, to know beyond doubt that she had not been turned, but he needed something more positive than the fact that he was in love with her to know the answer to that question. They didn't say another word to each other until they were in the loft above the barn.

Dane said, 'I suppose you have got the message for London?'

Garnett looked at her sharply. 'What made you say that?' he said quickly.

'Well, I get the impression that I am not the reason you came here.'

'Don't bet on it.'

She smiled. 'I'm glad.'

'I've got a long message.'

'All right, I'll get my pad out.'

'First, I want to know the frequencies you are using this evening.'

The smile faded. 'You don't have to know.'

'Oh, but I do. You see, you are not transmitting to London.'

Her eyes opened wide. 'What are you talking about?'

'I don't know who you are transmitting to at 1800 but it certainly isn't London. London is getting you loud and clear at 2300 hours.'

'That's impossible.'

'They say there is no doubt about it. They have positively identified your touch.'

'I don't understand.'

'Don't you?' he said harshly. 'Well, I'll paint the picture for you. They think you have gone over to the other side.'

'They must be mad, why would I do that?'

'Because you were in on the Parkhurst job and the pressure was put on you.'

'I wasn't the only one to be involved in that affair. You were for one, and so was Endicott. Look how close he must have sailed to the wind to provide you with your cover story.'

Garnett said, 'In case you forgot, you were the only one to go to prison. London thinks you were identified while you were inside, and that Soviet counter-intelligence made a deal with you.'

The colour left her face, beads of sweat showed on her forehead. 'Do you believe what they say?' she whispered.

'Would I be here if I did?'

'Good God, how do I know?' She bit her lip and her eyes blinked rapidly. 'What am I going to do?'

'You are going to let me have the frequencies.'

'All right,' she said faintly, 'if that is what you want. They are fifty-five decimal four, sixty-one decimal one, forty-nine decimal eight and fifty decimal zero.'

'In that order?'

'In that order,' she repeated dully.

Garnett lit a cigarette. 'I want you to send this message. Are you ready?'

She picked up her pad and pencil and nodded her head. 'Right. The message reads: First stop Have reason to believe Henry has been eliminated stop Please confirm this is correct stop You will appreciate that since Robert was lost in the abortive ambush comma it is necessary to find a new successor to Henry stop This will take time stop.' Garnett paused.

'Have you got all that?'

'Yes, you can go faster if you want.'

'Okay, message continues: Second stop Investigation into abortive ambush would indicate we were betrayed by truck driver stop Efforts to trace this driver have failed so far stop Am in contact with his parent group and have given orders he is to be terminated soonest stop Third stop Await your further orders stop.'

Garnett stubbed his cigarette out against one of the supporting beams. 'Encode it and send it on schedule,' he said.

Garnett moved to the other side of the loft, fished the mitre out of his jacket pocket, and set it up on channel

Charlie. At 1755 hours he called Norris and gave him the frequencies. He then moved back to Dane, borrowed a spare headset and listened in on her transmissions. Each part of the message was acknowledged, and that was enough for Norris' team to get a fix on the unknown station. At 1820 Dane signed off, and, after the bogus station had inferred that London would send them further instructions on the next schedule, packed up the transmitter.

Garnett said, 'Some while ago, you told me your frequencies and schedules had been changed.'

Dane stood up and brushed the dust off the seat of her skirt.

'That's right,' she said, 'a man called on me.'

'What did he look like?'

'Oh, well he was shorter than you, brown hair, eyes to match. His hair was brushed forward.' She shrugged her shoulders. 'I'm not very good at describing people, but if you come over to my room, I think I could sketch his features pretty accurately.'

It was on the tip of his tongue to ask her why she couldn't do the sketch in the loft, but then he thought better of it.

'I didn't know you were an artist,' he said.

Dane pulled a face. 'I wouldn't put my talent that high.'

He grinned at her and said, 'Do you know, if you could only cook, I think I would marry you.'

'Do you know,' she said blandly, 'given time and practice, I think I might even find I had a talent for that too.'

He followed her down the ladder, across the yard, and up to her room. She sat down on the edge of the bed, balanced a large sketch-pad on her knees, chewed on her pencil thoughtfully for a minute or two, and then with a frown of concentration began to sketch rapidly. Garnett was standing at an angle and had an oblique view of the face which was gradually taking shape. The face was lean, hard and vicious; the hair was brushed forward in a cowlick over the left eyebrow, and, as a final touch, she added two tiny black marks to the left nostril. Dane handed him the finished sketch. 'There,' she said, 'that's the best I can do.'

Garnett tore the page from the pad, folded it carefully into four, and slipped it into the breast pocket of his jacket.

'You're brilliant,' he said, 'the face is Frank Harvey.'

'Who?'

'Harvey—McDonald's right hand man.' Garnett laughed sourly. 'He has a wife, strips under the name of Lorraine Odell. I tried to use her as bait. God, that must have given them a laugh.'

'What happens now?'

'I have to meet a contact.'

'I see.'

'But not right away.'

Garnett caught her by the hands and gently drew her to her feet. He had no doubts now, and it was a wonderful feeling. She came willingly into his arms and kissed him. His fingers caressed the nape of her neck and she pressed her mouth urgently against his. Still holding her close against him, his hands travelled unhurriedly down her back, freeing the buttons of her blouse. He moved his hands across the velvety skin of her back and shoulders before unhooking the bra. Dane's arms left his neck long enough to unzip the skirt and discard the small triangle of nylon. 'I love you,' he said, as he drew her on to the bed, and he meant it, and not for the first time, people like Vickers and Endicott and Seagrave and Dinkmeyer and Norris seemed unimportant, and the war was a million light years away.

And then, when he was still in that other more peaceful world, Dane said, 'What time is it, darling?' And the bloody war was no longer a million light years away, but right there with them in that small room, and, cursing, he dressed quickly and left the room like some lover avoiding the cuckolded husband in the wings. He ran out of the house, crossed the yard, dragged the Norton out of the barn, and kicked it into life.

The George Inn was built about 1223, and he could well believe the claim that it had scarcely changed structurally in seven centuries. On 27 June, 1685, in a moment of fatal hesitation, the Duke of Monmouth, knowing that the cities of Bath and Bristol were held by the King's followers, encamped his army at Norton St Philip and set up his headquarters in the George Inn. Later that same day, the Duke of Grafton with the Life Guards Dragoons and five hundred foot-soldiers fell upon Monmouth, and an engagement was fought in the lanes and fields around the village which lasted until nightfall, when the King's forces withdrew to Bradford-on-Avon, leaving eighty dead on the field. Monmouth had won a skirmish but lost the war. A more superstitious man might have avoided using the inn as a rendezvous, but Garnett had no intention of following Monmouth's fate.

He left the Norton in the car park, went through the inn, crossed the courtyard, and walked down the stone steps to the Dungeon Bar. He was relieved to see that there were at least fifteen other people in the room, because it was always easier to make a contact in a crowd. There was no sign of Norris but that didn't bother him. Garnett found a place at the bar where he could watch the entrance, and then ordered himself a beer. He had a nose for policemen, but no one in the bar even set his nostrils twitching.

Norris showed up about a quarter of an hour later, when Garnett was on his second beer. It needed a sharp, alert eye to notice the index finger which Garnett had placed in a curve around the rim of his tankard, but Norris caught the signal and knew he was cleared to make contact. He made his way across the room, and found a place at the bar within touching distance of Garnett. He ordered a gin and tonic and sipped it slowly, while casting around for an innocuous opening remark. He found inspiration—it wasn't original, but at least it was innocent and safe enough.

He said, 'This is a very old pub.'

'Thirteenth century,' said Garnett.

'About as old as the Shambles then.'

'Do you come from York?'

'Yes, do you?'

'I've been there,' said Garnett.

Norris looked genuinely interested. 'Where did you stay?'

'The Cavendish.'

'You didn't like it?'

'It was a lousy hotel, all moth-eaten stuffed deer-heads, cobwebs and stained panels and Brown Windsor soup.'

Norris laughed. 'Try Savages Hotel next time you're up that way.'

'I'll bear it in mind,' said Garnett. He finished his beer, said good night to the bar tender, and left.

He walked round to the car park, found Norris' Mini-van and got inside. Dusk was beginning to close in on a rain-washed sky. A chill breeze ensured that no one was drinking outside in the walled garden. A few minutes later, Norris joined him in the van.'

Garnett said, 'Let's make this short.'

'Suits me.'

'Suppose you tell me how you made out.'

'Technically, it was no problem. We had two detector vans, and we knew the frequencies and the schedule. Unfortunately, we were sold a lemon. They are smart, very smart. Four changes of frequencies, four acknow-ledgements, eight bearings leading to four perfect inter-sections, giving us four perfect fixes.' Norris paused and then said, 'The only trouble was that they were all different. Your friend was sending to a mobile station. In short, we don't have any idea where their base is. I sent a squirt to London telling them it was no go.'

'You're getting a bit above yourself, aren't you?'

'I had my orders,' Norris said woodenly.

Garnett fished the drawing out of his breast pocket. 'We have this,' he said.

Norris glanced at the drawing. 'He's not exactly Mr Universe. Where does he fit in?'

'He is going to lead us to them.'

'Does he have a name?'

'Frank Harvey, McDonald's aide. He's the one who told Dane about the change of frequencies and different schedule.'

'Perhaps he is working with her.'

Garnett lit a cigarette. 'He has a wife; she's a stripper, works the clubs around these parts. That is how he makes contact with them.'

'You've lost me.'

'I'm just thinking aloud. When McDonald and Olds split up, Harvey came across with Sykes and the Cromptons, and they were killed but he survived. He survived because he fingered them.'

'You're guessing.'

'Of course I am, but I happen to be guessing right. We are going to lean on Harvey and he is going to finger his contact for us, and then we are going to follow his contact back to the nest.'

'We are?'

'You and a couple of helpers. I want a three car hookup and a disposal unit arranged for tomorrow night. I also want a car available for my own use from ten o'clock tomorrow morning.'

'Jesus, you don't want much do you.'

'I'll call you channel alpha 8:30 on the dot, and you can tell me where to pick the car up. We will make one other check call at 5:20 on channel bravo, and then I'll tell you where the stake out is.' Garnett wound down the window and tossed the cigarette out of the van. 'Any questions?' he said.

'Yes, two. Do you know where to find this Harvey?'

'Dinkmeyer can put me on to him. What's the other question?'

'Who drew the picture?'

'Dane.'

'Could be a neat move on her part. Perhaps she has

decided to change sides again, but I expect that idea has already occurred to you.'

It hadn't, and for a moment Garnett had a nasty feeling in the pit of his stomach, but then he dismissed the idea. It was, he thought, about time he started trusting Dane again. He opened the door and was half-way out of the van when he remembered one final detail. Turning to face Norris, Garnett said, 'I shall want an image intensification device left in the car.'

'What for?'

'Because I want to see in the dark, and I don't believe a bunch of carrots is necessarily going to improve my night vision.'

16

GARNETT SAT IN the corner café nursing a cup of tea. The sub-post office and grocery shop was just across the street and, from where he sat, he was able to see who went in and out. It was pretty much like any other village shop, but with one exception—this one was managed by Frank Harvey. The idea that a man like Harvey was both a shopkeeper and a sub-postmaster was hard to take. He just didn't look the part, but then he didn't look the type of man a girl like Lorraine Odell would want to share her bed with either. He figured Harvey must have hidden depths, in more ways than one. He had managed to hoodwink McDonald for months, not that that had been a particularly difficult task—if you've got a bigot who wants to believe the lies you are pushing at him, the battle is half won anyway.

He slipped his hand into his jacket pocket and fingered the tiny bugging device which Dinkmeyer had made up for him. Dinkmeyer, he thought, was an electronic wizard, and without his help it would be impossible to keep a close watch on Harvey. Garnett checked his wristwatch, pushed the cup of lukewarm tea to one side, and left the café.

He walked straight across the road and entered the sub-post office. He had chosen the time well, because Harvey was about to close up for the lunch hour, and they were alone in the shop except for Odell. She looked faintly surprised to see Garnett; Harvey's reaction was different—he simply looked astounded. His mouth opened and closed repeatedly and reminded Garnett of the goldfish he had seen in the tank at the Go Go Go Club.

Garnett looked at Odell and said, 'Lock the door.'

She bridled instantly. 'Who do you think you're talking to?' she snapped.

'Just do as I say,' Garnett said wearily, 'and give your mouth a rest.'

Harvey shaped up as if he meant to hurl himself at Garnett, and then he thought better of it. Harvey was all right as long as he had surprise on his side, but he could read the danger signs as well as the next man. One look at Garnett and he knew that, if he was going to get anywhere, he would have to wait until the taller man was off guard.

Odell said, 'Are you going to let him talk to me like that?'

'Do as he says and shut your row.'

'I'm not going to stand for that from you or anyone else,' she said angrily.

Harvey lifted his right hand and lightly tapped her across the face. 'I don't want any trouble with you, girl,' he said venomously.

Odell didn't argue the point. She stalked across the shop and locked the door. 'Now what?' she said.

'I want to have a talk with you both.'

'Nobody's stopping you,' she said.

'Not here.'

'How about the store room?' Harvey suggested.

'It'll do. You lead the way.'

Harvey's mood had changed, he was being reasonable, and it wasn't in his nature to be so. His eyes gave nothing away, but Garnett had the feeling that he was going to try something. Garnett lifted the flap and stepped behind the counter. Harvey stepped back a pace and allowed Odell to walk ahead. 'My word,' she said, 'we are remembering our manners today, aren't we?'

He caught the brief look of annoyance which flashed across Harvey's face, and knew that Odell had unintentionally let the cat out of the bag, and whatever it was

Harvey was cooking up involved the store room. Fore-warned, he should have been forearmed, and there was really no excuse for him to be caught on the hop, but Harvey still managed to fool him. As they went into the store room, Harvey grabbed a tin of soup off the shelf on his left, and flipped it over his shoulder. The tin came at Garnett head high, and instinctively he ducked and swayed to one side. As he did so, Harvey grabbed a second tin, spun round and let fly. It missed the left side of his face by a hair's breadth, sailed out into the shop and brought down the pyramid of bitter-lemon bottles displayed on the counter.

Odell shouted, 'Kill him, Frank.'

He was moving in close to use his feet when Garnett came out of the crouch like a coiled spring, and smashed his right hand into the pit of Harvey's stomach. All of his weight was behind that punch, and Harvey was also running on to it. He made a sound like a punctured tyre and collapsed in a heap over a sack of sugar. Odell stared at Garnett; her eyes narrowed and took on a speculative look, and then a smile slowly appeared at the corners of her mouth. He got the distinct impression she liked her men to be violent—perhaps that was the attraction Harvey had for her.

Harvey retched, moaned a couple of times, and then managed to get up on all fours. He shook his head, clutched hold of the rack for support and dragged himself to his feet. With a note of scorn in her voice, Odell said, 'You were a fat lot of good.'

Garnett said, 'Save it, you can have your fight when I've gone.' He leaned against the racking and lit a cigarette. 'Well Harvey,' he said, 'it's been one of those days, hasn't it old lad? As soon as I came into the shop, you said to yourself, here comes trouble, and how right you were, because make no mistake, you are in trouble right up to those blackheads on your nose. As of now I'd say your life wasn't worth a dud penny.'

Harvey caught his breath. 'You can go and get fucked,' he said.

Garnett shook his head sadly. 'I was hoping for a more articulate rebuttal.' His tone suddenly became cold. 'You really have been giving me the run around, Harvey. All this talk about Amos Lee being one of Olds' men. He's a Russian, Harvey, like Lenny, like all the other people you contact at the clubs.'

'I don't know what the hell you are talking about.'

'They sent you to contact Dane, and that was their big mistake. They gave you the dirty end of the stick there, Harvey, because now you are known.'

Odell had a puzzled expression on her face. She glanced at Harvey and then at Garnett before switching back again, looking like a spectator watching a slow baseline rally at Wimbledon. Her feeling of frustration mounted until finally, in a loud voice she said, 'Will somebody tell me what is going on?'

Garnett said, 'It's simple, Frank is working for the Russians. He passes information to them. He told them about Sykes, and the Cromptons and all the others who were killed, and then he did a good job poisoning McDonald's mind, to the state where McDonald was convinced his people were being murdered by Olds.'

'It's not true,' Harvey hissed.

Garnett dropped his cigarette on to the floor and trod on it. 'I want you to be clear about this, Frank,' he said quietly, 'we think you are guilty and that's enough. It isn't necessary to prove the case beyond doubt because we are not answerable to any judge, jury or court of law. If I walk out of here without getting what I came for, you're a dead man. Everybody but everybody, will be looking for you. You can run, but you can't hide for ever. Don't count on the Russians to protect you—once you've outlived your usefulness to them, they won't be interested.'

'What's your pitch?' Harvey said cautiously.

'If you help me, I'll do more than guarantee your safety, I will see you are fed into the escape pipeline.'

Garnett didn't push the offer because there was no need to. Harvey was a drowning man ready to clutch at any

161

straw, however improbable. If there had been any redeeming feature about the man, Garnett would have felt a pang of conscience, but where Harvey was concerned he was prepared to lie to him right up to the last minute.

'What do you want me to do?'

Odell said, 'Now, wait a minute, what about me? I'm not going to be left here on my own. If Frank goes, I go.'

Garnett looked at Harvey and raised an eyebrow. 'What about it, Frank?'

'You heard her.'

'All right, you're both insured.'

'So what do I do then?'

'There are a couple of things I want to know.'

'You're carrying the ball,' said Harvey.

'About Olds.'

'What about him?'

'How well did you know him?'

'He's a name, I never met him, I don't know what he looks like, or where he lives or what he does.'

'I find that hard to believe.'

'Listen, before the split, I worked under McDonald. I knew the head man was called "Henry", and it was a long time before I found out that Olds was "Henry", and that was no help because there are an awful lot of people called Olds in the south-west. The only thing I could give the Russians was the name of the man called "Henry".'

He spoke in a matter of fact voice, and if his conscience bothered him at all, Harvey did a good job of concealing it. If anything, he betrayed a note of pride, and although his audience was small, it flattered his ego to be the centre of attraction.

Garnett said, 'How did they turn you?'

'I was shopped. We used this place as a temporary cache for weapons in transit. I had just taken delivery of a load of jelly. It was in a margarine box and it came with the regular shipment of groceries. I hadn't had the stuff in the shop a couple of hours before they arrived and turned the place over. They knew exactly where to look, they made straight for this store room. I knew I was for the chop, but then they said I could save my neck if I helped them, and so I agreed. They had a pretty fair idea about our set-up, and they knew all about the split between McDonald and Olds. They said they weren't so much interested in knocking us all off, as setting us at each other's throats. They wanted names, so I gave them some.' Harvey paused and shrugged his shoulders. 'I figured they were as good as dead anyway. I mean, the Russians would have got them sooner or later without any help from me. I sort of speeded things up like.'

'You fed them information over a period of time?'

'I didn't tell them any more than I had to, if that's what you mean. I thought they would be satisfied after I had given them a few names, but they were always on at me for more.'

'And they paid you well?'

Harvey snorted. 'Paid me?' he echoed, his voice rising. 'Listen, if they had, I wouldn't let her work the clubs, now would I? I mean, it's no joke I can tell you, listening to all those randy bastards kidding each other on what they would do to her if they got a chance.'

'But you can regularly meet your contacts at these clubs, so they serve a purpose, don't they?'

'There is nothing regular about it. Contact is made if they know I have something for them, or sometimes they approach me. I don't always know I am going to meet anyone, see?'

'How do they know when you have something for them?'

'I put a sign in the shop window.' A sly smile appeared on Harvey's face. 'Somebody in the village tells them. You think you've been very clever, Mr Abel, but like as not they already know you've been to see me. Well now,' he said, 'what are you going to do about that, Einstein?'

Garnett said, 'After I have left, you are to put the sign in the window. When you meet your contact in the High Life Club you will scratch the right nostril as if you had an itch there. You will tell your friend that I have been to see you again, and that you think I am on to you. You will say that I made a funny remark about it being a coincidence that you knew Sykes and the Cromptons, but don't overdo it, we don't want to put the wind up them. The last floor show is scheduled for 11:30, and as soon as your wife has finished her spot, you will leave the club and drive out of Marlborough on the road to Burbage. One hundred metres short of the turn-off to Savernake, you will pull off the road and wait. You've got exactly five minutes leeway because I want you there between midnight and five minutes past. At seven minutes past twelve, a large refrigerated truck belonging to Igloo Foods will pull up in front of you; there will be two men in the truck, one of whom will get out and tell you what the next move will be. As long as you follow their instructions you've got nothing to worry about.'

Odell said, 'Can we take anything with us?'

'You travel light, we don't want anyone in the village to know you are leaving for good.'

'London must be proud of you,' Harvey said sarcastically, 'you think of everything, don't you? Well, I'll tell you something, mate, you may get lucky and find the Russian cell, you may even put them out of business, but one thing you'll never do is put the Resistance back on its feet. They've killed it, mate. It doesn't exist any more, all you've got left is a shell. Look, there hasn't been a curfew in months, and you know why? Because there hasn't been any Resistance activity, that's why.'

'Have you finished?' Garnett said quietly.

'You haven't heard a word I've said.'

'I have news for you, Frank,' said Garnett, 'nobody is going to hear from you. I am going to bug your phone in the shop, and smash the one you've got upstairs in the flat, and if you try to get clever, neither of you will see tomorrow out.'

'He won't do anything silly,' said Odell, 'I'll see to that.'

'He won't get the chance, because we shall be listening in on every call, and if he tries to remove the transmitter we'll know because it will set up a screech. We shall be watching the shop too, so don't take a walk, and if anything, but anything, goes wrong tonight, we will kill you.'

Harvey affected a sneer. 'Big deal,' he said.

'The biggest,' said Garnett, 'your life, you know anything bigger than that?'

Harvey didn't. He helped Garnett to bug the phone in the shop, and even went so far as to lend him a hammer so that he could make a thorough job of smashing the one upstairs in the flat. Harvey, Garnett decided, could change colour quicker than a chameleon, and was still about as lovable as a puff adder.

Garnett left the shop shortly after 1:30. The village looked half asleep in the warm sunlight, but somewhere in that rustic setting, someone was alert and watchful. There was a strong temptation to take avoiding action, but in the lunch hour with the streets almost deserted, he knew this would only draw attention to himself. He therefore strolled back to the car trying to look unconcerned.

The grey Ford Escort was still parked in the narrow unmade-up lane behind the church where he had left it over three hours ago. Some kid who fancied himself as an artist had used the film of dust on the bodywork to draw two matchstick figures locked in an embrace—underneath he had scrawled 'Jimmy loves Mary'. Garnett unlocked the car, found a duster, and wiped the coachwork clean. He then got into the car, started up and drove towards the outskirts of the village.

The house, a solid Victorian red-brick wrapped in ivy, was right at the end of the village, and sat back from the road peeping coyly over the top of a very high privet hedge. Set into this hedge, and hardly noticeable, was a brass name-plate bearing the tarnished inscription—Dr A. Munro-Park, MD. Garnett spotted the notice at the last minute, braked hard, and just managed to miss one of the sagging, dirty white gate-posts as he swung into the weed-choked gravel drive which struggled through the encroaching lawn up to the front porch. He made a U-turn at the top of the drive, parked the car and got out. To the left of the front door was a large iron bell-pull. He gave it a firm jerk and waited.

The door was opened by a diminutive young woman in a white smock. Grey expressionless eyes regarded him coldly out of a narrow elfin-like face. In a waspish voice, she said,

'Can I help you?'

'Are you Doctor Munro-Park?'

'I'm his receptionist.'

'I wondered if I might see him?'

'The doctor is on his rounds. Are you one of his patients?'

It was quite obvious to Garnett that she knew he wasn't. He smiled hesitantly. 'I'm a visitor,' he said, as if that explained everything. 'May I come in and wait?'

He had sidled past her into the hall before she had a chance to stop him. The girl sighed audibly, opened the door of the waiting room and showed him inside. Almost as an afterthought she said, 'May I have your particulars?'

'Abel,' said Garnett, 'George Abel, 36, Tavistock Gardens, Ealing, West 13. My social security number is TFX96859.' The girl barely thanked him.

The waiting room was crowded with furniture. There was the usual settee down at one corner with one arm-rest about to part company with the back, three bone-hard springless armchairs, two of which actually matched, a round oak table bearing the scratch marks left by a countless number of toy cars wheeled across its surface, and a pile of magazines from the previous decade on the seat of one of the assortment of dining chairs. He caught a glimpse of himself in the mirror on the wall above the boarded-up fireplace, and saw a dog-tired ageing face looking at him. The crows'-feet were getting as deep around his eyes as were the lines around his mouth. The white of the left eye was criss-crossed in a spider's web of fine pink lines. If the pressure lasted much longer, he thought, the time wasn't too far off before his eyes resembled one of Thurber's bull-terriers.

He took one of the magazines from the pile and sat down in an armchair. A painfully thin blonde with enormous eyes was featured on the front cover, wearing calf-length white plastic boots and a sleeveless dress, the top half of which appeared to be made of cellophane—underneath was the caption, 'The See-through Look, Will It Last?'. It hadn't. Since then fashion had flirted with midi-skirts, square shoulders and high collars in deference to the puritan influence of the Russians, but that hadn't been a success either.

He tossed the dog-eared magazine on to the table, crossed one leg over the other, and closed his eyes.

Ten minutes later he was woken up by the sound of tyres crunching on the gravel outside. A brake squealed, a door slammed with a tinny clang, a key slid into a Yale lock, and there were heavy footsteps in the hall followed by a subdued murmur of voices. A Scots voice said testily, 'Oh, very well, give me a couple of minutes and then show him in.'

Exactly two minutes later the receptionist came into the waiting room, favoured Garnett with a tight-lipped smile, and ushered him into the surgery. Munro-Park was a large, shaggy, grey-haired bear of a man with tufts growing out of both ears. The eyes were watery blue, and, like Garnett's, faintly bloodshot. He spoke as though he had a mouthful of burrs.

'Well now,' he growled, 'what's the matter with you, Mr Abel?'

Garnett said, 'Dinkmeyer recommended you to me.'

The watery eyes blinked rapidly. He took a spotted handkerchief out of his trouser pocket and blew his nose loudly.

'Hay fever,' said Munro-Park, 'always get it at this time of the year.'

The desk was covered with a confusing mass of paper. Munro-Park rifled through a wire basket, tossed a sheaf of forms to one side, and then grunted in satisfaction as his meaty hands encountered a small prescription-pad. He looked down at his chest and took a ball point from the battery of pens in the top pocket of his jacket. 'You're run down,' he said, scribbling rapidly on the pad, 'that's your trouble.' He tore the prescription form off the pad and pushed it across the desk. 'Take one of those every four hours for the next three days and you will be as right as rain.'

Garnett slipped the prescription into his pocket and in exchange pushed a button, the size of a hearing aid, back at Munro-Park. Munro-Park eyed it suspiciously. 'What am I to do with this?' he said warily.

'Wear it, like a deaf aid.'

Munro-Park tapped the ball point on the desk to a slow regular beat. Presently he said, 'I told Dinkmeyer I was getting too old to continue in this game. I'm nearly sixty-seven you see, ought to have retired long ago.' He sighed. 'If we do as you ask, will I be letting myself in for something I'll come to regret?'

'I don't think so.'

'Call it an old man's selfishness if you like, but when my time is up I would prefer to die in bed if possible.'

'The risk is negligible. This button is a listening device. I'm anxious that a particular person in this village should not communicate with the other side.'

'Who is this person?'

'Frank Harvey.'

He nodded his head sagely. 'I never did trust that feller.'

Garnett said, 'He may try to use veiled speech. If he says anything at all which sounds odd to you, ring Dinkmeyer STD.'

'What do I say?'

'Either Dinkmeyer or Tate will answer, and you will ask if that is the hospital, and they will reply, "No, this is Salisbury 295880", and then you will close the conversation by saying, "I'm sorry, I have the wrong number".'

'And Dinkmeyer will know what to do?'

'Of course.'

'It doesn't sound very difficult.'

'It isn't, and it will be over by 8:30 pm.' Garnett paused and then said, 'You're not leaving the village this afternoon by any chance?'

'Only in an emergency.'

'The button can only pick up transmissions within a radius of one kilometre.'

'I'll bear that in mind, Mr Abel,' he said gravely. He cleared his throat. 'It occurs to me that Harvey might well use other means to pass a message if he has a mind to.'

'We've taken care of that.'

It was a bare-faced lie because, apart from himself, no one was available to keep the shop under surveillance, and anyway, to be really sure nothing was passed, the observer would have to be inside the shop. A set-up like that was a non-starter from the word go. The top and bottom of it was that Garnett was trusting to luck—either Harvey would go along with him or he would pass the word to his contact. Munro-Park was no fool, the expression on his face showed that he had come to the same conclusion. The watery eyes blinked again. 'Aye, well,' he said slowly, 'I'll away to lunch then. Don't forget to take those pills, you're looking very run down, laddie.'

It was the first time in years that anyone had called him laddie. Garnett stood up, shook hands with Munro-Park, and left. The receptionist was sitting in her tiny office off the hall, her nose buried in a book, a sandwich held genteelly in her right hand. She didn't even look up as he let himself out.

He left the village and headed out towards Devizes. He drove without haste, keeping a weather-eye out for a lay-by. He found one eight kilometres out of the village and pulled into it. Sometime in the next three hours he would have to contact Norris and get Dane to send the usual message to London. Briefing Norris presented no problem, but the business with London was getting more and more complicated. He would have to say something about Harvey which would both substantiate what Harvey was going to tell his contact, and yet allay any suspicion which the other side might have that their set-up was blown. He mentally tried out any number of permutations before he got it right.

In the end, he decided he would say that, in his view, Harvey had a pernicious influence over McDonald and was largely responsible for the continuing rift between the two Resistance organisations. Garnett also decided he would stress the difficulty in finding a suitable replacement for Olds, inferring that he would have to be away from his base for a day or so, and as a final gesture, he would mention that he now had a car. He would express a hope that London would sanction the expense. He rather liked the last bit—agents were always haggling over money—it sort of added a folksy touch to the message.

He was beginning to feel desperately hungry, and opening the glove compartment, he found a small packet. Turning the packet over he read, 'Contents: This block is equivalent to approximately $7\frac{1}{2}$ ounces of raw boneless meat. The meat bar may be used for stew or as the basis for a soup. It can also be eaten dry as a munch. Ingredients—Freeze-dried minced beef, edible fat, monosodium glutamate.'

As he had no means of making either a stew or a soup, he followed their advice and ate it as a munch. No doubt, it was full of nutritional value, but it was like chewing balsa wood.

17

THE STRIDENT NOTES of Herb Alpert's Tijuana Brass
were gradually drowned under the rising chorus of cat-
calls, whistles, handclaps and stamping feet, as Odell
moved towards the climax of her act. Clad in thigh-
length silver boots, and wearing a black velvet jockey-cap,
she cavorted around the floor, cracking a riding crop
against each calf in turn.

Harvey was leaning against the bar holding a half-
empty glass in his hand. He looked as though he didn't
have a care in the world, which made Norris feel unhappy. Considering the spot he was in, Norris thought
Harvey had no right to appear so unconcerned. He did
not have to check his watch to know that the club would
be closing in less than an hour, and there was still no
sign of this contact man whom Garnett had talked so
glibly about. For the umpteenth time Norris turned his
head towards the spiral staircase willing the bloody man
to come into the club. It was, of course, a bad mistake,
and he was pretty sure that Harvey had noticed his
anxiety, because Norris had caught him staring in his
direction on a couple of occasions. The chances were
that Harvey already had him spotted, and he recalled
Garnett's last words on the subject. He had said, 'I don't
trust that bastard, if he finds out that you are his watch-
dog, he might just finger you to the opposition.' Norris
drank the rest of his beer thoughtfully.

He was suddenly aware that the floor show had ended
and people were beginning to drift back to the bar, and
he lowered his glass and scanned the room looking for
Harvey in the throng. He didn't notice the girl until

she said, 'Will you buy me a drink?' Turning, he saw a pale drawn face shrouded by fine, shoulder-length black hair looking at him pleadingly. A pick up, he thought, that's all I needed. He looked away hurriedly because this was no time to get involved with a cheap little bint on the make. Claw-like fingers clutched his wrist.

'Please buy me a drink,' she whispered urgently.

'What are you celebrating?'

'I don't know, the fifth anniversary if you like.'

'The fifth anniversary of what?'

'The end of the war, it happened five years ago to-morrow.'

She waited to see if he would come across, and when nothing happened, she whispered, 'I'm supposed to encourage people to drink.'

'Oh?' he said vaguely.

'The bar-tender's been watching me all night, nobody has bought me a drink.'

'Bad luck,' he said, not looking at her.

'Do you want me to lose my job?'

Harvey had his back towards Norris and appeared to be shielding someone from view. It began to look as though Garnett had been right; at any minute the little sod would turn round and point him out, and then that would be that. The girl said, 'Please, please help me, I can't afford to lose this job.'

At that moment, Harvey turned, stared straight at Norris, and then quite slowly and deliberately rubbed the side of his nose. In that instant, Norris saw a shortish man in grey flannel trousers and sports jacket making his way towards the spiral staircase. As he rose out of his chair, the girl grabbed his arm and tried to drag him back. Norris twisted free, tossed a 50NP piece on to the table, and walked quickly across the floor. He scarcely heard the girl saying, 'Thank you, oh thank you.' He was out of the door seconds after his quarry had left the High Street.

Norris forced himself to walk unhurriedly even though visual contact had been lost. For all he knew, the Russian could have been hiding up in a shop doorway waiting to see if anyone had followed him out of the club. He sauntered along the street, hoping like hell that his man had made straight for the car park round the back. As he reached the corner, a Land-Rover shot out into the road and turned away from him in the direction of the traffic lights at the top of the side street. He only caught a brief glimpse of the driver, but it was enough to allay the sinking feeling that he had lost the Russian.

Norris ran to the Mini-van, scrambled inside, and gunned the engine into life. He came out of the car park, turned left and shot up the street to find the lights against him and no sign of the Land-Rover. He could have screamed with frustration. All their careful planning now amounted to nothing because he didn't know whether to turn left or right or go straight on. The lights went from red to amber to green. He turned left on a pure hunch.

Forced to move at 50 kph through the town, he decided to alert the other two cars which were covering the exits to Chippenham and Pewsey. He picked up the mitre set from the shelf under the instrument panel, thumbed the switch to ON, and said, 'Red one for two and three; look out for Land-Rover MW 617 AZ.' He had to be satisfied with a couple of grunts in reply.

Norris travelled in an easterly direction for nearly five minutes without once sighting the Land-Rover. He was convinced the Russian had slipped him, and without realising it, he began to excuse his failure. There were five major routes out of Marlborough—you could go north up the A345 to Swindon, east along the A4 to London, west to Chippenham, south-west to Pewsey, or south-east along the A346. It was all very well of Garnett to insist that the other two cars should be positioned on the outskirts, but if it had been left to him, Norris would have stationed them closer in to the club, accepting the risk that they might be spotted as they pulled out in pursuit of their quarry.

A faint voice said, 'Red two, I have him moving south-west along the A345.'

Norris sighed with relief. He pulled into the side of the road, grabbed an AA handbook out of the side pocket, and flipped it open. A quick glance at the map showed him that it was possible to hold one car on a parallel route to the Land-Rover at least as far as the lateral road connecting Upavon and Ludgershall. He picked up the mitre again and told Red three to move south-east along the A346. Norris made a U-turn, headed back into Marlborough, and then took the A345 to Pewsey.

The trick was to keep changing the cars over in case the Russian suspected he was being tailed. It called for a cool brain and intelligent anticipation. If Norris guessed wrong, he could end up with his cars heading in the wrong direction and out of radio touch with one another.

South of Pewsey, Norris sent Red two east on the B3087 to join up with Red three, while he took over the job of shadowing the Russian. It was a still, clear night, and not surprisingly, since it was past twelve, there was scarcely another vehicle on the road. The Land-Rover was moving at a sedate 70 kph, and round about three kilometres short of Upavon, Norris was suddenly aware that the distance between the two vehicles was closing rapidly, and then he knew that the sod had been watching his lights in the wing mirrors and had grown suspicious. His heart skipped several beats, and then Norris started swearing with all the eloquence of an ex-boy soldier, because he had no option but to overtake the Land-Rover. He dropped down into third, accelerated, flashed his lights a couple of times, and then changing back into top, went past the Russian as though glad of the opportunity to get out from behind.

Norris watched the main beams of the Land-Rover receding in his rear view mirror until they were no more than tiny pinheads of light. So long as the Ivan kept on coming he wasn't worried. He planned to turn east on the A342 below Upavon and change places with Red three.

Without the mitre radio sets they would have been stuck, but on the other hand, by making use of them they ran the risk of being monitored. Norris frankly didn't give a damn about security any more, he got on to Red three and told him what he had in mind.

It was, of course, a nightmare. The Russian went on his serene unhurried way, while Norris was using the parallel and lateral roads to switch the tail cars around, and this went on until they reached the Amesbury Bypass when they ran out of laterals, and the Russian turned west for the A303, and then, with a sick feeling inside his stomach, Norris realised he would have to change his tactics.

It was not a warm night but Norris was bathed in sweat. His mouth felt tinder dry and he would have given his right arm for a drink if only to moisten his lips which were gummed together by strips of white tacky saliva. He was at his wits end, and like an inveterate gambler, he threw caution to the wind and staked everything on a two car cut-out. He decided to throw out two longstops by sending Red two up to Tilshead and sending Red three ahead to the junction of the A303 and A36 at Deptford, while he stayed back.

In the end, the other two cars played no further part in the proceedings. The Land-Rover swung on to the A360, went through Shrewton and then turned off on to the A344 towards the Army Training Area. Norris followed him all the way to the farm on the edge of the Range Boundary. The last part had been so easy it was almost an anti-climax. As Norris went on to rendezvous with Garnett, the buoyant feeling left him leaving him curiously deflated. Twenty minutes later he pulled into a lay-by and found Garnett waiting for him.

Garnett opened the door of the Mini-van and got inside. He lit two cigarettes and gave one to Norris. 'Well,' he said, 'did you make out okay?'

'It wasn't easy.'

'I didn't expect it to be.'

You bastard, thought Norris, you ice-cold bloody

whore-son bastard, you had it easy, you sat back and let me do the sweating for you. Angrily, he rummaged through the set of maps in the side pocket until he found the 1/25000. He flicked on the courtesy light, checked that he had the right map sheet, and then opened it out on his knees and pointed to the farm. 'There's your wolf's lair,' he said, 'right on the edge of the Training Area. Clever, aren't they? They are practically surrounded by British and Russian troops exercising on the Plain. They've got all the security they need.'

Garnett said, 'It can work both ways. I want a strong assault team and two Land-Rovers embossed with Unit Tactical signs. The team will be dressed in combat kit because they are going to look just like the Militia. I want everyone assembled for briefing at 10:30 am on the dot, and make sure you get the right mix of weapons and explosives.'

'You've got a hope.'

'Hope doesn't enter into it, your job is to make sure everything is ready on time.' Garnett paused and then said, 'I see the Harveys were picked up all right.'

'You were there?'

'Oh yes. Only one thing bothers me—both of them got into the truck. I thought I made it clear nothing was to happen to the girl?'

Norris started guiltily. The truth was that he had forgotten to tell them about the girl, and it was on the tip of his tongue to say so when he suddenly thought better of it.

In a flat level voice he said, 'They know what to do.'

'I hope they do.' Garnett opened the door, glanced at Norris and said, 'You did all right, don't give the Harveys another thought.' He got out of the Mini-van, slammed the door behind him, and walked back to the Ford Escort.

Norris heard the other car start up, and then the headlights of the Escort briefly filled his rear view mirror as it drew out of the lay-by. He sat there for some minutes thinking about Garnett's parting remark, and he couldn't help worrying about the Harveys. The 'Doctor' and the 'Italian' were in charge of that particular detail and that was reason enough to worry.

They were rolling east along the A338 to join up with the A4 at Hungerford, and the 'Italian' was behind the wheel. The truck was moving at a steady eighty kilometres an hour with its headlights on full beam. The road was empty, but they both knew that at any moment in time, a cruising police car might happen on the scene, and the crew might be just curious enough to flag them down and ask to see their papers, and this made the 'Italian' nervous and set his jaw working overtime on a piece of gum.

The 'Doctor', in contrast, appeared totally unconcerned. He sat with one foot resting on the panel while the other tapped out a monotonous rhythm on the steel floor of the cab.

From time to time he looked up at the handle above his head. The 'Italian', as if reading his thoughts, said, 'He didn't say anything about the girl.'

'She's in the back, isn't she?'

The 'Italian' licked his lips. 'It doesn't follow she is to get the same treatment.'

'You want that we should stop and let her out?'

'It might be an idea.'

'It would be a damn bad one. Where would she go? I'll tell you—the nearest police station. We've taken enough risks for one day. Now's as good a time as any, wouldn't you say?'

'I suppose so.'

'Of course it is.'

The 'Doctor' reached up and tugged on the handle, which in turn, triggered a cylinder of hydrogen cyanide inside the airtight freight compartment. In two minutes there was a lethal concentration. In less than five minutes Odell and Harvey were dead. It took another forty minutes to slowly disperse the agent cloud inside the freight compartment, and even then there was still a faint smell of almonds.

18

HE LAY THERE in the tiny copse overlooking the farmhouse and its outbuildings some eight hundred metres
away. The moon was partially obscured by a belt of low-
lying cloud, but there was enough ambient light around
for the starlight scope to function properly.

The farmhouse was sideways on to the road, and was
flanked by a Dutch barn and an outhouse on either side,
so that the overall configuration resembled the letter U
with an umlaut. An unsurfaced track led in from the
main road between the arms of the U and the umlaut.
The yard measured a good twenty by fifteen metres, and
he noticed that there was a fence of sorts between the
two outhouses. There was not a sign of life anywhere,
but that didn't mean a sentry had not been posted. It
would be like them to put an infra-red fence around
the property as an additional insurance.

Behind him, in the direction of the deserted village of
Imber, eight parachute flares went up into the night
sky, one after the other, to bathe the countryside in a
ghostly light. It was only the closing stages of some
Militia Night Exercise, but it reminded Garnett of another time and place . . .

They had been running for eight days, abandoning
one hastily prepared position after another, often before
contact had been made with the enemy. For them, the
enemy was a silver speck in the sky one minute, and the
next, it was a giant bird of prey which filled the horizon
as it screamed down your throat at 450 knots, and left
a trail of carnage in its wake. He was tired of digging in,

tired of falling back, tired of trying to maintain contact with flanking units, and tired of trying to act on orders which bore no relation to the situation by the time he got them. In the end, it was a relief to know that his company was to hold Sharnbrook at all costs.

And so they had held Sharnbrook and brewed up the platoon of three PT 76 reconnaissance tanks, which was the only enemy force to come their way, because the Ivans swung south and went through Bedford, and then swung northwards again to drive on Northampton. And then it was unnaturally quiet because the war had passed them by, and they were out of radio touch with their headquarters once more, and there were these rumours that a ten megaton SCRAGG missile had landed on Bath, or was it Bristol? And Garnett thought, Christ, I hope it's Bath because Liz and the boy are at Keynsham, and if it is Bristol they will be right in it. He remembered that the company clerk had produced a transistor set and they had listened in to the BBC News Bulletins which were being put out every hour on the hour. And on the six pm newscast, they heard the SCRAGG had definitely hit Bristol, and the bottom fell out of his world.

Three hours later, they were told that hostilities were to end at midnight, and he had walked out of the Command Post to visit the outlying platoons, and night had fallen and he could hear the sound of tracked movement in the distance, and he went past the burnt-out PT 76 scarcely noticing the blackened corpse draped across the turret hatch, and then the left forward platoon began to put up a string of parachute flares, and a nervous sentry had shot at him as he approached the platoon area, and that just about made his day.

And he remembered the way individuals had reacted when he told them the news, a few had actually cheered but most had looked stunned and apathetic, and the Colour Sergeant began to fuss about his stores because he thought it essential they handed everything over to the Russians in good order, because from first to last he was a store-keeper at heart. And he had trudged back to the Command Post, taken one look at the lethargic occupants, and quietly walked out again. And Lethbridge, the lost officer who had joined up with them on the first day of the war because he could not find Brigade Headquarters, had followed him, and on the outskirts of the village Garnett had stopped to tear off his badges of rank and had told Lethbridge to do likewise, because he believed the Russians would shoot them just as they had shot the Polish Officer Corps at Katyn in 1941. And they walked most of the night in a south-westerly direction, and towards dawn they ran into a Russian patrol outside Newport Pagnell who roughed them up and tied their hands behind their backs and removed their boots and made them walk barefoot to the PW Cage, and all that had happened exactly five long years ago to the day . . .

The earth felt like iron beneath him and his whole body was stiff. Garnett raised himself up on his elbows and moved each leg in turn, and then settled back into the small fold in the ground. The relief lasted a bare five minutes before the aches and pains came back. A thin streak of light was beginning to appear in the east behind Shrewton, and glancing at the luminous face of his wristwatch he saw it was 3:30 am, and suddenly he began to feel hungry and his stomach rumbled in protest. He found a boiled sweet in the pocket of his anorak but his stomach wasn't satisfied with that. To take his mind off the hunger, he trained the scope on the farm buildings and fell to wondering what they kept inside the Dutch barns. Cattle?—he didn't believe they ran a dairy herd because there was no sign of a loading platform for the milk churns—but then he was no farming expert.

The more he studied the place the less he liked it. They could drive into the yard dressed in militia uniform, and for a moment or so, the occupants might think they were a bunch of soldiers who had taken the wrong turning, but from then on, once surprise had been lost—and it was going to be lost as soon as they started shooting—they were faced with the task of clearing five separate buildings, and that was going to take time. There was a chance the locals would believe it was just another exercise, and so they would gain time there, but, and it was a big but, they would have to make sure the Russians didn't call for help. They could fix any telephone line before they went in, but dealing with their radio communications was going to be a problem because it could be anywhere in the complex. It would be nice to think they could sneak up on them and bring off a silent coup, but he knew that was sheer wishful thinking.

The light was up now, and he could see the farmhouse clearly without the aid of the scope. The kitchen door looked solid, but then it wouldn't be locked except perhaps at night when the occupants were asleep, and the windows on either side of the door were big enough for a man to get through if he had to. The nearest telegraph pole was almost within throwing distance on the blind side of the house, and as he looked closely he could see a line stretching from the gables to the pole.

A man appeared out of the shadow of the nearest Dutch barn and walked across the yard to the farmhouse. He stopped by the back door, stretched his arms above his head, and then went inside. Bit by bit, the farm gradually came to life, and over the next three hours, Garnett came to the conclusion that the Russian intelligence cell numbered at least eight men, amongst whom he recognised Amos Lee and the man he knew as Lenny.

Cautiously he backed out of the fold in the ground and crawled into the centre of the copse. Protected by the belt of trees, Garnett stood up, brushed the earth off his slacks, and then moved off in a westerly direction. There was a re-entrant behind the copse which was in dead ground to the farmhouse, and he was able to walk upright without fear of being seen. He had left the car in a disused barn about two kilometres south-west of the copse and there was, of course, the remote possibility that someone might have stumbled across it. In the event, he found the car as he had left it, and even in daylight, it was difficult to spot the Ford Escort through the pile of old planks which he had leaned against it.

Garnett moved the camouflage to one side, got into the Escort and moved out of the barn. He drove across the field and then turned into the lane. Ten minutes later he was on the main road to Salisbury.

19

It was a bright sunny morning and Garnett was still feeling elated. He was idling along at a sedate seventy kilometres with pop music on the car radio for background noise. Ahead of him, the road was a thin straight ribbon of tarmac as far as the eye could see. He was clean-shaven, and a long soak in a hot bath had taken the tiredness out of his body, and the knowledge that the job would be over in a couple of hours as far as he was concerned, acted like a tonic. For once, someone else was going to do the killing.

A steady procession passed him going in the opposite direction. The traffic was not as heavy as it would have been pre-war, but there were a lot more private cars on the road than there had been a month ago, and a whole lot of people were going to be more favourably disposed towards the Government because of that monthly ration of fifty litres of petrol. Garnett thought they would only have to take chocolate off the ration to have the entire population eating out of their hand. His mood of elation began to evaporate.

The garage was handily placed at a crossroads in the middle of nowhere. It boasted a breakdown service and four petrol pumps. Only two pumps were in use at any one time because the fuel allocation didn't warrant the use of all four. A number of assorted cars were piled on top of one another in an untidy heap on a piece of wasteland opposite the garage. At first sight it might have been supposed they had been wrecked in a multiple crash, but on closer inspection you could see that they were merely worn out and had been abandoned by their owners.

Garnett drove into the forecourt and stopped outside the shed which housed the workshops. A man sauntered out of the shed and looked closely at the Escort before giving a thumbs down sign. Garnett raised an eyebrow questioningly, but all he got was a shrug as the man disappeared back inside. It didn't convey anything to Garnett; he left the car and went after the man and found him leaning against a work bench stirring a mug of stewed tea.

Garnett said, 'What was all that supposed to mean?'

The man didn't look up, but concentrated on stirring the tea with a long yellow tooth-marked pencil, and when he spoke his lips barely moved. He said, 'Norris is out looking for your friends.'

'What about the stuff?'

'We only managed to get hold of one Land-Rover; had to do a paint job on it in the early hours of this morning. It's drying off out there under that pile of junked cars.'

'How about the hardware?'

'I wouldn't know about that, ask your friend, he'll know. The uniforms are in the office, and the sooner you take them off me the better I'll like it.' The man looked up and stared at Garnett. 'Why don't you wait outside for your friend?' he said. 'I don't like being too close to you people, you've caused me enough trouble already.'

A car drew up outside, a door opened and then slammed, and footsteps crunched across the gravel.

A voice which he recognised as Norris' said, 'Is anyone at home?'

Garnett strolled to the door. 'I am,' he said.

To say Norris looked pale was an understatement. He did not have the ability to keep a poker face, if something was wrong he showed it. He looked positively ill.

Garnett lit two cigarettes and gave one to Norris. 'All right,' he said quietly, 'let's have it.'

Norris exhaled a thin spiral of tobacco smoke. 'It's off,' he said abruptly, 'no go, finish.'

'What are you talking about?'

'The team didn't make it. I've just seen what is left of their Dormobile. They must have had a blow-out as they were overtaking a coach. They got sandwiched between the coach and a pantechnicon coming in the opposite direction. I hear two were killed outright, the rest are in hospital.'

'Where did this happen?'

'About eight kilometres east of here.' He puffed on the cigarette nervously. 'They failed to show up on time, so I went looking for them.' He paused and then said, 'I've been in touch with London. They say we are to drop the whole thing and get out fast.'

'Like hell.'

Norris stared at him open-mouthed. 'You're not thinking of going it alone, are you?' he said slowly.

'No, there will be four of us, you included.'

'You've got to be joking.'

'I was never more serious in my life.'

'Look, we've probably been rumbled.'

'You said it was an accident, and they were travelling clean, weren't they?'

'Of course they were.'

'Well then, there's nothing to worry about.'

Norris dropped his cigarette and trod on it. 'You're not asking me to volunteer, are you?'

'No,' said Garnett, 'you've been drafted.'

'That's what I thought.' A lopsided smile appeared on his face. 'You don't have to worry about the girl, London says they will give her the benefit of the doubt. So what are we trying to prove? Why are we sticking our necks out?'

'Because the cell is too bloody malignant to be left alone. Understand?'

'No, but I don't suppose it is going to make any difference. You'll go ahead no matter what I think. You'd better tell me what you want done.'

Garnett stubbed his cigarette out against the door. 'Get on to London again and say we need a recovery organisation set up fast. Tell them we shall be ready for them around 9 pm. Then see about that Land-Rover which is hidden under the pile of junk—we must be able to get it out quickly in daylight and without arousing a lot of undesirable curiosity. Get the key to the garage office, because we need somewhere to change into uniform, and then when you have picked up the hardware, I want you to make up a charge strong enough to chop a telegraph pole down. And don't hang around this place. Go anywhere you like, but be back here at 6:30 pm. Okay?'

'Oh sure,' Norris said sarcastically, 'what you have in mind couldn't be more simple.'

The last thing he wanted to do was to lose his temper with Norris. Swallowing hard, he said, 'Well, okay, I'll be seeing you.' He started to walk away and then stopped because he felt he ought somehow to snap Norris out of his despondent mood. 'Don't worry about it,' he said, 'we'll pull it off, I feel it in my bones.'

'How many are there of them?'

'I counted eight.'

'Eight?'

'Well, there may be one or two more I didn't see.'

'It's that extra one or two that worries me.'

Garnett smiled. 'Listen,' he said, 'if they were more than ten in number they would be sleeping two to a bed, and they are not a bunch of fairies.' He got into the Escort and drove off before Norris had time to come up with another gloomy question.

He drove with practised ease, intent on getting to Salisbury as quickly as possible while not appearing to be in a hurry. He kept within the speed limit, using the gear box to give him that extra burst to get by the slower traffic. In these last few hours, it was vital not to break an established pattern of behaviour, and since he had never taken lunch at the guest house, Garnett needed to contact Dinkmeyer before he left the office. He kept glancing at his wristwatch, watching the minute hand getting closer and closer to one o'clock, knowing that if he arrived after that time, Dinkmeyer would be gone and he would be forced to break the pattern.

Lunch-time traffic in Castle Street robbed him of precious minutes as he tried to turn across the stream to get into the car park, and he barely made it. He caught Dinkmeyer as he was about to open the street door, and hustled him back into the office.

Dinkmeyer said, 'Can't it wait, I was just on my way to lunch.'

'No, it can't.' Garnett lit a cigarette and looked up at the ceiling. 'How bright is Sue?'

'What are you getting at?'

'I've got eyes in my head.'

'Well, try looking at me with them.' Dinkmeyer waved his hands wildly. 'You make me sick,' he snarled, 'why don't you say straight out you think she is a half-wit.'

'All right,' Garnett snapped, 'is she a half-wit or not?'

'She has a low IQ and wouldn't find it easy to get a job. If she was left to make her own way in the world, she would cut a pretty sorry figure.'

'How well can Sue follow simple instructions?'

'She can do most things as long as they are not too complicated.' Dinkmeyer opened a drawer in the desk, took out one of his long thin Cuban cigars and struck a match against the wall. He looked at Garnett closely, trying to read the other man's thoughts. 'Things have changed since you saw me this morning, right?'

'Yes.'

The match was still halfway to the cigar and he dropped it hurriedly as the flame licked his fingers. 'In what way?' he said.

'We'll have to do the job ourselves.'

'What happened to the team?'

'They were in a traffic accident.'

'And I am one of those elected to take their place?'

'Any objections?'

Dinkmeyer shrugged his shoulders. 'What's the point. We're depending on you to get us out, so you can write your own terms.'

'The other man wanted to know why we were going through with it.'

'You can save the speech,' Dinkmeyer said wearily, 'I don't care enough to want to know the reason why. Just tell me what I have to do.'

Garnett stubbed out his cigarette in an ashtray. 'Go home, tell Sue she is going to the cinema this afternoon. She is to leave the cinema at 4:30 and catch a bus to Southampton. She is to go to the restaurant in the Odeon Cinema and order herself a meal. Three-quarters of an hour later, she will go down to the foyer where Tate will meet her and take over. Do you think she can follow those instructions?'

Dinkmeyer struck a second match and this time lit the cigar.

'Only one problem,' he said, 'Sue has never met Tate.'

'All right, tell her she will be met by a lady who will have a snapshot of her. I suppose you have got a recent snapshot of Sue?'

'Sure. Is that all?'

'It is as far as Sue is concerned.'

'And the rest?'

'I'll tell you later.'

'You do that.'

'On your way out, ask Tate to pop in.'

Dinkmeyer threw him a salute. 'Yes sir, General,' he said, 'right away, is there anything else the General wants?' He walked out of the office and slammed the door behind him.

The newspaper was lying in the out-tray where Dinkmeyer had left it after drawing a neat circle around the Stop Press. It caught Garnett's eye, and he picked it up and read it. The flash reported that a Karen Olds was helping the police with enquiries ... It was a nice way of saying she had been detained. It was no more than he expected, but it was just one more thing to worry about. He tossed the paper back into the tray as the office door opened.

The moment Tate walked into the office he could

see she was nervous. She was wearing a brittle stiff-upper-lip, I-won't-give-way expression on her face. A stiff drink would have done her no harm, but he didn't possess a hip flask, and it was no good offering Tate a cigarette because she didn't smoke. He wondered how such a nervous old maid ever got herself involved with the Resistance in the first place. He pulled a chair forward for her and smiled. 'It's nearly over,' he said. She nodded thankfully. 'I have never asked you this before, but whereabouts do you live?'

'I have a bed-sitter in Canadian Avenue,' she said quietly.

'That's just off the Wilton Road, isn't it?' She nodded her head again. 'How do you get home?'

'By bus, or sometimes, if it is a nice evening and I am not feeling too tired, I walk.'

'Do you get the bus from the depot?'

'Occasionally.'

'You are not going home tonight, but instead you are going to take a bus to Southampton from the depot. You are leaving Salisbury and you are never coming back, does that worry you?'

'No. I'll be glad to leave, these last three days have been a strain.'

Garnett said, 'You'll walk out of here in the clothes you stand up in. There is no question of going back to your rooms to pack a few things, because, you see, we have to fool those men across the street who are watching us. It may be that they have your rooms under surveillance as well, and it would look rather odd if you went back home, and then reappeared carrying a suitcase, wouldn't it?'

'I suppose so,' she said doubtfully.

'You take it from me, it most certainly would. When you get to Southampton, I want you to go straight to the Odeon and pick up Sue. Mr Dinkmeyer will give you a snapshot so that you can recognise her.' He drummed his fingers lightly on the desk. 'Do you know anybody who would give you shelter?'

'I'm not without friends,' she said quietly, 'but I would not want to get them into trouble.'

She was lying, but she did so with such quiet dignity that Garnett admired her for it. She was a middle-aged spinster, alone in the world and friendless, but she was never going to admit it unless someone tricked the admission out of her, and Garnett drew the line at that.

'I should have thought of that,' he said. 'If your friends are not connected with the Resistance, it would be wrong to involve them. I think the best thing is for you to take Sue to London, and ring 891 40625 as soon as you get there. Tell whoever answers, that you have come up from the country, and Mr Abel said you would know of suitable accommodation. Can you remember the number?'

'Yes.'

'Good. Now, here is another fail safe number which you can use in the Winchester area—56995. Whatever you do, don't get the two numbers confused. I don't want you to use the Winchester number unless Southampton railway station is crawling with policemen. All right?'

'I think so.'

He wrote the details on a slip of paper and gave it to Tate. He smiled and said, 'Once you've memorised the telephone numbers, make absolutely sure to burn it.'

There had been a number of people like Tate in the early days of the Resistance, but most of them hadn't lasted. He thought it a small miracle that Tate had survived five years. There must have been other occasions when she had been in danger, and somehow she must have found the courage to hang on. He hoped she had enough nerve left in the bank to hang on for a few more hours.

He cast around for another topic of conversation to take her mind off the present. He didn't come up with anything original. He said, 'Where are you lunching?'

'I've brought some sandwiches to eat in the office.'

'Come and have lunch with me.'

'No, really, it's very kind of you to offer, but I would prefer to stay here.'

'Can I bring you back a stiff drink?'

'No, thank you, I don't drink,' she said primly.

He walked to the door, looked back at Tate and said, 'Sure you won't change your mind about lunch?'

'Quite sure.'

'Well, all right,' he said, 'I'll be at the Tap Room if anyone wants me.' He walked out leaving Tate to close the door behind him.

And now it was purely a question of waiting for time to pass, and that wasn't easy, because the mind had nothing else to do but dwell on the risks. If the Dormobile hadn't been smashed up, the Russians would have been dealt with already, but this enforced delay opened up all sorts of possibilities.

As Garnett sat there, picking at a Cornish pasty which was half-buried under a mound of watery cabbage and mashed potatoes, he tried to put himself in their shoes. After what had happened last night, they would check up on Harvey and find that the pair of them had flown the coop. That much was a dead cert, but what their next step would be was anybody's guess. As he saw it, the Soviets could come to one of two conclusions. Either they figured that Harvey was right and they were close to being rumbled, or else they might think Harvey merely had the wind up and was lying low for a few days. If they came to the former conclusion, the Soviets would shut the game down and they were as good as dead.

The Cornish pasty looked even less appetising now. Garnett pushed the plate to one side, finished his drink, and then left. The clock in the Market Square showed a quarter to three. There was two hours fifteen minutes to go.

The office was as solemn as a funeral parlour. Garnett and Dinkmeyer sat at the desk playing Canasta with a pack of dog-eared cards while they both chain smoked. Garnett disliked all card games, but at least it helped to pass the time and, to a small extent, it took his mind off the present. They had six callers between three and four thirty, and all of them were after a job, but each time the street door opened, Dinkmeyer and Garnett froze. It wouldn't have surprised Garnett if Tate had cracked under the strain, but somehow she held out.

The last half hour crawled by at a snail's pace. Periodically, Dinkmeyer would look up at the ceiling and voice his fears about Sue, and Garnett would sigh and light yet another cigarette adding to the thick pall of grey-blue smoke. He thought five o'clock would never come, and then suddenly it was on them. Tate was the first to leave the office, and they watched her progress down Castle Street until she was out of sight. No one approached her, nothing happened.

Dinkmeyer and Garnett left together, locked up the office, and walked round to the car park. Garnett let Dinkmeyer have a head start and then, instead of following him, he turned left on Castle Street, went up to the roundabout and turned left again to hit Fisherton Street above the railway station. Continuing on a left-hand circuit, he came back to the city centre and followed the signs for Southampton. The detour was necessary to give Dinkmeyer time in which to park the Volkswagen in Wimbourne Street, go through the house, hop over the privet hedge at the back, persuade the neighbours to let him through their house on some pretext or other, and emerge on Calshot Avenue. Garnett thought it possible that the Russians would be watching Dinkmeyer's house from a vantage point across the street, but he hoped they didn't have enough men to cover the back as well. If he was wrong on that count, it was just too bad.

Garnett drove up Fowler Hill, shot past the bottom of Wimbourne Street and turned into Calshot Avenue. Dinkmeyer appeared out of someone's front garden, strode across the pavement, and jumped into the car as Garnett slowed down to a walking pace. When they turned the corner at the bottom of Calshot Avenue, Dinkmeyer slid over the front seat and curled himself up on the floor so that he was below the window level. For a heavily built man he took up surprisingly little room.

Dinkmeyer said, 'What are you going to do about McDonald?'

'I don't know.'

'Shouldn't you warn him? He's in just as much danger as we are.'

'More so,' Garnett said tersely, 'because of Harvey, the Russians can pick him up any time they choose. Maybe they already have him.'

'You can't leave him out in the cold.'

Garnett swung on to the Wilton Road and marginally increased his speed. 'If all goes well, I'll warn him after the job is finished.'

'Not before?'

'Not before. We don't want to alarm the Ivans.'

'Getting them means more to you than McDonald's safety?'

'Yes.'

'And the lives of all the men he might betray when he is interrogated?'

'Yes.'

'You are a bastard,' Dinkmeyer said quietly. 'You and Vickers are two of a kind, don't kid yourself you are any different.' It suddenly came home to him that Dinkmeyer was right. He was behaving exactly as Vickers would have done if he had been running the show, and it left a nasty taste in his mouth. On impulse, he stopped being rational. 'All right,' he said, 'I've changed my mind, I'll call him from the farm.' Dinkmeyer didn't say a word.

Twenty minutes later Garnett turned into Brocken-hurst Farm, and there was Dane waiting for him. She was wearing the faded, oil-stained jeans and the tartan shirt again, and she came running across the yard to meet him. He told Dinkmeyer to stay down out of sight, and then got out of the car to meet her.

'We're getting out,' he said simply.

'After we've put the Ivans out of business,' he added.

'You've found them?'

'We found them, now we have to kill them.'

'I was afraid that would be the case,' she said listlessly.

'Do you mean that literally?'

'Of course I'm damn well frightened,' she said, 'only a moron likes fighting. I suppose we have to do it? I mean, isn't anyone else available?'

'We're a real happy band of warriors,' he said savagely. 'We all want to run and hide from the enemy.'

She flushed and scuffed her foot in the dirt. 'You would have made a brilliant recruiting sergeant in the old days,' she said.

'I want to send a last message to London, it might help to keep the Russians happy.'

'I'll get my pad.'

'There's no need to, it's really very simple. We will tell London we have found a suitable head of operations, code name Roger. Personal details to follow by courier tomorrow. All right?' She nodded her head. 'Okay, send it, and then go and put on a skirt and blouse, and then tell Brockenhurst I want to see him.'

She ran a hand through her short blonde hair. 'You don't want much, do you?' She turned and walked towards the barn. Garnett got back inside the Escort.

Dinkmeyer said, 'You were rough on her.'

'Yes. I'm going to be rough with Brockenhurst too. I am going to give him the option of going to ground or staying put. If he chooses the latter, I shall advise him to turn informer, it's about his only hope.'

'You're the boss.'

'Don't remind me.'

'You haven't forgotten about McDonald, have you?'

'No,' Garnett said wearily, 'I haven't forgotten him. I'll give him a ring—what's his number?'

'What are you going to say to him?'

'I'll tell him he ought to follow Harvey's example and take a holiday. Now, do I get his number or not?'

20

HE STOOD AT the crossroads with his back to the garage, waiting until the main road was clear of traffic. The casual observer saw a figure dressed in olive-drab combat kit and mottled camouflaged smock, wearing a Soviet pattern steel helmet and carrying a Kalashnikov 7·62mm (AKM) assault rifle slung over his right shoulder. If they had been going slowly and were sharp-eyed enough, they might also have spotted the tiny sergeant's chevrons on the right sleeve. Most people didn't give Garnett a second glance; they simply took him for a Militia soldier on exercise. Some might have wondered what he was doing at the crossroads, the more knowledgeable assumed he was on point duty.

Dinkmeyer was behind him, tucked away in rear of the garage and out of sight from the passing traffic. From time to time, he gave a series of short blasts on his whistle to let Garnett know that he had seen something moving up the road towards the intersection. From where he stood, Dinkmeyer could just see Norris lying in a prone position behind the hedgerow on the opposite side of the road, where he was watching Dinkmeyer through a gap he had made in the undergrowth.

Dane was sitting in the Land-Rover, boxed in by a pile of scrapped cars, and was just able to see Norris out of the corner of her eye by looking through the side windows of a battered Morris Oxford, provided of course he adopted a kneeling position. Stacked in rear of the Land-Rover was a pile of worn-out tyres which they hoped would topple out of the way when she reversed into them. Dane did not look very prepossessing, but then she wasn't supposed to be. The combat suit swamped her and the boots were several sizes too big. The steel helmet almost masked her eyes, and she had been forced to adjust the straps until they almost choked her, in order to make sure the blasted thing stayed on her head. An armoured flak jacket worn loosely over the top of the camouflaged smock completed the picture of a pudding-shaped soldier and obliterated the curve of her breasts. To give her face a more rounded look, she had been forced to plug her cheeks with foam rubber, with the result that she was unable to speak.

She had been sitting there like a hen cooped up in a battery layer for over half an hour, and she was beginning to think she would be there all night when, out of the corner of her eye, she saw Norris on his knees waving frantically. Leaning forward, Dane switched on the ignition and pressed the starter button, and felt a surge of relief as the engine fired into life. She banged the gear stick into reverse, revved up, and let the clutch in fast. Starting from cold, the engine wouldn't take it. The Land-Rover hit the pile of tyres and immediately stalled. Like manna from heaven, the tyres rained down on top of Dane turning her into an ad for Michelin X.

Dane freed herself from the couple of tyres which were hanging round her neck like giant-sized life jackets, and re-started the engine. This time she intended to make sure the Land-Rover didn't stall, and she accelerated viciously over the pile of tyres. The vehicle took off, and then hit the ground again with a spine-shuddering crash which pitched her forward against the steering wheel. The helmet came down over her eyes, the breath went out of her body, her foot slipped off the pedal, and in consequence the Land-Rover stalled yet again. Norris ran towards her, gesticulating madly. 'You stupid little bitch,' he shouted, 'what the hell are you playing at? Can't you drive?'

Keyed up and frustrated, she cursed and spat the foam rubber out of her mouth. 'Don't you bloody well swear at me.'

As Norris jumped into the back, she re-started the engine and shot forward, yanking the wheel hard over to avoid hitting the Morris Oxford. She had to come hard right again to make the gap in the hedgerow, which was in front of the abandoned cars, and she took the ditch far too fast. The Land-Rover bounced, hit the road with a thud, and to her horror, she saw they were heading straight for the petrol pumps in the forecourt. Dane trod on the brakes, frantically put on a right lock, and went into a broadside skid. Somehow she avoided a pile-up and managed to halt the Land-Rover five metres short of the crossroads. Dinkmeyer and Garnett ran towards the vehicle from opposite directions, and leapt aboard. Garnett said, 'That was a damn fool thing to do. What on earth got into you?'

Close to panic, Dane pounded her fists on the steering wheel.

'Shut up,' she yelled, 'shut up, I've had more than enough.'

He squeezed her shoulder gently. 'It's going to be all right,' he said in a soothing voice, 'it won't last much longer, and I know you can do it.'

She rubbed her forehead with the back of her hand, and then drove forward to the crossroads, where she waited for a break in the traffic before turning left. There was just about two hours of daylight left, but there were storm clouds building up in the west, and it looked as if it might rain before dark.

Garnett cleared his throat and said, 'What did London say about recovery?'

Norris said, 'They gave us the address of a safe house in Basingstoke; they also said we were on our own until we got there.'

It didn't need a high IQ to read the implications. Garnett was pretty certain that a comprehensive recovery plan had been laid on for the original team, and London had seen fit to cancel it, and he had Norris to thank for that. If Norris had delayed reporting the traffic accident, he might have persuaded London to let the arrangements stand. Now, it began to look as though Vickers, having washed his hands of the affair, had been forced to make a last-minute change in plan. He wondered how many of the others had come to the same conclusion. He looked round at Norris and said, 'What's the address?'

'65, Cornwall Drive, it's near the station.'

They were on the Amesbury Bypass now and less than fifteen minutes from their destination, and he debated whether or not to take them over their separate tasks again step by step. One glance at Dane's tense face convinced him that it was not a good idea. It was also on the tip of his tongue to ask her what she had done with the foam rubber inserts, but that didn't seem a very good idea either. Nobody was going to take much notice of her now, and if they did get a second glance at Dane, they might take her for an effeminate-looking youth. He settled back in his seat and tried to relax.

The clouds were much darker now, and he thought it wouldn't be long before the storm broke. He was right about that. They entered Shrewton to a clap of thunder, and seconds later the heavens opened. They turned on to the road leading to Warminster with the rain lashing into their faces, and in a short time, they were soaked through to the skin. The combat kit was supposed to be waterproof, but the suits they were wearing had been in store for too long and were no longer resistant. Dane switched on the headlights, but they were more of a safety factor than an aid to vision, and because her eyes were screwed up against the driving rain, she would have overshot the telegraph pole if Garnett hadn't punched her on the arm.

Norris went over the back as the Land-Rover slowed down. He was carrying the necklace, primer and battery in the crook of the left arm, the cable was piniioned under his right arm, and his right hand clutched the wires trailing from the end of the electric detonator. He hit the ground awkwardly, almost lost his balance, and felt the necklace slipping out of his arm. Instinctively, the right arm started to move across his chest to trap the slipping necklace. He stopped the movement just in time. A split second later and the trailing leads of the detonator would have touched the battery terminals to complete the circuit, and he would have been so much offal hanging on the trees. The necklace, battery and primer fell into the gutter. Norris carefully placed the cable and detonator to one side on the kerb, recovered the necklace, battery and primer, and then methodically started to sort them out in the order he wanted.

As they turned into the lane leading to the farm, Garnett caught a final glimpse of Norris crouching over his demolition kit, and noticed that he had inadvertently left his Kalashnikov in the Land-Rover, but it was too late then to do anything about it. Dane slipped into third gear and made a left-hand circuit of the yard. As she passed the barn on their left, she noticed a man standing in the entrance.

A voice shouted, 'Where the hell do you think you're going?'

Garnett swung round in his seat, and holding the Kalashnikov at hip height, hosed the barn with a long burst. The bullets stitched an untidy pattern across the wall and left the man unharmed. The stranger threw himself flat and rolled over and over seeking to put some sort of cover between himself and Garnett.

As Dane stopped the Land-Rover opposite the farm-house, Lenny appeared in the back door and peered out into the yard. He recognised Garnett immediately, and turned about to shout a warning. They were less than five metres apart, and a more prudent man would have thrown himself flat and let the others take their chance, but he was not a man to put his own safety above all else. The high velocity bullets broke his spine and slammed him forward on to his face. Garnett sprang out of the Land-Rover and ran into the house followed by Dinkmeyer.

Norris wrapped the necklace around the telegraph pole and tied it in place. He was rather pleased with the neck-lace, and mentally he congratulated himself on having

199

the foresight to fashion it from a tool wallet. He had shaped the plastic explosive to fit into the various recesses provided for the spanners, which ensured that the charges stayed in place when he tied the wallet to the telegraph pole. Working calmly, he inserted the primer into the PE, slipped the detonator into the primer sleeve and connected the wires to the cable. He walked backwards paying out the cable until he reached the spot where he had left the battery. He then bared the cable, bent down and placed the wires across the battery terminals.

The charge felled the telegraph pole across the road with the precision of a lumber-jack. Norris had been so engrossed with his task that he had not heard the initial burst of gunfire, and he ran towards the farm buildings unaware that the enemy had been alerted. His one concern was to recover his rifle before the fighting started. He turned into the yard, spotted the Land-Rover outside the house, and ran blindly towards it.

Dane had been slow to get off the mark because she had to free the automatic rifle which had become wedged between the driver's seat and the transmission tunnel. By the time she started moving, the man Garnett had shot at and missed had got himself a pump action, repeating shotgun. In the excitement, his first shot had gone high and to the right. Dane hadn't given him a chance to correct his aim. Turning quickly, she had dived headlong into the mud, and slithering on her stomach, had crawled behind the Land-Rover as the shotgun boomed twice in rapid succession behind her.

She had just got into a position where she could fire back at the gunman in the barn, when she caught sight of Norris rushing towards her. She shouted a warning. but either he didn't hear her or else he misunderstood, because he ran straight into the line of fire, and the shotgun started booming again. All three rounds of buckshot hit Norris, knocking him flat on to his face. Blood began to seep through his clothing from neck to buttocks as he tried to drag himself towards the house.

The gunman was still hovering in the entrance to the barn as Dane brought the rifle up into her shoulder, put the change lever to semi-automatic, and let go with four quick shots. One round took the man in the head, and she saw pieces of shattered bone fly off from his skull. Suddenly, the total destructive effect of her marksmanship came home to Dane, and she backed away from the two prone figures in the yard. As revulsion mounted, she turned and ran into the other barn. Holding the Kalashnikov at the trail, she leaned against a stall and waited for the feeling of nausea to pass. A lonely, frightened voice in the yard called out to her, 'Help me. Don't leave me, please don't leave me.'

Dinkmeyer left Garnett to clear the downstairs rooms while he made for the bedrooms. There were nine steps in the first flight, and then the staircase turned through a hundred and eighty degrees, and he couldn't see the landing, but he had a feeling that someone was up there waiting for him. Speed, he decided, was essential. He took the stairs two at a time whilst firing the rifle above his head like some trick marksman in a circus. It could have been a waste of ammunition, but there was someone up there waiting for him, and the unaimed, prophylactic fire forced the man to move further back along the landing.

Dinkmeyer hit the top step, hurled himself round the banister post, and threw himself flat as he snapped off two shots in rapid succession. He could have got it wrong and found himself facing in the wrong direction with the enemy behind him, but luck was favouring Dinkmeyer. One round smashed into the man's kneecap and knocked him over on to his back. A door at the end of the corridor opened a fraction of an inch and a gun barrel appeared in the crack. Dinkmeyer put the Kalashnikov on to full automatic and fired a long burst. The impact knocked the door open and Amos Lee toppled out on to the landing, his hands clasped round the tea-cup-sized hole in his stomach. The man with the smashed kneecap was still trying to recover the Stechkyn machine-pistol which had fallen from his hand, when Dinkmeyer stood up and fired a short burst into his back.

As suddenly as it had begun, the brief exchange of fire ceased. In the silence which followed, Dinkmeyer heard Garnett moving about downstairs checking out each room in turn, and it jogged him into action. Maybe Garnett was trying to conserve ammunition, but for himself he had no intention of going into a room unannounced. His drill was simple in the extreme. He fired a short burst through each door before he went into the room. Fourteen rounds and five rooms later, he had yet to encounter further opposition. He retraced his steps, and was about to go downstairs, when he noticed that there was a room at the other end of the corridor which he had not checked out. He followed the same drill as before, only this time someone screamed and water slopped on to the floor.

He stepped inside the room, and saw a pair of slim but hairy legs dangling over the side of the bath. The legs didn't look muscular enough to go with the hair, and as he drew closer he found the answer. The woman's head was sunk down on to her chest, and pinky brown water lapped gently against her breasts. She was, of course, unarmed.

Garnett drew a blank in the kitchen, and he went out into the hall to clear the other rooms on the ground floor. He was moving quickly, and in consequence, he failed to notice the door under the stairs which led to the cellars below. He checked the dining room and moved cautiously through the connecting door and, finding both rooms empty, stepped out into the hall again. There was an office of sorts across the hall from the lounge, and he was half-way towards it, when he saw the reflection in the oak-framed mirror on the wall to his right. He threw himself headlong, turning a complete somersault in mid-air before the Russian had a chance to take a deliberate aim. Behind him, the bullets gouged deep pockmarks in the plaster walls and shattered the mirror.

Garnett landed heavily on the balls of his feet and, unable to keep his balance, pitched forward and dug his nose into the stair carpet. The blood streamed from both nostrils, ran down over his chin and spotted the camouflaged smock. Partially screened by the banister post, he made the best use of such cover as he had by holding the Kalashnikov as though he was left-handed, and poking it in the general direction, let go with a burst of eight rounds. Garnett didn't hit anything, but the Russian didn't stay for a repeat performance; instead he opted to go back into the cellar.

Garnett sat on the stairs listening to the sound of footsteps fading to nothing. He got up, wiped the blood from his face with a handkerchief, and walked towards the cellar. The door was ajar and, through the crack, a beam of light beckoned invitingly. He pushed the door open wide and immediately flattened himself against the wall. Nobody shot at him, but somewhere down there, beyond the pool of light, someone could be waiting for him. Cat-like, he crept down the stairs.

Six steps from the bottom and he still had no idea what the lay-out of the cellar was. He froze, trying to catch the slightest sound of any movement, but the only thing he heard was the pounding of his own heart. If he jumped the rest of the way and then went left or right, there was an even chance he would be wrong. Garnett decided he would stand a better chance in the dark. He put the Kalashnikov on to single shot, took a steady aim, and shattered the light in the ceiling. There was no reaction.

He took off his steel helmet and lobbed it into the cellar as he slithered down the remaining steps. The steel helmet clattered across the floor and sparked off the reaction he wanted. A sub-machine-gun stuttered briefly, and he spotted the muzzle flash to his left. He swung round and fired three shots in quick succession. He didn't know it at the time, but the first round hit the Russian in the jaw and blew the back of his head off; the other two rounds went high and ricocheted off the walls. For good measure, he wheeled about and let go with another three. In that confined space, each shot sounded like a cannon and he was almost deafened. Gradually it dawned on him that there was a tunnel leading off from the cellar, but he decided not to explore it until his eyes became more accustomed to the darkness.

The feeling of revulsion was still with Dane, and she could not summon up enough willpower to get on with her task of clearing the barns and outhouses. To add to her discomfort, the stifling atmosphere inside the barn made her sweat freely. She rubbed the sleeve of her camouflaged smock over her face, and suddenly, there they were—two men who had appeared out of the floor. For a moment, she stared at their backs open-mouthed, and then she stooped, grabbed the rifle and brought it up into her shoulder. The sudden movement was heard by both men who turned round, saw Dane and scattered. She fired twice at each man and was convinced she had killed them both. On any other occasion, she would have been more cautious, but the adrenalin made her careless of her own safety. Holding the rifle across her body at the port, she walked forward. The man on her left raised himself up, and she saw, to her horror, that there was a Makarov 9mm pistol aimed at her heart. At a range of ten paces he couldn't very well miss. The bullet smashed into the flak jacket and knocked Dane back a couple of paces. If she had never had much faith in the heavy armoured jacket before, she had then.

The man's eyes widened in surprise; by rights she should have been dead, and yet there she was still on her feet and apparently unharmed. He took aim again, but of course he was far too slow; his finger was still curling round the trigger of the Makarov when Dane shot him. She went over to the second man and nudged him with her foot, but he didn't come to life. She turned and started back to the stall. At the last moment Dane noticed the trap door, and then only because it had been raised just that fraction so that the hidden sniper could aim his rifle. In a pure reflex, she sprang out of the line of fire and simultaneously flicked to automatic and loosed off a short burst. The rifle disappeared, the trap door closed hastily.

The rattle of gunfire, which died slowly like a train receding into the distance, almost muffled the metallic clatter. For a moment Garnett was puzzled by the noise, and then it dawned on him that the man had dropped his rifle when he fell back into the tunnel. Time was not on his side, but Garnett was cool enough not to open fire. The man who won this duel would be the one whose eyes adjusted first to the prevailing light, and since the other man had been exposed to the brighter light above, Garnett thought he had the edge on him.

Gradually a blurred outline of a crouching figure came into focus, and in slow motion Garnett brought the Kalashnikov up into the shoulder. Keeping both eyes open in shotgun style, he sited the weapon on to the target and took up the trigger pressure. The noise of the explosion was deafening. He squeezed the trigger again and there was a dull click as the working parts slid forward on to a now empty magazine. He scrambled forward, intending to club the man about the head with the gun butt, but as he got closer, he saw there was no need to do anything.

The bullet had opened up a hole in the Russian's chest and the blood was trickling out of his mouth. He tried to align his rifle but the effort brought on a paroxysm of coughing, and Garnett was able to take the Kalashnikov out of his limp grasp with almost contemptuous ease. A glimmer of recognition flickered in his eyes and he smiled painfully. 'Hullo George,' he whispered, 'remember me—Alan?—we met in the Amusement Arcade in Bournemouth.'

Garnett said, 'You certainly fooled me that day.'

'Oh, no,' he said faintly, 'you fooled us in the long run. I told Valentine Teroshkova it was too good to last.'

He started coughing again, and the blood vomited out of his mouth, and his eyes took on a glazed look. He lapsed into a babble of Russian and then he died.

Dinkmeyer ran quickly down the stairs, went through the hall, paused briefly at the top of the steps leading down to the cellar to stare into the darkness below, and, since everything was quiet, came to the conclusion that Garnett had already gone. He had no wish to be left behind and so he ran through the kitchen and came out into the back yard. He saw an empty Land-Rover and Norris lying face down in the mud with a dead man nearby, but there was no sign of either Dane or Garnett. He began to wonder if he was the only survivor.

'Is anyone there?' he shouted.

A small voice answered him, and turning, he saw Dane standing in the entrance of the barn. He pointed the Kalashnikov in the direction of the two outhouses and the other barn and said,

'Have you checked them out?'

'No,' she said faintly, 'I haven't had the time.'

He knew that she had had the time all right, what she lacked was the inclination, and he was on the point of telling her so, when he realised it would not register because the girl had reached the limit of her endurance. Even at that distance, he could see she was trembling, and there was no sense in driving her like a sacrificial lamb to the slaughter.

'Okay,' he said, 'I'll check them out, you see to Norris.'

Without waiting for a reply, he ran across the yard and disappeared into the other barn. Dane moved like a sleep-walker. She went up to the Land-Rover, placed the rifle carefully in the back, and then knelt down beside Norris and gently turned him over.

There was something wrong with his eyes because everything was a blur, but gradually the face came into focus, and he recognised Dane. He was numb from the kidneys down and he knew he was dying, and it was all her fault, and he wanted to tell her to her face that she wasn't bloody well worth it, but when he tried to speak, the words were a rattle in his throat. But he didn't have to speak, because the hate was there in his eyes and she knew it was directed at her, and the tears began to course down her cheeks. And he died with his head over on one side, and the rain washing the fringe of straw-coloured hair showing beneath his helmet and plastering it to his forehead in spiky fingers, and the upturned button nose was caked in mud, and the once absurdly young-looking freckled face didn't look young any more. She sat there holding his hand until Dinkmeyer returned and told her roughly to get into the Land-Rover.

Garnett had managed to find three candles in the cellar, which gave him some light to work by while he went through the two chest-high steel filing-cabinets which held the Russian card index system. With the zeal of civil servants they had meticulously committed to paper every detail they had learned about the suspects they had under surveillance. They had kept intricate records of informers and double agents on their payroll, and apparently, had attempted to assess their reliability and cost effectiveness, although Garnett couldn't be too sure about the latter because his knowledge of Russian wasn't all that good.

He went through both cabinets, selecting those cards which he thought would be of interest, and packing them into an old fibre suitcase he had found in the cellar. The rejected cards he tossed on to the growing pile on the floor. They were well-provided with travel documents, blank social security cards and money. He thought it prudent to help himself to a little of everything, because there was no knowing what he might need in the future. He was so engrossed in his task that he wasn't aware that someone had joined him.

Dinkmeyer said, 'Are you planning to stay all night?'

Garnett jumped. 'For God's sake,' he said, 'don't do that again.'

'What the hell are you doing?'

'Looting,' Garnett said cheerfully. He closed the locks on the fibre case and, stooping, set fire to the pile of paper on the floor.

'What good will that do? They will have a duplicate set of records.'

'I don't think so, because the one thing which every Secret Service has in common, is a marked reluctance to share their information with other agencies.' He picked up the case, slung the Kalashnikov over his shoulder, took one last look round the cellar and then left. Dinkmeyer was close on his heels.

Garnett ran out into the yard, saw Dane sitting hunched up in the back of the Land-Rover and hesitated for a moment before slinging his rifle and the fibre case in with her. He jumped into the driving seat, started up the engine and drove swiftly out of the yard. He had no choice but to turn right on the main road and, glancing back over his shoulder, he saw a small knot of people standing by the felled telegraph pole. Sooner or later, at least one of those spectators was going to take a closer look at the farm, and then the trouble would start.

Dinkmeyer said, 'We're going deeper into the Training Area.'

'We don't have any choice.'

'No, I guess we don't.'

Garnett had the accelerator flat on the floorboards, but the Land-Rover wasn't responding because the engine was too clapped out to give more than a sluggish seventy-five kilometres an hour. The road ahead was like a switchback, and the loss of power on each incline reduced their speed appreciably. In the distance, he spotted a procession of three Army Land-Rovers coming their way and Garnett began to sweat. It could be that the Russians had, after all, succeeded in calling for help and the same thought had occurred to Dinkmeyer, who began to reach for his rifle. Garnett put out a restraining hand and gently shook his head.

He watched the oncoming vehicles with his heart in his mouth, conscious that nothing could be more conspicuous than an open Land-Rover in the rain, and knowing it was too late to do anything about it now. When they were fifty metres apart, the leading vehicle flashed its headlights at them, and for a moment he wasn't sure what they were getting at, and then he realised it was just a friendly greeting and he flicked his headlights on and off in reply. One by one, the Land-Rovers passed them without incident.

Dinkmeyer sighed loudly. 'Jesus,' he said, 'now I can breathe again.'

They ran down the steep hill into Chitterne, and the knowledge that they were still heading in the wrong direction stretched his nerves tauter than a piano wire. He turned left in the middle of the village and took the road to Codford, knowing that it would bring them out on to the main road for Salisbury. His one aim was to get out of the immediate area before it was sealed off by police road blocks.

The rain was easing off, but as they were already soaked it made little difference to them. The Land-Rover wasn't cornering too well, and at first he put it down to the worn tyres and the wet surface of the road, but then it began to affect the steering and it dawned on him that they had a slow puncture. They hit the A36 and turned in the direction for Salisbury, and the drag on the steering became more pronounced. He desperately wanted to be the other side of the county boundary before the police reacted in force, but at the back of his mind was the knowledge that he could not shelve the problem of changing the wheel for much longer. Reluctant to stop, Garnett tried to convince himself that the tyre was good for a few more kilometres.

In a calm but quiet voice, Dane said, 'There is a police car behind us; it's been on our tail ever since we joined this main road.'

'Does he seem interested?'

'He's watching us, I think they are curious.'

'Could be our flat tyre,' said Dinkmeyer.

Dane caught her breath. 'He is pulling out to overtake us.' Garnett glanced at Dinkmeyer's Kalashnikov which was propped against the battery box beside him. 'Is that thing empty?' he asked.

'Near enough, there may be six or seven rounds left in the magazine.'

The White Zephyr went past them with the police sign flashing. An arm appeared out of the nearside window and waved them down as the car slowed to a halt at a blocking angle in front of the Land-Rover. A uniformed policeman got out of the nearside door and walked slowly towards them. He was wearing a black leather Sam Browne and pistol holster, and there was something vaguely familiar about him. Garnett had the feeling he had met him before somewhere, and then in a flash, it came to him that this was the bastard with the narrow unblinking hazel eyes who had searched him, when he had called in to the Police Headquarters for a residential permit. Casually, he picked up the Kalashnikov, got out of the vehicle and sauntered forward to meet the other man.

The policeman said, 'Don't you people know you've got a flat?'

Garnett was holding the Kalashnikov in his left hand with the barrel pointing downwards, but it needed only the slighest adjustment to line it up on the other man's stomach.

Garnett said, 'And you should know that you will get a hole in the belly if you make any trouble.'

The man stared at him open-mouthed. 'You,' he said, as recognition dawned.

'Me,' Garnett agreed. 'I'm hitching a lift with you. Now, walk back to the car.'

Dinkmeyer watched Garnett get into the Zephyr and wondered what he had in mind. He'd seen enough to know that the police were being intimidated, and it occurred to him that there was something to be said for lifting a police car. The Zephyr moved off while Dinkmeyer was still scrambling across the seats to get behind the wheel, and by the time he had started the Land-Rover, a coach had overtaken him and slid in behind the police car. Fortunately, it didn't stay there for long—at the first opportunity it overtook the Zephyr.

Garnett sat behind the two policemen, resting the muzzle of the Kalashnikov on the back of the front seat. So far, nothing had been sent over the police radio net to indicate that the alarm had been given, but he knew the honeymoon couldn't last. It didn't, it ended there and then. An excited voice brought all Sierra Romeos to Red Alert and asked for locations. He heard Control acknowledge each car in turn, and then the excited voice revealed a trace of anger when they failed to come up.

Control said, 'Sierra Romeo 9 this is Zero, did you get my last?'

Garnett jabbed the muzzle of the rifle into the co-driver's neck. 'Answer up,' he snarled. 'Tell them where we are and don't try any tricks.'

The man did as he was told. He said, 'Zero, this is Sierra Romeo 9 on patrol approaching Deptford.'

Control was not to be mollified, the voice was still curt. 'Roger, Sierra Romeo 9. In future, answer up first time. All Sierra Romeos are to watch out for open Army Land-Rover with three armed occupants in militia uniform. Do not attempt arrest, shadow and report. Standard road blocks will be effective within next fifteen minutes; out.'

Garnett said, 'Just what are standard road blocks?'

The driver opened his mouth, and then closed it abruptly when his companion dug a sharp elbow into his ribs. This time Garnett was not so gentle; he rammed the barrel into the co-driver's skull and opened up a crescent shaped cut. 'Suppose you let your friend do the talking,' he said nastily.

'You fucker.'

Garnett jabbed him again. 'It's your friend I want to hear from, not you.' He glanced sideways at the other man. 'Well,' he said, 'what about it?'

The man hesitated briefly, and then said, 'They send them out from Salisbury to Alderbury, Fordingbridge, Coombe Bisset, Wilton, Amesbury and Winterslow to block every road leading out of the city.'

They were now about eleven kilometres from Salisbury,

and Garnett knew they would have to get off the main road very soon before they ran into the road block at Wilton. As they crossed the bridge over the stream and started to climb the hill in a curve, he noticed a road branching off to the left. On impulse, he ordered them to take it.

The flat tyre was now having a marked effect on the steering, and Dinkmeyer was forced to drag the Land-Rover round each curve. He was having a hard time staying up with the Zephyr and he doubted whether he would be able to do so for much longer. He followed the Zephyr when it turned off the main road, but he was caught on the hop when, with no warning, the police car swung off the road to turn into a field of stubble and disappear behind the hedgerow. Dinkmeyer shot past the turning into the field, and had to reverse back down the road. By the time he had driven the Land-Rover into the field and tucked it up against the hedge, Garnett had got the two men out of the Zephyr. Both policemen were standing at an angle to the car with their hands resting on the roof and their legs splayed apart. Garnett was standing a few paces to their rear covering them with the Kalashnikov. Dinkmeyer got out and walked across to the Zephyr.

Garnett said, 'We're ditching the Land-Rover. You get changed into your civilian clothes and tell Dane to do the same. Don't take all day.'

His face was white and set in tense lines, and Dinkmeyer thought, 'Jesus, we've got another one ready to crack.' Ordinarily, he would have snapped back, but this time he swallowed his anger and walked back to the Land-Rover.

They worked quickly, and for the most part, in silence; they followed Garnett's clipped instructions without hesitation, content to let him do the thinking for them, unaware that he was steadily losing confidence in his ability to think clearly any more. He made the driver strip down to his underwear, and then donned his uniform, leaving Dane to handcuff the driver's wrists behind him, while Dinkmeyer held the Kalashnikov on the other man.

In a harsh voice, Garnett said, 'Gag the driver and put him in the boot, I'll watch the other one.'

Dinkmeyer said, 'He'll suffocate.'

'Well, for God's sake,' Garnett shouted, 'who fucking cares. We've just killed nine people, what's one more between friends?'

Dane opened the boot. 'We could punch a hole through the partition and the back seat,' she said thoughtfully.

'Christ, if it makes you feel any better, do what you bloody like, only stop jawing about it.'

The hazel-eyed policeman shook his head and laughed softly.

'Look at you,' he said, 'fighting amongst yourselves now. You really don't stand a chance.'

Garnett said, 'I have news for you, friend, you are going to give us that chance. We need you to answer the calls on the radio, because we don't want Control to cotton on to the fact that Sierra Romeo 9 has fallen into the wrong hands, do we?'

'Suppose I refuse to help you?'

'I'll kill you, you can rely on that, friend.' Garnett looked at Dinkmeyer. 'Haven't you got that man into the boot yet?' he said irritably.

Dinkmeyer closed the lid. 'We have now,' he said.

Garnett took the .38 Lee Enfield pistol out of the holster and tossed it to Dinkmeyer. 'Here,' he said, 'I won't need it, I'm driving.'

They kept to the back roads, forced to work their way steadily northwards to get round the immediate road blocks. The police radio net helped them, inasmuch as they knew where the other mobiles were, and they fed back false location reports of their own position. It was Dane who had the brainwave of sending in a false contact report to draw the other cars away from the vicinity, and it worked beautifully until they were out of voice range with Salisbury Control. And then it dawned on them that Control would become suspicious once they could no longer contact Sierra Romeo 9, and it was only a short step for them to reach the conclusion that Sierra Romeo 9 had been stolen, and suddenly the Zephyr had lost its attraction, and the policemen were a liability to be got rid of as quickly as possible.

The rain had almost stopped, and they were heading south from Wantage, having completed a great semicircle, and the light was fading when Garnett spotted an isolated copse standing back from the main road. He pulled off on to the verge, doused the lights, and leaving Dane in the car, he and Dinkmeyer dragged the policemen across the open field to the copse. It would, he knew, have been prudent to execute both men, but he couldn't bring himself to do it, and it was no use asking Dinkmeyer to do it for him, because he couldn't live with that on his conscience. And so he took the easy way out and hand-cuffed both men to a birch tree, knowing that he had left behind two witnesses who would be able to identify him if ever he was arrested.

It was now imperative that they got rid of the car at the first opportunity, and this time it was Dinkmeyer who came up with the solution to their problem. He noticed the isolated house and told Garnett to stop. He had seen the garage tacked on to the side of the house, and concluded that where there was a garage there ought to be a car, and since lights were showing in the house, someone was at home.

There were, in fact, three people at home—the man, his wife and their unmarried daughter; and they weren't expecting any callers; and, 'Yes,' they said, 'we do have a car, but there isn't very much petrol in the tank'; and, 'Yes, there is a phone, it's in the hall'; and, 'Who do you think you are that you can burst into our home like this?'; and, 'We shall report you to your superior officer if you don't leave at once'. And then Dinkmeyer waved the pistol in front of their faces, and then the penny dropped that they were not dealing with a couple of obstreperous police constables, but people who were much more dangerous. And then the man asked them what they wanted, and they said, 'Your car and your silence for the next few hours.'

And so they tied the man and his wife and daughter to the dining chairs, and they cut the telephone wires, and Garnett borrowed a suit because his was still in the grip and too crumpled to wear, and they took the car and left the Zephyr in the garage where it was out of sight.

And as they left, Dinkmeyer said, 'What's the difference between us and the criminal fringe?'

And Garnett couldn't think of an answer, because at that precise moment in time, there was no difference.

They approached Basingstoke from the north, and abandoned the car outside Kingslere, so that the police were faced with the possibility that they might have gone off in any one of three different directions. And so they separated, leaving Dinkmeyer to travel on his own, and Garnett and Dane arrived in Basingstoke and nobody took any notice of the couple who got off the bus and walked down the street with their arms around each other's waists, the man carrying a shabby fibre suitcase in his free hand. And they made the safe house without further incident.

The man from Recovery was very surprised to see them.

21

THE INVITATION CARD read: Anthony and Laura Bloom invite you to a party to celebrate the publication of Jeffrey Hunter's new book, *Bloody Monday*.

Garnett looked up from the card at the number on the gate and checked that he had the right address. There were only half a dozen cars parked outside on the street; either they were early or most people had come by Tube. The house, pseudo-Georgian, was in the better part of Hampstead with a view over the Heath. He walked up the short drive with Dane on his arm, and rang the bell.

To say that Dane was different was a masterful understatement. She was wearing a black sleeveless cocktail dress cut on simple lines, high-heeled black sandals and smoky coloured tights. A small brooch, pinned below the left shoulder, which might have been a paste imitation but was equally likely to be the real thing, added to the striking effect of the dress. The wig was an exact match, and if he hadn't known to the contrary, he would have sworn it was her own hair now back to its former length. His mind reached for a word to describe her, but such overworked and debased adjectives as beautiful or magnificent were totally inadequate. She was a figure from Greek mythology, a goddess down from Olympian heights to taunt the mortals.

She caught Garnett looking at her and smiled. 'I find it hard to believe too,' she said. 'Before we left, I kept looking in the mirror to make sure it really was me standing there.'

She shivered. 'I should have brought my coat with me instead of leaving it in the car. Don't you feel cold?'

'I'll go back for it.'

'Don't bother. We can slip away without causing a hiatus if I haven't got a coat.'

He rang the bell again. 'I don't think they can have heard us.'

'I'm not surprised, it sounds pretty noisy in there.'

He meant to tell her to stay close to him when they went inside, but he didn't get the chance. The door was opened by a dark-haired petite woman who said, 'I'm Laura Bloom, you must be James and Diana Garside, do please come in.'

She spoke rapidly and without pause, like a runaway machine-gun gobbling up an endless belt of ammunition, and he didn't get a chance to correct her about the names. Still chattering gaily, she ushered them into a crowded room, introduced Dane to a bored-looking young man lounging by the door, who ceased to be bored the moment he laid eyes on her, and then, before Garnett could protest, steered him towards another group clustered round the bar at the far end of the room.

She leaned across the bar and tapped a slim balding man on the shoulder, and said, 'Anthony, darling, this is James Garside.'

'Actually,' said Garnett, 'my name is Abel, George Abel.'

'Of course,' said Bloom, 'you must forgive Laura, she has a habit of confusing names.'

'I've even tried Pelmanism,' Laura said brightly, 'but it was no good. I just haven't got a head for names.' She wandered away, a chirpy bird-like woman, seemingly without a brain in her head.

Bloom smiled and said, 'What do you do for a living?'

'I was a solicitor, but now I'm what you might call an insurance agent.'

'Really?' he said without enthusiasm. 'How interesting. What would you like to drink—gin, whisky or sherry?'

'Whisky, with soda.'

217

Bloom found a tumbler, poured a generous measure of whisky into it, and placed the glass and syphon in front of Garnett. 'Help yourself to soda,' he said, pointing to the syphon. He lit a king-sized cigarette. 'Have you read any of Jeffrey Hunter's books?'

'No, I can't say I have. What's his theme?'

'Suspense. He's just written a topical novel about the struggle between the police and the Resistance. The police are the heroes, which practically guarantees we will get a subsidy from the Ministry of Culture. It's almost bound to be a best-seller too. I only wish my publishing house had a few more authors like Jeffrey Hunter.'

'But there are not many of his calibre around?' Garnett suggested politely.

'Unfortunately not,' said Bloom. He glanced about him. 'I'm neglecting my duties; a lady at the end of the bar has an empty glass. I'll be back, don't go away.'

It was, he supposed, not unlike some of the cocktail parties he had been to before the war. There were the usual tit-bits, caviar spread on soggy bits of toast, thin slices of smoked salmon on equally thin slices of brown bread, cubes of mousetrap cheese impaled on toothpicks, and the inevitable savoury dip. The background music from the radiogram was fighting the usual losing battle with the usual banal small-talk. An assertive woman at his elbow said, 'Well, of course, my dear, what else can you expect, she has absolutely no taste.' And behind him, a man said, 'I ran into Stephen Bailey the other day, I must say I thought he was beginning to look his age.' And a reedy, opinionated voice said, 'He should have retired years ago. He's no longer up to it, and because he is totally unable to cope with present-day Government controls we're losing out to our competitors hand over fist.'

Garnett turned about and looked for Dane in the crowded room. She had circled round the young man, and was now standing with her back towards Garnett. But the young man wasn't going to be left high and dry, where she went, he was determined to follow, and all the time, his eyes flicked over Dane, mentally undressing her. Garnett decided it was time he rescued her. He started to move away from the bar, but a hand clutched his arm and he turned to see who it was. Bloom pushed an ice bucket across the bar. 'I'm running out of ice,' he said, 'would you mind being a good chap and get some more from the fridge in the kitchen?'

'Where's the kitchen?'

Bloom pointed across the room. 'That way,' he said, 'you can't miss it.'

Garnett picked up the bucket and eased his way through the crowd. He opened the kitchen door and stepped inside.

Vickers said, 'Please close the door behind you, we're not expecting anyone else.'

Garnett looked round the functional kitchen, and it struck him how out of place they all looked. Endicott, in an old grey pinstripe suit, sat at the table smoking his pipe and filling the room with evil-smelling blue smoke. Opposite him was Seagrave, looking matronly in a floral printed dress. Vickers managed to look suave in a char-coal-grey suit. double-breasted and out of fashion, of course, but he could have worn a sack and still got past the doorman at the Savoy. As usual, he was smoking a cigarette in that long black holder of his, which was almost a badge of office. While he could have walked into the adjoining room and joined the party without attract-ing comment, the same could not be said of the fourth member of the select party, a young man in his early twenties, who looked as though he might have been one of the founder members of the skinheads. Aggression oozed out of every pore.

'Who's the stranger?' said Garnett.

'Martin,' said Vickers. 'He is here to see we are not disturbed.'

'I hope he came in by the back.'

'Why?'

'He might have frightened the guests.'

The pale brown eyes narrowed to pinpoints of hostility.

Martin rocked backwards and forwards on his heels, alternately clenching and unclenching his enormous hands. Garnett could see that he was just itching to have a go at him.

Vickers said, 'You requested this meeting, David, and I'm sure you've got a good reason. I don't suppose you got me here merely to congratulate you?'

'I thought you would want to hear about the end result.'

Vickers looked at his watch. 'Will it take long?' he said.

Garnett said, 'I'll be brief.' He lit a cigarette. 'You had it right when you briefed me, we were being penetrated by a Russian cell—a hand picked team, selected and led by Valentine Teroshkova, the brain behind the set-up. If it had been successful, they would have expanded their field of operations. You were wrong in thinking they were out to destroy us—that wasn't their primary aim. They set out to drive a wedge between the Resistance and the civil population and between each Resistance organisation. They knew we would come after them, and they wanted us to do just that, because that gave them the opportunity to undermine the confidence existing between the local Resistance leaders and the Central Committee in London. You almost convinced me that Dane had been turned and was deliberately feeding London with false information, but we proved that theory didn't hold water, didn't we?'

'If you say so.'

'I'm dealing with facts, General, not theories. Dane wasn't turned, she was used. All right, if she was used, they had to know where she was, and who she was. They had to know everything about her radio frequencies and schedules. And, when they made contact with Dane, they had to convince her they were genuine. Someone had to provide them with the necessary cover story.'

He paused. No one said a word. Endicott examined his pipe to see if it had gone out; he held it by the bowl, gave it a couple of vigorous shakes, and stuck it back in his mouth. Spittle bubbled in the stem as he drew on the pipe.

Garnett cleared his throat and went on, 'You thought Dane had been turned while she was in prison because someone had connected her with the Parkhurst affair. It was a reasonable assumption at the time. You know what Dane said? She said, "Why me? Why not Endicott?—after all he had to sail pretty close to the wind to make sure you had a good enough cover story to get inside the prison".'

Endicott removed his pipe from his mouth. 'Is this a joke?' he said calmly. 'Because if it is, I think it is a bad one.' Garnett took a key out of his trouser pocket and tossed it to Vickers. Vickers caught it effortlessly.

'How dramatic,' he said dryly. 'What do I want this key for?'

'Left luggage, Paddington station. You'd better collect it within twenty-four hours.'

Vickers raised an eyebrow. 'Oh?' he said languidly.

'You will find a fibre case inside the locker. You see, Valentine Teroshkova believed in keeping records—a sort of card index system. I shoved the most interesting cards into that case—it should be quite a windfall for your Intelligence boys. Of course, my Russian isn't up to all that much, but I do know the Russian for agents and informers. Endicott is listed as an informer. I had a funny feeling about him, General; you see, they knew where to find Dane, they had Katz taped, and they were waiting for me to show up at the farm. Apart from you, only Endicott could have fed them that kind of information.'

Endicott didn't move a muscle. He sat there, almost as if he was in a trance, while the others waited for him to say something. The least they expected was a violent denial, but this silence was uncanny.

Vickers moistened his lips and said, 'Why, Endicott, for God's sake, why?'

A twisted smile appeared on Endicott's face. 'Why?' he said bitterly, 'you ask me why? Because you asked too much of me, that's why. You pushed me too far, and my cover was blown, and then I had no choice but to co-operate with them.'

Garnett walked towards the door and then stopped. 'Oh, by the way,' he said, 'I'm leaving Tate, Dinkmeyer and his daughter in your hands, Vickers, and I expect you to look after them. You don't have to worry about Dane and me, because we are opting out of the Resistance and your bloody non-existent escape pipeline.'

'You're being very foolish, neither of you stand a chance without my help.'

'We'll manage. You see, that Russian cell was well provided with all kinds of documents and money. I helped myself to a bit of everything.'

Garnett walked out of the kitchen and no one made a move to stop him. He found Dane standing near the assertive woman, and he rescued her unobtrusively. As they left the party, the last thing they heard was the assertive woman still holding forth— '... at least this Government has got all those unkempt demonstrators off the streets. Harry used to call them long-haired freaks hawking their consciences around in search of a cause ...'

EPILOGUE

FROST CARPETED THE stubby grass, clung tenaciously to the bare trees, and decorated the evergreen hedges like sugar icing on a cake. A blood-coloured sun peeped through the low-lying haze, but failed to raise the temperature above freezing point. Autumn had come early and winter was breathing on its heels.

The man thought he had a thankless task. Sitting in a cemetery watching a stonemason at work, was not his idea of how a Special Branch agent should be employed, but those were his orders, and he always obeyed orders without question.

There wasn't much in the paper to occupy him, apart from the Prime Minister's speech, and he had seen that live on television the night before. He had thought then, that what the PM had left unsaid, was of greater significance than what he had actually said in his broadcast. For some months now he had heard rumours that there was trouble on the Sino-Soviet border, but he hadn't paid much attention to it because it seemed to be limited to patrol clashes. And yet, the Prime Minister had seen fit to mention these clashes when he announced that the Soviets were scaling down their army of occupation to a mere three divisions. And that pledge to maintain law and order had a sting in the tail too—universal conscription instead of Selective Service, and active duty extended from eighteen months to two and a half years, in order to raise those additional militia divisions needed to plug the gap left by the withdrawal of Soviet units. He thought the militia was unreliable enough now, but God knows what they would be like once the expansion got underway. As sure as anything, a hell of a lot of their equipment was going to end up in the hands of the Resistance.

He thought about the dead man in the grave, and despite what his superiors said, he personally didn't think they would ever get to the bottom of that affair. The dead man had been seen to enter the block where he lived at 10:30 pm, and had then apparently taken the lift up to the eighth floor where he had a flat. At ten past eleven, another resident had entered the block of flats and, finding the lift stuck on the eighth floor, had pressed the recall button. When the lift arrived at the ground floor and the doors opened, there was a body lying curled up in the corner. The police doctor could find no cause of death other than heart failure. Nobody in Special Branch believed it.

He watched the stonemason pack up his tools and leave the cemetery, and then, out of curiosity, the Special Branch agent walked up to the grave and studied the headstone. The inscription was simple—'In loving memory of my dear husband, Richard Endicott.'

He walked back along the narrow gravel path between the graves and sat down on a bench. Keeping a watch on the grave was a bloody silly idea because nobody was going to turn up, least of all Mary Endicott. She had been tight-lipped from the moment they had broken the news of her husband's death. She hadn't cried then, and she wasn't going to cry now. In fact, looking back, it seemed to him that the news of his death hadn't come as a surprise to her, and he was not alone in thinking that the Resistance had got to her first.

Until yesterday, he would have said that the Resistance was on its last legs and wouldn't last another year, but now he wasn't so sure. The withdrawal of all but three Soviet divisions was going to give them a shot in the arm, and if the Sino-Soviet dispute really blew up, who could really say what would be the outcome? It occurred to him that he ought to store up some goodwill with the Resistance as a form of insurance. There was no telling when he might need it.

He turned up the collar on his coat and thrust his hands deep into the pockets. He noticed that there were a lot of berries on the holly bushes, and there was a saying that this was a sign of a hard winter to come. Looking up at the cold grey sky, it struck him that it was probably going to be a long hard winter in more ways than one.